Didn't Tori Ford think about anything but sex?

If answering the door wearing little more than a transparent robe over her lingerie was any indication, no, she did not. And that was bad news for Adam and his determination to remain strictly professional. He could pretend she was fully clothed—and hope she didn't do anything more outrageous.

"Shall I come back later?" he asked in a voice that didn't sound as raw-edged as he felt. Despite his intentions, his gaze drifted to her pouty lips pursed to kissable perfection. So tempting... He should have had the self-control to stop there.

He didn't. His gaze fell to her breasts, barely concealed by her silky bra, to her slim waist, to the scrap of fabric that hardly qualified as panties.

The blood drained from his head so fast he felt dizzy. He immediately raised his eyes, catching Tori's sexy smile.

"Actually, I need your help with the zipper of my dress." She turned and walked into the room, treating him to a remarkable view of her backside.

This was o

Blaze™

Dear Reader,

I hope you're enjoying my steamy miniseries FALLING INN BED... and the various ways that falling in bed can lead to falling in love.

After Laura and Dale (*Hot Sheets*, Blaze #153) finally gave in to their long-term lust, I decided to explore a case of "sparks at first sight." After all, falling in love should be fun, and I've never met a man more in need of lightening up than Adam Grant. As the assistant general manager of the "most romantic getaway," he has a responsibility to his guests, and *himself*, to get into the spirit of things.

Fortunately for Adam, reporter Tori Ford arrives to cover the Naughty Nuptials, and as it turns out, she's not content to report what's happening at Falling Inn Bed—she wants to experience the magic for herself. Now she just has to convince Adam to share that magic, too....

I hope you enjoy Tori and Adam's love story. Let me know. Drop me a line at www.JeanieLondon.com. And look for Miranda and Troy's story, *Pillow Chase*, Blaze #161, coming next month!

Very truly yours,

Jeanie London

Books by Jeanie London

HARLEQUIN BLAZE
28—SECRET GAMES
42—ONE-NIGHT MAN
53—ABOUT THAT NIGHT...
80—HOW TO HOST A SEDUCTION
90—BETWEEN THE SHEETS
110—OVER THE EDGE
128—WITH THIS FLING
153—HOT SHEETS*

*Falling Inn Bed...

RUN FOR COVERS

Jeanie London

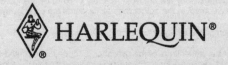

HARLEQUIN®

TORONTO • NEW YORK • LONDON
AMSTERDAM • PARIS • SYDNEY • HAMBURG
STOCKHOLM • ATHENS • TOKYO • MILAN • MADRID
PRAGUE • WARSAW • BUDAPEST • AUCKLAND

To Stephanie Kondas. Thirteen seems like forever ago (it was?!) and I've appreciated every day of your friendship since. Now repeat after me, "We're going to be *sskickin' little old ladies who know how to have fun...in the *very* distant future!"

ISBN 0-373-79161-5

RUN FOR COVERS

Copyright © 2004 by Jeanie LeGendre.

This edition published by arrangement with Harlequin Books S.A.

® and TM are trademarks of the publisher. Trademarks indicated with ® are registered in the United States Patent and Trademark Office, the Canadian Trade Marks Office and in other countries.

www.eHarlequin.com

Printed in U.S.A.

Prologue

SEXUAL CHEMISTRY wasn't a thing like champagne.

Tori Ford always knew what to expect when she poured a flute of her favorite beverage—perfectly chilled, a sugar cube tossed in because more fizz made that first sip burst over her tongue like tiny orgasms.

With sexual chemistry, on the other hand, she never knew quite what to expect. Fortunately, Tori liked surprises because her latest assignment had started off with a bang. She *never* expected to walk through the grand entrance of Falling Inn Bed, and Breakfast, known locally as Falling Inn Bed, and get caught up in the spirit of this romance resort so quickly.

Oh, she knew all about the place. No one who lived in Niagara Falls could have missed the rebirth of this historic property from failing hotel to winner of the prestigious Most Romantic Getaway Award, lauded by hospitality magazines and industry periodicals worldwide.

With a philosophy that translated into something like "Life belongs to lovers and lovers belong naked," Falling Inn Bed backed up their stance with romance-themed suites designed to get couples feeling amorous. They even let staff members with titles such as the *bedding consultant* loose on their guests.

While a big proponent of anything promoting *l'amour*,

Tori reserved opinion on the inn's bedding consultant. She reserved opinion on a few things about her latest reporting assignment, actually—including walking through the door to a powerful case of lust at first sight. Yet one look at Adam Grant, the too-attractive assistant general manager, and the bulb on her lust-o-meter popped like a cork from a champagne bottle.

That the man looked like someone her family would approve of came as another surprise. Tori usually went for the rough-around-the-edges, daring and dangerous types who wouldn't be welcomed within five miles of the family mansion.

But her family would have flung the doors wide for this one, with his neat sable hair and black eyes. His custom-tailored suit hugged his body like a glove. He was tall, handsome and *too* conservative with a composed air of self-assurance.

Adam made her itch to rough up the veneer of powerful male he wore along with his intense expression. And while his businesslike appearance and serious demeanor didn't interest her, everything simmering below it did.

As a reporter, Tori's observation skills were top notch. She recognized the calm deliberation in his gaze, the calculating mind, the tension in the impressive body that convinced her he was equally aware of her. But instead of checking her out, this guy locked his sex appeal tight under lock and key.

And then she knew exactly what it was about Adam Grant that interested her...well, besides his handsome face.

They were kindred souls.

Once upon a time, Tori's every waking moment had been spent trying to live up to her family's expectations. While her surname might be Ford, she was a member of the prestigious Prescott family compliments of her mother, and being a Prescott meant keeping up appearances at all costs. But she'd eventually realized that life was too precious to spend all her time worrying about living up to other people's expectations.

She'd gotten smart.

People weren't perfect—except for her mother and sister, who'd mastered the art of appearing that way. But at what cost? They didn't take time to enjoy their lives. They always wore a smile for the press and never did anything that would risk starting any gossip. They never had any fun, and it was sucking the joy right out of them.

So she'd washed her hands of trying to live up to everyone else's expectations and decided the only person she needed to satisfy was herself.

And that was why Adam had resonated so strongly with her—he clearly hadn't learned yet that life was for living. They shared all this incredible chemistry, yet he wore his professionalism like armor.

Could she help him lighten up and enjoy himself?

Tori wanted to answer that question, along with a number of others about what was taking place behind the scenes at Falling Inn Bed. She finally had a chance to prove herself a competent reporter to her managing editor, who'd previously buried her on the municipal beat because she was the senator's granddaughter.

Until meeting this too-composed man who made her mouth water, she wasn't sure just how to prove herself, but now Tori knew exactly what she needed to do.

She needed to live the magic of Falling Inn Bed for herself. Then she'd report to her readers and bowl this town over with her journalistic skill and ability to sell newspapers.

And whom better to experience that magic with than the inn's assistant general manager?

"If you'll join me, Ms. Ford," Adam Grant said in a rich, smoothly polished voice that rippled through her like the first sip of *really* fizzy champagne. "I'll introduce you to the rest of the management team and bring you up to speed with where we are in the schedule of grand opening events."

"It'll be my pleasure to join you, Mr. Grant," she said with just enough innuendo to blast his cool professionalism straight into personal.

One sable brow lifted before he schooled his expression. But control wasn't meant to be part of this equation. When he touched her elbow to guide her down a hallway marked Business Offices, Tori felt wired to the man with a current. A quick glance into his dark gaze assured her he felt it, too.

Sometimes, there was just no explaining chemistry. And most of the time, there was no resisting it.

Tori wondered if Adam Grant knew that.

Giving him a smile that said Run for cover!, she felt another thrill when a tiny frown appeared between his brows, a look that convinced her he was expecting the worst from her.

No, this assignment wasn't turning out to be anything at all like champagne....

DIDN'T TORI Ford think about anything but sex?

Adam Grant wished she would, but the local reporter who'd unexpectedly become his escort for the duration of this grand opening didn't seem interested in much else. She'd made it her life's quest to teach him to have fun, and sex apparently topped her list of fun pastimes.

While he generally appreciated ambitious, focused women, Tori Ford was beyond ambitious and focused. She was outrageous. Not only had she promised to do whatever it took to get her story, she wanted to experience that story for herself.

She wanted to live the magic of Falling Inn Bed, and Breakfast with *him*.

Adam didn't get personal with guests or co-workers, and in her current capacity, Tori Ford qualified as the latter.

So here he was, trying to run interference so the grand opening won good reviews, and this reporter's no-holds-barred tenacity went head-to-head with his no-holds-barred professionalism. Adam had a strict business ethic, honed at the knees of the elderly grandparents who'd raised him.

Business was business. Personal was personal.

By separating the two, his grandparents had run a successful manufacturing operation for over half a century while keeping their marriage equally successful.

He wouldn't mix business with pleasure. And certainly not with a woman only interested in *living her story*.

Unfortunately, keeping business and pleasure separated during this grand opening was proving to be a problem. The promotional event inaugurating the new Wedding Wing had been dubbed the Naughty Nuptials for good reason. Every function was designed exclusively for couples, with sex front and center.

The harder he tried to keep their relationship professional in the face of all that sex, the more Tori Ford kept trying to get personal. She saw everything as an opportunity to taunt him into joining the fun.

Like now, for example. While the featured bridal couple posed for photos after the ceremony, Tori had slipped away to her suite to freshen her makeup.

Or so she'd said.

Most women Adam knew didn't undress to put on mascara, and when he returned to accompany her to the reception, Tori opened her door about as undressed as she could be short of greeting him in the buff. The beaded gown she'd worn to the wedding had been replaced by a transparent robe.

Equally transparent was her ploy to breach the boundaries of professional behavior. Looking back, Adam supposed any request to visit her suite should have been suspect. She'd been using these ploys often enough in the two days of their acquaintance, each time upping the stakes.

Tori Ford scored a big hit this time.

She even looked like sex. All creamy skin and vibrant red hair, she tempted him with slim curves covered in barely there undergarments. The robe only reached the top of her thighs and hung open to reveal more than it concealed.

He was thinking personal now. Despite himself, his gaze dropped from the tumble of bright hair to the beautiful face where midnight-blue eyes watched him and pouty lips pursed to kissable perfection.

She wore a necklace of unusual design. Swirls of gold encircled her neck, with a solitary teardrop emerald dangling toward her cleavage. The silky bra clung to her breasts, muting blush-colored nipples but doing nothing to hide the tight tips pointing to needy little peaks.

He should have had enough self-control to stop there.

He didn't. Adam tortured himself further by skimming his gaze down that expanse of slim waist and smooth stomach to the scrap of matching fabric that hardly qualified as panties. The filmy triangle rode low, directing his attention to the juncture of sleek thighs, where he could detect the faintest hint of golden-red hair beneath.

The blood drained from his head so fast he felt dizzy.

And still Adam couldn't stop. He was human, after all, and even worse, he hadn't had sex since his ex-fiancée had broken off their engagement, prompting his move across the country to take this management position at Falling Inn Bed, and Breakfast.

Right now he wished he'd never left Seattle.

Yet the career move had seemed a good opportunity at the time, *before* he faced Tori's shapely legs showcased on strappy high heels and her determination to get him into bed.

Sweeping his gaze over her again, he said in a voice that didn't sound as raw-edged as he felt, "Shall I come back later?"

He would *not* let her know she'd scored a hit.

"No need. I was just taking a breather. Don't let anyone ever tell you beaded gowns aren't heavy." She fanned herself with a manicured hand. "It's warm in here. How is it out there?"

"The temperature's fine, Ms. Ford." Nothing wrong with the inn's climate control system, despite the summer heat.

His body temperature proved a different matter.

"I keep asking you to call me Tori." She flashed him an exasperated smile. "Why don't you come in? I won't take long."

Though she issued her invitation casually, Adam recognized this maneuver for what it was—another move toward personal.

If she could get him inside the Wedding Knight Suite, they'd be a step closer to the bed. And with her looking the way she did, she'd keep him awake all night.

The memory of her in that robe would keep him awake tonight anyway, but he wouldn't tip his hand to Tori. Not when he'd declined to participate in her contest of wills. Regardless of how much his body urged him otherwise.

"I'll wait out here for you."

"In the hallway?"

He inclined his head, not offering further explanation. He'd already established where he stood on this issue, and wouldn't play her game by rationalizing his decision. To do so would only imply she might sway him the other way. She couldn't.

Leaving the door open wide, she turned and walked away, treating him to a remarkable view of her backside. The see-through robe made it impossible not to notice how the T-back panties disappeared between her shapely cheeks, and combined with those nicely toned thighs… His body heat went on the rise again.

Letting his eyes drift shut, Adam inhaled deeply and willed his body to behave, implementing a cleansing tech-

nique he used before working out. Karate was his sport of
choice and at the moment, he appreciated the strict discipline it demanded. Another deep breath tempered the memory of a half-naked Tori Ford. Slowly the tension receded,
and his body came firmly back into his grasp.

Opening his eyes, Adam straightened his tie and waited,
as prepared for her next move as he'd ever be. Reformu-
lating his game plan proved more difficult. He simply
didn't understand this woman. Why she thought he needed
rescuing from a dreary existence was a mystery. True,
work had taken up most of his time since he'd made the
move to Niagara Falls, but that was normal when es-
tablishing a new career path.

And he'd done nothing to encourage her interest. In
fact, he'd resisted her every attempt to engage him—and
she'd made many. Since they'd met, she'd been teasing him
and trying to provoke a reaction. Yes, they had chemistry,
but that didn't mean they had to act on it.

Unfortunately, the *not acting* kept getting tougher. He
couldn't help wondering what Tori's next move would be,
and they were only a couple of days into this grand opening. Naughty Nuptials comprised three *weeks* of events.
When Wild, Wild Weddings concluded after tonight's reception, he still had to survive Risqué Receptions and Hottest Honeymoons.

Somehow, Adam would manage. Tori Ford might be determined to get her scoop on the inn, but he was equally
determined to prove this establishment, despite its status
as a romance resort, conducted business on the level. Promoting romance between couples wasn't synonymous with
orgies in the main lobby, and Adam would make sure she
understood the difference.

Of course, he wasn't always clear on the difference

himself…especially since the focus of the Naughty Nuptials was sex, which likely explained why he reacted to this woman with a need testing his restraint.

And almost as if she wanted to prove the point, Tori reappeared, looking sultry in a beaded green gown that clung lazily to her curves. Spangles flashed with every step, and he inhaled another cleansing breath to shore up his defenses.

Even with her clothes on, this woman looked like sex.

"Will you give me a hand?" She turned and presented her back with its open zipper. Lifting her hair, she moved close enough to bombard him with her subtly spicy fragrance. "Do you mind?"

Yes.

Clearly this was another power play—one he wouldn't let her win. Not when he came face-to-face with all that bare skin. Not when he knew she'd managed to get her zipper down without assistance in the first place. He wouldn't let her see how that one touch made his every thought zero in on his fingertips.

Chemistry practically crackled between them. Every sense honed in on the texture of her skin. Every nerve kicked into hyperalert and only his skill at self-discipline saved him from a reaction that otherwise would have leveled him.

He dragged the zipper up, an action that felt like an intimacy they shouldn't be sharing. But not according to Tori, who clearly enjoyed liquefying professional boundaries with her suggestive smiles and constant innuendo.

Adam knew better than to show this woman weakness. One slip and she'd move in for the kill. He didn't care to test his ability to resist her under extreme conditions.

More extreme than these, anyway.

Tugging the zipper into place, he put a much-needed step

between them and felt a lot more relief than he should have for a man who'd decided not to play her seduction game.

"Did you fasten the eye hook?" she asked, her voice a hushed whisper between them.

If Adam hadn't been struggling so hard to rein back, he might have enjoyed knowing he wasn't the only one feeling the effects of her little game.

He was working hard to keep his expression neutral when she peeked a sultry gaze from beneath the fall of wild hair.

"If you don't fasten the eye hook, the zipper will creep down. I might wind up flashing everyone at the reception."

Now there was another vision to haunt him. This beautiful woman swaying to the music on the dance floor. The heavily beaded gown slithering into a puddle at her feet. Those filmy undergarments and all that skin…and two hundred surprised guests enjoying the show.

As Adam wasn't partial to exhibition fetishes—or any fetishes at all, for that matter—he reached for the eye hook.

The fastener proved a test for his supersize fingers. What should have been a fast fix became a series of awkward efforts that brought more skin against skin until his careful expression melted into a scowl.

Tori pulled her hair higher and leaned into the light to assist his efforts, but all she did was flood his senses with the scent of her hair and that underlying spicy fragrance.

She distracted him and, in the process, undermined his efforts to finish this task and make his getaway. By the time he forced the microscopic hook through the metal loop, his fingers had grown stiff with frustration.

"There you go." Not even his usual rock-steady discipline could keep the triumph, and relief, from his voice.

If Adam expected Tori to gloat, he miscalculated her response. She leaped on her advantage by firing again.

Shaking her hair out, she tumbled cloudlike waves over her shoulders and sent another blast of enticing fragrance his way. "Thank you."

He only nodded and stepped farther into the hallway, as much to clear his senses of her provocative scent as to prompt her to action. Right now, he needed two hundred reception guests to remind him he should be working. He made a mental note to avoid being alone with this woman again.

"What's on the agenda this afternoon?" He steered the conversation where it belonged. "And more importantly, how can I facilitate your work?"

"Helping me dress was a big help."

She issued *that* with such a straight face he felt the urge to smile. Pulling the suite door closed, Tori sidled close and slipped her arm through his.

"We're going to have fun today, Adam. You have heard that word before, haven't you?"

She gazed up into his face with those big blue eyes but never gave him a chance to reply. "We're going to drink champagne and dance and watch other people drink champagne and dance. We're going to toast your honorary couple, and, with any luck, I'll catch the bouquet and you'll catch the garter. Will you slide it up my leg with your teeth, if you do?"

"*Work* fits in where exactly? I was under the impression you had a scoop to find and daily deadlines to keep."

"I do, but my job is to report on your grand opening functions. To do that, I have to interact with your guests. Didn't you read my article in this morning's paper?"

"I did. You reported on last night's rehearsal dinner. You played up the excitement of the event and the romance of how our featured bridal couple became engaged while they built the Wedding Wing." Directing her toward the elevator, he disentangled his arm to press the button, then clasped his hands behind his back to wait.

Tori frowned, assuring him that she hadn't missed his getaway. "I also explained that today's wedding would conclude the first week of your grand opening and officially start the second. Since I'll have the feature in tomorrow's paper, I left my readership hanging to find out what happens."

"Is that why you mentioned our unexpected guests?" he asked, referring to her parents' last-minute addition to the rehearsal dinner guest list.

"My parents weren't the only gate-crashers. Your bedding consultant's parents showed up, too, which meant I had area news of interest to report." She must have seen something in his expression because she asked, "You don't agree?"

"No, I don't."

She gave a slight shrug that made those red waves shimmer in the overhead light. "That might explain why you're a hotel manager and not a reporter."

He didn't get a chance to respond before the elevator beeped and the door slid open. They entered beside another couple Adam recognized as wedding guests.

"Heading back to the wedding?" he asked.

The man nodded, and Adam inquired about their accommodations, dissuading Tori from continuing their discussion until they were alone again.

When the doors opened, the Wedding Wing lobby appeared before them. He held the door while the guests exited before joining Tori, who picked up right where they'd left off.

"You're not from Niagara Falls. Trust me when I say your unexpected guests last night are news around here.

People gobble up any mention of my family. Take a look at our society page someday. Every other paragraph has the name Prescott in it. It's a side effect of being related to politicians. When my family and your bedding consultant's family are together in the same room, it's news. I was simply writing to my audience."

She motioned to the life-size painting showcased in the lobby. "Your bedding consultant knows how to use the press to her advantage, too. That's why she arranged the loan of the *Falling Woman* from Westfalls. To create spin. She told me so herself."

Adam followed her gaze, unable to argue the point because his co-worker Laura Granger—the inn's bedding consultant and the woman who'd conceptualized the Wedding Wing—had acquired the painting to stir up interest in the Naughty Nuptials.

This had been a noteworthy acquisition because the artist, a French woman named Mireille Marceaux, was apparently a local mystery. Adam glanced at the painting, a woman surrounded by a summer-green forest and mist from the falls.

"I still can't believe she managed to get this painting on loan. Talk about using personal connections," Tori said, referring to Laura's status as friend to the headmistress of the exclusive preparatory school that owned the painting.

Adam nodded, but as he gazed at the painting he noticed something he hadn't before. The redheaded semi-nude reminded him of the brash young reporter standing by his side. Something about the way the red hair, refined facial features and delicate curves came together struck him as similar.

Of course, this shouldn't come as a surprise. The sight of Tori Ford in that skimpy robe still burned in his brain. Like the *Falling Woman*, she was the stuff fantasies were made of and he wasn't likely to forget the sight any time soon.

"Laura's acquisition of this painting was a promotional stunt, but I don't believe it falls under the same heading as gossiping about our guests in print."

"Gossiping? Don't you think that's a little harsh?"

He shook his head. "You're capitalizing on a decades-old feud between your family and Laura's, as well as your connection to the senator. That strikes me as sensationalism."

"It's Laura's job to create public interest in her Wedding Wing. It's my job to create public interest so my readers buy newspapers. People around here *enjoy* reading about our families, so where's the difference?"

If Tori didn't understand, Adam wasn't about to debate the point. He would have thought Senator Prescott's youngest granddaughter would have been more concerned about where she directed her media attention. Apparently not.

But while he was entitled to his opinion, Adam wouldn't purposely antagonize the woman responsible for the reviews on the Naughty Nuptials. Upon learning the *Niagara Falls Journal* would be sending her estranged cousin to cover the events, Laura, his normally professional, if somewhat quirky co-worker, had told management about her troubled history with the senator's family. These families were so estranged, in fact, that Laura had feared coverage would be biased as a result.

Falling Inn Bed, and Breakfast needed rave reviews, so Adam was doing his best to earn them. Unfortunately, he hadn't been assigned to this job because he was the best fit, but because he was the only male on the executive management staff who could escort Tori Ford to couple events.

He intended to enforce what damage control he could

and, at the very least, not make matters worse. But he hadn't counted on Tori turning him into her pet project, either.

"We'd prefer the inn to attract interest on its own merit," he said to segue through the stiff moment. "Surely you can understand that."

While Tori might have understood, he could tell by the way she notched her chin that she didn't agree. And he didn't give her a chance to embroil him in another debate. Touching her elbow, he guided her toward the grand ballroom, where the Wallace/Marsh reception currently was taking place. She moved along by his side without further comment, and he greeted the ushers posted at the main entrance before escorting her inside.

Laura had indeed outdone herself with this event. The ballroom boasted a sweeping wall of doors that opened onto a forest. With the June sun streaming through, the wedding party and guests looked like a scene on a postcard in the inn's novelty shop.

Adam had been on the property for over ten months now, yet sometimes the place still caught him by surprise with its unique combination of nineteenth-century grandeur and atmosphere.

And *sex*.

It was subtle, but everywhere. Glancing up at the ornate friezes separating lofty ceilings from gleaming white walls, he recognized the whimsical sculptures depicting couples with limbs entwined. Mouths and hips thrusting. Rubenesque women in varying degrees of nudity looking dreamy and sated as they pleasured their equally nude men.

Then again, perhaps the sex around here wasn't always so subtle. Adam thought about the restaurant's grand opening specialty menu with its bold header scrawled across the front—*Inter Courses*. And the inn's promotional materials weren't much better. The lineup of romance-themed suites in the main hotel boasted names like the Demimondaine's Boudoir and the Wild West Brothel. The new Wedding Wing had followed tradition with honeymoon suites called the Egyptian Pleasure Pyramid and the Castaway Honeymoon Isle.

His current charge had been installed in the Wedding Knight Suite, which reminded Adam of a sex dungeon with its Dark Ages furnishings and handy supply of bondage gadgets. Even the bed had a choose-your-pleasure theme, with specialty sheets like the *Kama Sutra* Sports Set and the Fetish Collection.

"Looks like the receiving line has finished and the bridal couple are gearing up for their first dance," Adam said. "So where to first, Ms. Ford?"

Tori scanned the crowd, her gaze darting from her photographer, who snapped shots of the bridal couple, to the sidelines, where Laura stood applauding with the Wedding Wing architect. "To the bar. I can't mingle without champagne."

Together they skirted the edges of the crowd, and Adam greeted the elderly bartender. "Hello, Clyde. Ms. Ford would like a drink."

Clyde had a head full of cottony hair and a quick smile that flashed against his wrinkled black skin. "What's your pleasure today?" he asked Tori.

"I'm a champagne cocktail classicist. What can you do for me?"

"I can fix you up right. Just tell me whether you want to visit the Alps, the Mediterranean or head south to Cuba."

Tori laughed, a bright sound that managed to spiral through him as if it were alive. A reminder of their chemistry that he didn't need.

"I knew I liked you from the moment we met, Clyde," she said. "I'm in the Mediterranean mood today. Just can't resist those beaches. And please double my order, so I can share."

Adam wasn't sure what a champagne cocktail classicist was, but the look Tori shot his way told him he would soon find out.

Accepting a flute, she passed Adam a second, then accompanied him from the bar.

"Mediterranean?" he asked.

"Bubbly with a dash of pomegranate and orange liqueur."

They wound their way to a spot in the crowd where they could view the proceedings before Tori tipped back her first sip. Her eyes fluttered shut, and she sighed appreciatively.

"I love that man. And I'll give you one thing around here, Adam—you know how to pick staff. Clyde's the perfect man for his job. And Laura…the *bedding* consultant." She chuckled, and he wondered what she found so amusing. He didn't ask.

"You're the only one I haven't been able to figure out yet, Adam. What do you bring to this place?"

He would have said *sanity* but as he hadn't accomplished that ambitious goal yet, he said, "You've formulated your opinions of our staff quickly."

"I work fast."

No doubt there. "And you have a lock on everyone but me?"

"It's been two days," she said as if that explained it. Then she glanced back at the bar. "Take Clyde for example. He's a retired businessman who took the job as your head bartender because his wife died." She tipped her flute in salute. "I thought his devotion to your hotel might be to avoid being home alone. So I asked him. You know what he told me?"

"No idea."

"That he came to Falling Inn Bed because the romance around here helps remind him of all the years he had with his Alice. Isn't that sweet?"

Adam nodded, surprised. While he would expect a reporter of Tori's caliber to dig up intimate details on a man's life, he hadn't expected her to be influenced by them. A thoughtful smile played around her mouth, and there was a softness to her voice he'd never heard before.

"Are you impressed?" she asked.

"I am. You learned more about Clyde in two days than I have in the past ten months."

Not that it had ever occurred to him to ask personal questions. Clyde did a superb job running the house bar, and Adam hadn't needed to know anything else about the man.

Tori flashed him a high-beam smile that told him his praise had pleased her. She tapped her flute against his in a tinkle of crystal. "Now drink up, Adam. Think of this as an adventure. You'll always be able to say you tried one."

He wasn't sure who would care whether he'd tried a champagne cocktail, but he'd rather taste it than engage in another debate on the importance of adventuring in life. He sipped. He swallowed. He said, "Good."

Her frown suggested she'd guessed he was humoring her, but he was spared from further debate when the emcee invited couples to join the bride and groom on the dance floor.

Taking a long drink of her champagne, Tori deposited the glass on the tray of a passing waiter. "Come on. Dancing is a divine way to loosen up and have a good time. It gets the blood flowing and the heart racing—a fun way to stay healthy."

Adam wouldn't mention that to make up for the personal life he'd left back on the West Coast, he'd nearly doubled his normal workout schedule. Staying healthy was not an issue when he was training with a martial arts master five days a week.

So he disposed his glass and led her onto the dance floor, reconciled. As her escort, his life for the next two weeks would be subject to her whim. After the way she'd greeted him in her suite a short time ago, he'd pick his battles.

As the band slid into a slow tune, Adam twined his fingers through hers and slipped his hand around her waist. Tori melted against him until he could feel the brush of her curves everywhere, and he found himself remembering the way she'd looked without her gown, all creamy curves and bold challenge. The effect was double-barreled, forcing him to call upon every ounce of his will to keep his body behaving appropriately.

She wanted a reaction. He wouldn't give her one.

"What makes you so convinced there's a scoop to be had around here, Ms. Ford?"

"Would the Worldwide Travel Association send a photojournalist with Tyler Tripp's credentials to film a documentary if there wasn't a story?"

"You are aware that Tyler has a connection to our inn."

"I know, I know," she said snuggling closer. "Once upon a time, he covered the inn for WTA's annual contest. His coverage earned you the Most Romantic Getaway Award and a substantial promotional package. Tyler's been very forthcoming. But he and I are looking for different things in our stories."

"What's so different, Ms. Ford?"

"He's filming an industry documentary on your bedding consultant and the Naughty Nuptials. He'll showcase what Falling Inn Bed does as a way of helping other hotels to find their niche market and capitalize on it. He's already sold on this place—"

"But you're not?"

"Oh, no, I'm sold. I live in town, remember? But I want more. I want to know how you serve romance to your guests and why it works. People are fascinated with this inn. I intend to answer all my readers' questions, and to do that, I have to experience the magic firsthand."

She glanced up at him, her expression suddenly serious. "You know, that gives me an idea…."

To Adam's surprise, she stepped out of his arms. He let her go, appreciating a reprieve from all those taunting curves while she rummaged through her purse and pulled out a small electronic device. Bringing it to her lips, she depressed a button and said, "What about an FAQ section? Frequently asked questions for readers who are just tuning in. It'll be the perfect way to keep readers up to speed while welcoming new readers. Three weeks is a long time to keep everyone's attention."

Adam watched, shielding her from the dancers while she stood unselfconsciously talking into her recorder.

She finally dropped the device back in her purse. "Sorry. I have to get my ideas down when they happen or I forget them."

Nodding, he guided her back into his embrace again, only this time keeping her at arm's length. "Now I have a question for you, Ms. Ford."

"Shoot."

"Why do you think you need to get personal?"

She peered up at him with a smile playing around her mouth, and he couldn't help but drag his gaze over her face, taking in her delicate features one by one. Smooth skin. Deep blue eyes. Thickly fringed lashes that looked dusted in gold. She was an incredibly beautiful woman. *Too* beautiful for his peace of mind.

"I've got two reasons, Adam."

"And they are?"

"I like you. You've got this wonderful old hotel with all these sexy suites and all you want to do is work, work, work. I happen to know that your boss ordered the management team to participate in the Naughty Nuptials and have fun. You've got a unique opportunity here, and I like you enough to help you make the most of it. When will you ever get another chance to be a part of a special event like this one?"

Never, if he got lucky. "I can safely say there won't be another Naughty Nuptials campaign happening for some time."

"My point exactly." Tori flashed him a grin and melted bonelessly against him.

Suddenly responsible for holding her upright, Adam could feel her breasts press close and her stomach cradle what was about to become a raging erection.

He gritted his teeth.

She sighed.

"And the other reason?" he asked to distract himself.

"For the record, I don't want to get personal so you'll give me the hotel's deep dark secrets. Contrary to what my managing editor believes, I happen to be a very competent reporter. As long as you let me behind the scenes, I'll get those secrets myself."

Tipping her head back, she met his gaze. "I want to get personal because I'm attracted to you. *Very* attracted. I want to experience the Falling Inn Bed magic and I can't do that all by my lonesome. Admittedly, you're not the type of man I usually date, but then there's no accounting for chemistry."

Truer words had never been spoken.

He wondered what type of man she usually dated and would not even entertain asking the question.

"So, Adam, there you have it. I think sex is a great way to relax and have fun. And I happen to have a suite filled with sexy goodies that we could experiment with together. But that means you'll have to come inside and get naked."

His chest constricted tighter with every word she spoke and he couldn't decide whether the breathless quality in her voice or her boldness nailed him like a sucker punch.

Bottom line—it didn't matter.

He was in for a *long* two weeks if he couldn't come up with a way to deal with this woman and keep his clothes on.

2

TORI SLIPPED INTO the seat that the namesake of Bruno's Place held for her. "I'm being seated to breakfast by a five-star chef. Is this VIP treatment for your local reporter or do you usually seat all your guests on Sunday mornings?"

"The VIP treatment, of course. If I played waiter too often, I'd have no time to cook, and that would be a crime," the burly chef said with a grin. "You're in my world now, Ms. Ford, and I take my press seriously."

"Is that how you manage to keep in our food critic's good graces? She's known to be tough, yet you manage to stay on her top shelf week after week."

"No mystery there. Your food critic is tough, but she's good. She recognizes I'm *that* good."

With a laugh, Tori accepted the napkin he handed her. She appreciated honesty, preferring to know where she stood with people, good, bad or otherwise. And Bruno, a chef who was *that good*, would shine when his turn for an interview rolled around—as long as he continued to shoot straight with her.

This morning, however, he was off the hook. She had a breakfast interview with the infamous bedding consultant, who, Tori glanced at her watch as she accepted a menu, would be tardy in a mere two minutes.

"I want you to read through my dishes and pick whatever your little heart desires," he said. "If you want something special, I'll whip it up."

"Why, Bruno, you really are sucking up to me." She couldn't help but wish Adam Grant would be as accommodating. The thought of that hot man satisfying her every desire... *Mm-mm.*

"Of course I'm sucking up to you, Ms. Ford." The burly man with the balding head gave a hearty laugh. "The way to *my* success is through *your* stomach."

And he was off to a good start as he poured her a cup of much-needed coffee, explaining his specialties and otherwise entertaining her until the bedding consultant appeared at the hostess station with barely a minute to spare.

With her white-blond hair and blue eyes, Laura Granger wasn't only beautiful, but striking in a runway-model sort of way. Tall and slim, both features leant her a gracefulness as she wound her way through the tables, greeting guests and staff.

Tori couldn't help but remember how pea-green her older sister used to get about Laura while they'd been attending school at Westfalls Academy. While she'd been a few years behind them, she'd been privy to her sister's feelings on visits home.

As an adult—and an adult who made her living observing people and looking for stories—the situation made more sense. People in this town tended to compare her sister, Miranda, with Laura because of the connection between their two families.

But meeting Laura up close and personal convinced Tori that although both women were the same age, they couldn't have been more different if they'd tried.

Miranda was delicate and dark. Laura was taller and fair. Miranda had always been social and popular, Laura the shy outcast. Miranda excelled at whatever she did. Except for dance class at Westfalls, where Laura had stolen the spotlight.

Boy, could Laura Granger dance. Tori remembered how she'd get out on that big stage in Marshall Hall and wow the audience. Like Bruno in the kitchen, Laura had been *that* good. Tori wondered if she hadn't turned professional because her family couldn't afford to train her.

But Laura seemed to have found her niche at Falling Inn Bed. It wasn't every day that a hotel wedding coordinator had the Worldwide Travel Association send a photojournalist like Tyler Tripp. Then again, Laura wasn't an ordinary wedding consultant by any stretch; she was the one and only *bedding* consultant.

She marched to her own beat, while Miranda maintained the status quo at all costs. And Tori knew those costs were high.

She watched as Laura kissed Bruno's cheek when he told her he'd send along a waiter with espresso. Then she slipped into the chair across the table and told him they'd need some time before ordering.

"That'll work for you, Tori?" Laura asked.

"As long as the coffee keeps coming."

"It won't get a chance to cool," Bruno promised before strolling away, looking remarkably like a bull in a china shop among the turn-of-the-last-century antique tables and glassware.

Tori sipped her coffee, curious to gauge Laura's attitude to their first interview. They'd spoken since her arrival on the property, of course. Laura had even given her a tour of the new Wedding Wing. But today they were going to get personal and, with a family history like theirs, that was saying a bunch.

"Well, who'd have ever guessed that we'd be sitting together with only a few feet of table between us?" Tori said.

"Not in my wildest dreams." Laura smiled, and up close, her looks were even more striking.

Okay, maybe Tori should have been more sympathetic to Miranda's plight—she certainly wouldn't want to be compared to Laura Granger and her incredible good looks.

"So you were worried I was going to be biased," Tori said.

"Adam told you that?"

"I asked. I figured he'd have denied it if he could have."

"At first, perhaps," she admitted. "But you promised you wouldn't trash the Naughty Nuptials because of our family history, so I took you at your word. I also told everyone to take exceptional care of you or we wouldn't stand a chance."

Tori thought of Bruno and smiled. "So I heard. Why don't you mention it to Adam."

Laura arched an eyebrow. "Is there a problem?"

"Not really. He's very…professional." *Too* professional. "So what did you tell him about me?"

She needed to know everything she could to help this man have a little fun.

"Nothing more than the overview of our family history that I shared with all my co-workers. When I found out you were taking over our press. I didn't want them to be sandbagged either way."

"How is it they never heard about the rift between our families? I thought we were legend around Niagara Falls."

Laura smiled then greeted the approaching waiter. Accepting the steaming mug, she sipped appreciatively. "None of them come from around here. Think of the inn's management staff like a traveling circus troupe. My boss picked them up at the different properties she's managed throughout her career. Our maintenance supervisor has been with her for over twenty years at five different properties."

"That sort of loyalty is unusual, and impressive."

"Ms. J is an impressive woman."

"Okay, so official interview time." Reaching into her bag and grabbing her voice-activated recorder, Tori plunked it on the table and got to business. "For the record, what makes this hotel so special?"

"Falling Inn Bed is a place where couples can focus on romance. We're not a singles-type of resort, where men go to meet women or vice versa. We're a place that helps our couples focus on what's important—making the most of being in love."

"That's spin."

"It's true."

Impressed that Laura didn't hesitate to measure her words, Tori decided that the media-handling skills so rampant on her mother's side of the family weren't necessarily a side effect of living with politicians.

"Since none of this is in your promotional brochure, I'll take you at your word. You have a very romantic view of what you do around here."

Laura laughed. "I've been accused of being a romantic idealist."

"Really?" Romantic idealism had to come from somewhere and discovering where might be an important key to understanding the whole picture of the bedding consultant. "I imagine romantic idealism serves you very well on this job."

"Especially with the Wedding Wing. I create fantasies for my newlyweds. Each one's as individual as the couple itself."

"I've heard about some of the fantasies you create. What

I caught of your Wild, Wild Weddings campaign last week was impressive. The Sex Toy Shower. The Bad Bachelor/ette Parties. The Racy Rehearsal Dinner. Neat stuff. I'm sure your honorary bridal couple was impressed with the fantasy you created for them. Speaking of, what honeymoon suite did they spend their wedding night in?"

"The Shangri-la Paradise."

"Sounds romantic. I lucked out with the Wedding Knight Suite. All those bondage goodies to play with." The potential for fun was endless. *If* she could get Adam to play.

Laura smiled, looking quite pleased. "The Wedding Wing has a suite for every fantasy."

"So who came up with these ideas?"

"I did. My parents helped me conceptualize them, though, and you've met our architect, Dale Emerson. He and his company made everything a reality."

"Dale Emerson, your *date*."

She nodded and Tori noted a hint of color rise in her cheeks. "Yes, he's that, too."

"He's a lot more, from what I hear. I've got connections downtown, and I heard his firm pulled applications from the licensing department. Is he opening offices in town?"

Laura reached forward and turned the recorder off. She looked so serious that Tori's reporter's instincts went wild.

"If you want to discuss Dale," she said, "it'll have to be off the record. And I would like to know why you're interested in my personal life. You're covering the grand opening."

"But my slant is *you*, and what you're doing here. Tyler can go mainstream with his documentary, but I need to appeal to my readers. There's a local angle here that'll launch my story into the major leagues. I won't pass it up."

"Our family history."

"The Fords and the Grangers together for the first time since Westfalls. Not to mention a romance resort in town that our conservative grandfather has been curiously silent about."

"He's not *our* grandfather. He might technically be my mother's father, but I've never met the man. As far as *your* grandfather's concerned, I don't exist."

Tori considered that for a moment to decide on her line of questioning. The history between their families was as much a draw around here as erotic artist Mireille Marceaux was a mystery. Their family connection was another card in her hand that she could play to make her coverage something special, and since she intended to capitalize on this local angle, it wouldn't hurt to get Laura's read on the whole deal.

"I don't think that's entirely true," she said. "*Our* grandfather has acknowledged you."

"How?"

"By his silence."

Laura narrowed her crystal blue gaze. "The senator hasn't been silent. He made a statement a long time ago."

Tori shook her head. "The senator talked *around* you. He spouted stuff about supporting values of traditional couples and businesses that bring tourist dollars into our local economy. But that's not endorsing a romance resort. He didn't criticize it, either, and people noticed. I'm the municipal reporter in this town. I hear the gossip on my beat."

"The senator didn't attend Miranda's wedding," Laura pointed out. "I assumed that meant he didn't want people to mistakenly think he was in contact with a Granger."

"Grandfather didn't attend Miranda's wedding because the Senate got called into special session. He'd planned to come."

Laura set her cup on the table and sat back in her chair,

looking disbelieving. "Are you saying you think my in-
volvement here might have something to do with him not
taking a stand against the inn?"

"I think it's possible. Think about it, Laura. You might
be spinning sex from the romance angle, but you're still
spinning sex. There's a reason he's handling this inn the
way he is, and I think you're it."

Tori didn't give her a chance to think about the impli-
cations of that statement. She'd planted the seed and that
was enough for now. Hopefully, the seed would take root,
and Laura would want to talk some more about their family history. Until then, though, Tori had an opportunity to
steer the conversation in another direction.

"So tell me, if your *date* is pulling permits to open an
office in town, do I assume that means Falling Inn Bed has
worked its magic on you and Dale Emerson?"

Laura's careful expression melted away, and she got a
soft look in her eyes. "Dale says the magic's contagious,
and no one who walks through our doors is exempt. Not
our featured bridal couple. Not even the bedding consultant or the man who built the Wedding Wing."

"Contagious, hm? Now that's a theory I haven't heard
about."

But it was one that had promise. Tori could use all the
help she could get in her quest to get Adam to enjoy the
grand opening celebration. And when Laura waxed poetic
about marriage proposals on construction sites and falling
in love with her handsome architect, Tori thought she might
just stand a chance at helping the hunky assistant GM
catch some magic.

ADAM HADN'T STOPPED running since he'd opened his eyes
this morning, though Laura had left Sunday a free day in

their Naughty Nuptials schedule to give their newlyweds
a chance to rest after the excitement of the wedding day.
Guests had been checking out all morning, while the inn
staff had been regrouping for the week of Risqué Receptions events ahead.

Adam had been looking forward to working out and a
break from Tori Ford, but instead had found himself clev-
erly roped into giving her a tour of the hotel when he
caught up with her midmorning at Bruno's place.

In the time since he'd last seen her, Adam had mentally
reviewed all the reasons why he didn't want to involve himself with a woman who believed in fun for fun's sake, no
matter how much his body urged him otherwise. He believed this little exercise had done the trick.

That was, of course, until he'd set eyes on her in a sundress that left her shoulders bare and too much cleavage
swelling above the bodice. With red waves bouncing down
her back as she moved past the hostess station, Adam had
to admit that discipline wasn't holding up in the face of the
woman herself. Not when she caught sight of him, and her
expression lit up. His pulse took a huge leap in tempo.

Steeling his spine, he forced a smile and asked, "How
did your interview with Laura go?"

Slipping her arm through his, she moved close enough
to accelerate his pulse a few more beats. "Great, thanks,
but I'm stuffed. Remind me to stay out of this restaurant,
or your chef will do some serious damage. I don't want to
have to go shopping for bigger sized clothes."

Adam raked his gaze over her slim curves before he
could stop himself and gave a short laugh. Nothing but perfection there. "Never fear, Ms. Ford. The spa's cardiovas-
cular schedule runs seven days a week."

"Great minds and all that, Adam." She tipped her head

back to smile up at him and heaved a giant sigh that did amazing things to that swell of cleavage. "I'll bet we could burn off lots of calories together."

"Shall we go on a tour? Laura told me she took you through the Wedding Wing, but you haven't seen the main hotel yet. I'll be happy to show you."

She pursed her lips in an exasperated moue, and he was pleased to sidestep at least one indecent proposal today.

"Thank you," she said.

He directed her out onto the promenade. "I'm actually surprised Laura didn't tour you around the whole property when you first arrived."

"Oh, she offered, but I only let her show me the Wedding Wing. That's her cupcake, after all." Tori's big blue eyes sparkled. "But I'm dying to see the original hotel, though. My sister and her husband stayed in the Roman Bagnio on their wedding night and to hear Troy tell it, he'd have enjoyed spending a few more nights there before flying off to Hawaii for their honeymoon. Think you can arrange to tour me through any of the inn's original suites?"

Sure he could, but did he really want to be alone with her in suites with names like the Victorian Bordello, Sultan's Seraglio and Demimondaine's Boudoir?

No, yet he couldn't help but be impressed at how neatly she twisted the situation around to corner him. Strategy he could respect, even when it meant postponing his workout even longer.

The woman was clever, he'd definitely give her that.

"I haven't reviewed the audit reports yet, Ms. Ford, but we ran close to full occupancy last night. Seeing a suite might not be possible."

"Today's Sunday, and checkout was at noon. Surely some guests will have left by now. Can't you slip me in for a peek?"

"Housekeeping's scheduled after checkout."

With her arm still locked through his, she tugged him around so they were headed back in the direction of the front desk. "Just check, please. For me."

No wheedling, yet even so, Adam marveled at the way she managed to turn everything back around to what she wanted.

To be alone with him.

"I'll check." If only for a moment to put some distance between them and regain control of his pulse.

A trip behind the front desk almost did the trick until he found two suites recently vacated—the Red Light District and the Wild West Brothel. He considered claiming that none were available, but Adam wouldn't lie—not even to spare himself a visit with this woman to the Red Light District, complete with spotlight, stage and chair suitable for a sexy lap dance.

"We'll tour the Wild West Brothel."

With any luck, the historically themed furnishings would distract this woman from the overt sexuality of the suite.

Then again, Adam wouldn't get his hopes up. Not when Tori beamed at him across the counter and said, "Ride 'em, cowboy," then led him up to the fifth floor herself.

"You're familiar with the layout of the inn, I see," he said dryly when she brought him right to the door with the appropriate shiny gold nameplate.

She gave a casual shrug that drew his gaze yet again to the red waves spilling over her shoulders and the delicate curve of her throat. "Wouldn't be much of a reporter if I couldn't find my way around without help."

"No argument there." He'd never met a more determined woman and he still had the memory of her in that see-through robe burned in his brain to prove it. Withdrawing his master keycard, he inserted it into the mechanism, unlocked the door and stepped inside to hold the door for his curious reporter.

Tori smiled up at him as she walked past and said, "Was that a compliment or a criticism, Adam?"

"A compliment, of course." He injected some sincerity into his voice as the door shut with an absurd note of finality.

"Wouldn't do to criticize the reporter responsible for your reviews, hm?"

He didn't get a chance to reply before she came to an abrupt stop in the foyer and laughed. "Oh, my. Look at this place. This is as incredible as the Wedding Knight Suite. Not as elaborate, but, still, very impressive."

Stepping inside this suite always made Adam feel as if he were walking onto the set of a John Wayne western. A bar served as the dining area and a long mirror mounted with steer horns graced the wall above. Walls paneled in rustic wood bore vintage posters of lustful couples for a welcoming bunkhouse look.

All the furniture had been scaled in size for two, and the leather sex swing hanging from the ceiling was the focal point of the room. Adam knew the bedroom was set up with a wax warmer and specialty sheet set, so guests could engage in sexy branding.

Tori's observation skills were clearly on because there were indeed differences between this romance-themed suite, which had been fashioned to accommodate the original hotel structure, and those designed for the new Wedding Wing. Building from the ground up had given Laura and Dale the chance to create suites on a grand scale.

Creating fantasies, he'd heard Laura call it.

Which made Adam wonder—not for the first time—why he'd been so completely unprepared for the way sex affected the management around here. He'd researched Falling Inn Bed thoroughly before interviewing for the position. He'd seen all the press and had even toured the property. Yet he'd still not fully understood that the inn's sexy theme would change the requirements and attitudes for upper management.

In his mind, all properties had qualities targeting specific clienteles, but just because a hotel catered to an island vacation crowd didn't mean management worked in beachwear.

Maybe he'd just been too eager for a chance to become a stockholder in the Falling Inn Corporation. Or maybe he'd been so intent on leaving Seattle after his broken engagement that he hadn't paid close enough attention to what was really taking place at this inn.

And as he watched the sex-crazed reporter inspect the romance-themed suite, Adam couldn't help but think that his oversight in assessing the management—whatever the reason—was directly responsible for Tori Ford becoming the top item on his agenda.

"Did Laura design these suites, too?" she asked.

"Not to my knowledge. If memory serves, she came on the scene after Ms. J and her staff had acquired the property. Laura did tell me these suites inspired the ones in the Wedding Wing."

"Even bigger and better fantasies. Mm-mm." She took off into the bedroom, where he knew she'd find a bed with the Rope 'Em and Ride 'Em specialty sheets—complete with custom pockets filled with sex toys—and the bathroom that boasted a garden spa for couples.

Leaning against the bar, Adam passed on this part of the tour. No doubt Tori would use their close proximity to a bed to get a reaction from him, and he'd rather not give her another opportunity to play her game.

She didn't need his help. She was getting enough of a reaction by doing nothing more than crossing the room to peer out the windows that overlooked the forested park leading to the Falls. The noon sun threw her into sharp relief, and Adam imagined he could see the faint outline of her body through her sundress. The memory of all those luscious curves from yesterday's performance still burned too hot in his brain.

And then she scooted into the swing. The supple leather seat molded her shapely bottom as she started up another show…this time, one that prompted thoughts of what she'd feel like with her legs wrapped around him, weightless…

She pushed off, and her long bare legs stretched out as she rode backward in a smooth glide. Her body arced with the motion, her hair spilling out behind her, treating Adam to an image of what she might look like spread out horizontally for that calorie-burning exercise she'd mentioned earlier.

One of her sandals slipped off, clattering onto the wooden floor and drawing his gaze to the neatly manicured toes in some shade of ultrafeminine pink. She laughed, a carefree sound that contrasted sharply with the tension coiling tight inside him as his blood rushed hard in a direction in which it shouldn't be rushing.

"This is a wonderful suite. Sex swings and those sheets." She gave a low whistle. "I thought the set in my suite was wild. Have you ever played with restraints and warm wax, Adam?"

"No, Ms. Ford. I haven't."

She leaned back for another glide, this time arching her breasts high as the swing carried her backward. "Neither have I. Sounds like it might be fun." The innuendo was in there and being the bold woman she was, Tori glanced at him with a smile just to make sure he was watching.

Adam was watching, all right. And reacting.

He'd have to be dead not to react to this woman, and he was very alive, as was his libido, which he'd obviously ignored for way too long.

She must have recognized his struggle because she slipped out of the swing, collected her sandal and headed his way, all sultry smiles and sexy purpose.

Adam stood his ground, refusing any show of weakness, not even a simple step backward when she sauntered right up to him and took over his personal space.

Sliding her fingers around his tie, she loosened the knot with a few easy motions and said, "Don't you ever want to take a deep breath, Adam?"

"I can breathe just fine, Ms. Ford."

Lifting that midnight gaze, she searched his expression, a slight frown creasing her brow at what she found there. "Let me tell you a secret. My family comes with a lot of baggage. Not only our history with Laura's family, but a lot of visibility because my father and grandfather are politicians. It was all too easy to be sucked into trying to behave the way everyone expected me to behave."

"What are you saying, Ms. Ford?"

"That I was like you once, Adam." A soft smile touched her lips. "Surprise, surprise. I was all wrapped up in things that were keeping me from enjoying what was important in life."

This was insight he hadn't expected about her, and Adam wondered what had happened to make her turn that corner in her life. To transform from a woman of perfect decorum like her sister to this carefree spirit who only seemed focused on fun.

"You don't know me, Ms. Ford. It's presumptuous for you to think you know what I should find important in life."

"That's true. I don't know you. But I know what I see. You've got a celebration happening in a hotel filled with sexy suites and a woman you share some serious chemistry with. Yet you shut yourself off to the possibilities the instant you realized you were attracted to me."

To Adam's profound annoyance, he couldn't deny her claim, which left him to accept the hard reality. This woman had gotten under his skin no matter how much he had willed it otherwise.

3

AFTER THEIR BREAKFAST interview earlier, Laura Granger was about the last person Tori expected to see again when she appeared in the doorway of Falling Inn Bed's records room, dressed casually in jeans and sandals, with her long blond hair bound stylishly in a braid.

"Got a minute?" she asked, sounding tentative. "Adam told me he left you in here."

No doubt. After their tour of the main hotel, he'd brought her to this archive room and abandoned her here without a backward glance. She couldn't blame the guy, really. She'd obviously hit close to the bone, and there was a little part of her that felt downright guilty for pushing him so hard. Adam was right—she didn't know him. And she had no real idea why he was so determined to ignore their killer chemistry and all the unique possibilities of the Naughty Nuptials celebration.

Pushing herself up from the floor where she'd been searching through a filing cabinet that contained decades' worth of press releases from all the inn's various incarnations, she said, "Sure. I'm due a good stretch. What's up?"

Laura didn't answer, and Tori clasped her hands behind her back, stretching to ease muscles tight from crouching over that cabinet for too long.

She waited, wondering why Laura seemed nervous.

"Finding everything you need in here?" Laura asked.

Tori didn't think that was why she came, but nodded. "Since they sprang this assignment on me only a few days ago, I haven't had time to do my usual preliminary research on the inn's history."

"The history's important?"

"Helps me add color to my articles. Just another way to interest my readers." Cocking her hip against the table, she folded her arms across her chest. "So, are you here to interrogate me on my journalistic technique?"

Laura shook her head. "I've been thinking about our talk this morning and I wanted to ask you a question."

"Shoot."

"Did your mother ever tell you what started all the trouble between our families?"

Tori stifled a grin. She'd wanted to talk about what had led their grandfather to disown his eldest daughter and start a family rift, but she hadn't expected Laura to take the bait so quickly. "Not really. As the official nosy one in my family, I've tried picking her brain, but she just doesn't like to talk about what happened."

And she wasn't the only one. To Tori's knowledge her grandfather had never uttered one syllable about his eldest daughter, either, so the only thing she'd ever heard came by way of her sister, mostly gossip about how Laura's mother had run off with a hippie to live in a commune.

"How about you?" she asked. "What has your mother said?"

Laura perused a framed newspaper article on the wall, an early twentieth-century announcement from Tori's own paper about an upcoming slate of Christmas festivities. "Not much. She wanted to be an artist and open an artist retreat with my dad. The senator didn't approve and gave her a choice—my dad and her art, or her family."

"And she made her choice."

"She did."

"Two points for your mother for following her dreams." Tori could understand the need to break free. It seemed to be sort of a knee-jerk thing in her family. With the kind of pressure on everyone around the senator, one either complied or rebelled. While she'd been accused of a lot of things in her life, total compliance had never been one of them.

"So is she happy with her choice?" Tori asked.

"My mom and dad are the happiest couple I know."

"Which explains where your romantic streak comes from?"

Laura glanced over her shoulder. "I suppose. But following her dreams didn't come without a price."

There was subtext in that statement. Given what Tori remembered of their Westfalls years and how the Granger family had been ostracized by most of the town, she guessed that price had trickled down to Laura. "Your mom gets credit in my book. It must have taken guts to turn her back on everything."

Tori hadn't even managed to break away for college.

"My mom's got guts in spades, Tori. No doubt there."

"She must have, to give up her place in society."

"I don't think society was ever an issue. She's your typical artist, indifferent to social standing and all that. I think giving up her family was an issue, though."

"Really?" This was news. Tori always had the impression that everyone was content with the distance between the two families. At least, that was the way things seemed in the family mansion.

Laura turned back around and met Tori's gaze evenly.

"Something she said once has always stuck with me, and after talking with you this morning, I can't stop thinking about it."

"What'd she say?"

"That sometimes when someone dies, the people left behind are so hurt it's easier to drift apart rather than face the pain of their loss."

"Was she talking about our grandmother?"

Laura nodded.

"She died in that car accident when my mother was only six. I don't think she remembers much about her."

In fact, the only things Tori had ever heard about their grandmother had painted a picture of the perfect political wife and devoted parent whose tragic death had hit her family hard.

"What makes you think your mother had an issue with giving up her family?" Tori asked, curious.

"I was hoping you'd let me show you something."

"Laura, I'm here to cover the bedding consultant and her Naughty Nuptials. Remember?"

"Then let's go for broke." Laura reached for the radio affixed to her belt. "Come in, picture taker."

A few moments passed with the crackle of static between them before a male voice shot back, "Got a copy, bedding consultant. Go ahead."

"I need a ten-four."

"I'm soaking up the rays at your pool, babe."

Tori recognized Tyler Tripp's voice and listened to Laura sweet-talk him into leaving the pool to meet them in his room.

"Just wait," she said to Tori. "I promise what I have to show you will be worth the trip."

They caught up with Tyler on the third floor. He indeed

had come straight from the pool, with his surfer shorts and wet hair. Laura gave him a big hug and said, "I so appreciate this. I know I promised you a whole day off."

He flashed them a tolerant smile, his gaze raking lazily over Tori. "No rest for the wicked, babe. That's the nature of the game. Tori knows."

"Indeed." She raked an equally lazy gaze over Tyler.

Now here was a man who knew how to enjoy his life. Tanned. Buff. Gorgeous long hair she could wrap herself in. He was enjoying himself out at the pool on a sunny Sunday rather than holing up inside to work. His dark gaze spelled trouble, and the silver studs adorning his eyebrow and ears made her wonder if he had piercings in places she couldn't see without a research expedition into his surfer shorts.

His artistic mind had earned him the respect of the journalism community, and if he'd ever shown up on the doorstep of the family mansion, Rutger, her grandfather's butler, would have slammed shut the door and called security.

He was exactly the type of man Tori normally found herself attracted to—even better, because of their common interest in journalism—only this man didn't ignite even the teensiest spark.

No, everything she might have felt for this absolutely scrumptious man, she felt for the totally uptight and unsuitable assistant GM who wanted nothing to do with her.

Damn that chemistry, anyway. Maybe she should lay off Adam and reconcile herself to observing the magic instead of living it and writing a factual account of the Naughty Nuptials. Why should she care if the man chose to shrivel up inside that gorgeous body of his and ignore everything around her?

"Tyler's been pulling together his footage of the grand

opening events," Laura said. "I want him to show you something we came across the other night."

Tori followed her into a spacious suite that cornered the building on the third floor, a guest room comfortably furnished with living, dining and small kitchen areas sans the romance-themed grandeur of her own Wedding Knight Suite. Which just went to show that Laura had been serious about making her staff take good care of their local reporter. On the journalism food chain, Tori Ford was plankton compared to Tyler Tripp.

"So how's it going?" she asked him.

"It's going. I made a deal with myself to come back here every night and not sleep until I've transferred the day's footage. So far I'm on top of it."

"Good for you. My editor extended my daily deadline, but I'm still scrambling to write my article and post it on time."

"Nice spread today." Tyler moved into the office area that had been set up as a mini production studio, and Tori smiled. Considering the source, his words were high praise indeed. Now if she could just convince her managing editor…

"It won't be too difficult to find, will it?" Laura asked.

Tyler slung a pool towel over the back of a recliner. "No problem. We'll view it on my computer."

He booted his system, and the staccato beeps and blips ensued while they waited. When the monitor screen went live, Tyler sat down, opening programs and flipping through windows.

He forwarded through footage of what Tori recognized as the Racy Rehearsal Dinner event that had taken place on the night before the wedding, and when Laura cued him, he began clicking the images forward frame by frame. "Here you go."

Tori glanced at a table and recognized the people seated there. Her family. Her parents. Her sister and brother-in-law.

As the featured couple for the upcoming Hottest Honeymoon week, Miranda and Troy had been participating in all the festivities. When Laura's mother had been invited to the rehearsal dinner for a look at the Mireille Marceaux painting she'd helped arrange the loan of, Miranda had insisted her parents be invited as a show of force against the Grangers.

As a result, there'd been Fords and Grangers together in the same room for the first time in years. Tori had been able to slant this society bit for her feature. Successfully, too, as she'd been pleased to learn from her managing editor, even if Adam Grant had called her tactics sensationalism.

Damn man. Maybe he really was a hopeless case and she should just give up.

Tori scowled at the monitor, watching as the camera zoomed in on her mother, looking as beautiful as always. But the look on her face was one Tori hadn't seen before, an unguarded look that would have been fleeting without Tyler to play it out frame by frame. That look arced through a lot of emotions...all painful, all captured on film in aching clarity.

Then the angle of the camera shifted and panned in on Laura's mother.

Occasionally during her school years at Westfalls, Tori had seen Suzanne Granger in the business offices where the woman had worked as chief financial officer. Her wavy brown hair might be different than her own mother's red, but the similarities between the sisters were striking. Not only their features, but their expressions.

Tori didn't have to ask to know that these long-alienated sisters had been looking at each other across that crowded ballroom when this footage had been filmed.

"Why are you showing me this?" she asked.

"Because of what you said at breakfast. I think you're right. What happened between our moms isn't cut-and-dried."

Tyler slid his chair back. "If you don't need me anymore, ladies, I'll head back to the pool. Clyde promised to ply me with some serious alcohol so I don't notice the heat."

"Have him whip you up a Rum Demon. You'll forget your name." Laura tugged his ponytail. "Go have fun. I'll lock up."

He didn't need to be told twice. This man understood the importance of fun and, grabbing his towel, he took off, leaving Tori and Laura alone.

Dropping onto the arm of a recliner, Tori stared at the monitor where Suzanne Granger's hauntingly familiar face stared back. "Okay, Laura. I agree things aren't cut-and-dried between our mothers."

"I want to find out what happened and see if we can fix things. Doesn't seeing them like this make you sad?"

Sad was only part of it. Frustrated that her mother ran herself ragged being the perfect society woman was the other part. "It makes me wonder."

"About what happened to break them up?"

"About your sanity. We already know what broke up this family. Your mother ran off to a commune with an artist."

Laura shook her head. "That's what happened between my mom and the senator. Not what happened between our moms."

Tori thought about that for a moment and knew Laura was right. Their grandfather had disowned his eldest daughter, but that didn't explain why *her* mother hadn't made peace with her sister in the thirty years since. Then again, Tori knew her mother wasn't much for going against the senator.

Another side effect of trying to lead the perfect life.

"Are you looking for some big family reunion?" she asked. "If you are, you obviously don't know much about my family." They didn't have reunions, not even with family members they haven't been disowned.

"If a reunion's possible, why not?"

"Man, you really do deal in fantasy around here."

"Falling Inn Bed specializes in love, Tori. Why does that have to be only the romantic kind? You said it yourself—we've got the Grangers and the Prescotts together for the first time since Westfalls. I'd hate to miss an opportunity to fix things." She gave a wry smile. "For our moms. Personally, I'm content to live my life without you or your sister."

She couldn't help but smile. Had their circumstances been different growing up, she might have liked Laura Granger. As it was, she could only wonder if the time had come to bridge that distance, and if she would be the right person for the job.

She returned to Suzanne Granger's face staring at her from the monitor, a striking reminder of the way the past influenced the future, and proof that people could live the lives they dreamed of.

But not without a price.

There was always a catch, but when Tori thought of the expression on her own mother's face, she knew her mother had paid no less a price to remain home and live up to the family standards.

Tori had paid that price once, too, and had decided it was too high. Only unlike her estranged aunt, she hadn't been disowned.

Yet.

"How do you expect to do this, Laura?" she asked. "Our

mothers haven't made an effort to do anything about this situation for thirty years, so don't give me any sappy crap about it being easy to reunite sisters who miss each other. Unlike you, I wasn't kidnapped from the fold and raised by wolves. I'm a Prescott-Ford, and we don't deal in fantasies. Just cold, hard facts."

"I've got a few ideas." Laura folded her arms across her chest and eyed her with a twinkling gaze. "But since I only know half the story, I need someone from the other team to help me fill in the blanks and pull this all together."

Was it worth a shot? Should she go out on a limb to try and wipe that expression from her mother's face, or should she give up on her family the way she was about to give up on Adam Grant.

Tori gazed at this cousin she'd never known, a woman who was proving to be nothing at all like expected, and she realized that Laura was right about something else, too.

Tori only had one half of the story.

Not only about her family, but about Adam, too. Maybe he wasn't so hopeless after all….

"Okay, bedding consultant. I'll join your team. *If* you agree to join mine."

Laura eyed her curiously. "What do you have in mind?"

Tori inhaled a deep breath and went for it. "I could use a little help catching a man."

BETWEEN A HARD workout and a long visit to the Turkish steam room, Adam's attempt to exorcise visions of Tori Ford in a sex swing had consumed most of his Sunday afternoon off. He arrived at his massage appointment sore and in need of relief.

"Sandra's running behind," the spa host told him. "Just go in and make yourself comfortable. She won't be long."

With a nod, Adam stepped inside a private room, where the sound of ocean surf piped in through overhead speakers and the tranquil lighting combined to lull his drowsy senses. He'd sat in the Turkish steam room so long he could practically feel eucalyptus seeping from his pores, but the visit did exactly what he'd hoped—slowed his racing thoughts about the woman in hot pursuit.

He'd been racking his brain to come up with a new game plan for dealing with Tori Ford. Simply stating his disinterest should have been enough. And for any rational woman, a polite rejection *would* have been.

Rationality didn't seem to be part of Tori's equation. Today, she'd revealed herself to be a woman on a mission, and he couldn't stop wondering what had happened to commit her so firmly to her cause. Under normal circumstances, savoring life would have been an admirable goal, but these weren't normal circumstances. They were together during a function that celebrated sex, and Tori was no ordinary woman.

And when Adam got down to it, he really didn't want to know. She had him totally preoccupied as it was, dodging her moves by day and being too edgy to sleep by night.

He wanted to stop thinking about her.

His long workout this afternoon should have cleared his head. Long workouts and frequent massages were about the only indulgences he'd allowed himself since coming to Falling Inn Bed, and Breakfast. With friends and acquaintances back on the West Coast, Adam hadn't done much but work since his arrival in Niagara Falls. The focus had suited his mood. Or at least it had until now.

To his relief, though, as soon as he lay down and pulled a towel over him, the effect of his recent sleepless nights began to take effect. Drowsiness edged out visions of the attractive redhead he didn't want to think about.

He must have dozed because he had no idea how much time had passed before Sandra's voice intruded.

"I'm so sorry I took so long. Just go back to sleep. We're fine on time." Her fingers, slick and warm with oil, sank into the tight muscles of his neck and shoulders.

He grunted, too sleepy to open his eyes, and Sandra must have recognized his pitiful condition because she took mercy on him. Instead of her usual deep muscle massage, she worked him over with a gentle kneading that let sleep crowd his brain.

He dropped off again to the steady glide of her hands on his skin. Long pleasant moments of unconsciousness when he was aware of nothing but her strokes easing the tension from along his spine, his lower back, his butt, his thighs. Yet images of red waves spilling over creamy curves lingered in his mind, creeping in when his guard went down.

This drugged half sleep presented the perfect opportunity for Tori Ford to accomplish her objective—forcing him to give in to their potent chemistry. He was aware of her in a way he'd never been aware of any woman before. Not even his ex-fiancée. Tori had a power over him that he didn't understand as he lay here with visions of her heightening his senses, memories of her flashing gaze and quick smiles.

He found a much-needed distraction when Sandra paused to pour more oil. She warmed it in her palms before pulling her hands down his thighs in long strokes. Her light touch affected him in a way her more aggressive massages never did, and thoughts of another woman's hands lingered in his drowsy imagination. Forbidden thoughts about how *her* hands would feel on him. And all he had to do was stop resisting to find out if the reality would come close to the fantasy.

Adam guessed it would, which is why that stubborn voice reminded him to resist. Giving into that bold redhead would be playing with fire. Tori Ford was far from the solid, focused type of woman who respected what it took to successfully mix business with pleasure. And that was the kind of woman he wanted in his life, one with common goals and interests, not some fly-by-night wild child who wanted fun to be the be-all and end-all of her existence.

His ex-fiancée had already shown him that even a woman who seemed perfect might not be. Adam would be a lot more cautious the next time around.

And what was going on with his feet? He couldn't ever remember Sandra paying such careful attention to that part of his body before. Not that he was complaining. Not when she rolled his foot in slow circles, massaged his insteps and worked each toe for so long that warmth radiated up his leg….

Adam must have dozed again because when he awoke, she'd returned to his thighs, and damned if she hadn't awakened another part of his body, too. Those steady strokes rerouted his blood flow to a region that had no business waking up right now.

With a mild sense of disbelief, he willed away the sensation. He'd locked onto Sandra's services not long after his arrival in town and had been directly responsible for getting her the position as head massage therapist in the Wedding Wing's new spa. Not once in all the months she'd been providing her services had Adam ever become aroused.

But there it was, a familiar—and unwelcome—feeling rushing to his crotch, a precursor to an erection. Good thing he was lying on his stomach or he'd have been royally embarrassed.

This was Tori Ford's fault. If not for her relentless pursuit, he wouldn't have had sex on the brain when his defenses were down. And he didn't stand a chance of containing his arousal when slick fingers dipped between his thighs, a light touch that somehow teased and tempted.

It had been *way* too long since he'd had sex.

Exhaling heavily, he gave in to the inevitable and forced open his eyes. "Let's cut this short today, Sandra."

When she didn't reply or even slow down, Adam got his first clue that something wasn't right.

"Sandra?"

Still no reply, just that constant kneading into places more intimate than she'd ever gone before. And that was when he realized something else his drugged brain hadn't caught before.

Her hands were smaller, which explained the lightweight massage.

For someone who'd been lulled into a near coma, Adam's reflexes were dead-on when he twisted around to grab a slender wrist...and found himself facing a redheaded troublemaker.

"Having fun back there, Ms. Ford?" he asked, sounding a lot more in control than he felt.

With an iron grip on her wrist, he forced her to stop those teasing strokes and dragged her around to face him.

Not even the dim lighting concealed the flash of challenge in her eyes. "Yes, as a matter of fact, I was." She gave a tug to break his grip, but he didn't let go. "You've got nice biscuits. I'm in trouble now. You're going to haunt my dreams."

"I'm the one in trouble."

Her smile widened. "Why don't you just let go, Adam.

You're attracted to me and I'm attracted to you. We can have a good time together."

"You're a guest in my hotel."

Impulse demanded he get off this table and out of reach, but he swung around and sat up instead. His nakedness was her problem, not his. And as she'd been the one massaging him to near arousal…she could deal with the sight of *that*, too.

But Tori was ready for him. Starting her gaze at his feet, she worked her way up his body. The gleam in those midnight eyes grew brighter along the way.

"What part of 'no' don't you understand?" he asked.

"The part about why you're using the word. You seem to be enjoying yourself." She gazed pointedly at his crotch. "I want to understand why you stopped me."

"You mean aside from the fact that I thought you were my usual massage therapist having a very unusual effect on me?"

She nodded. "Am I moving too fast, Adam? Will it help if I slow down?"

"I don't mix business with pleasure, Ms. Ford."

She pursed her lips in a pouty expression that dragged his gaze from her flashing eyes to that delightful mouth. The urge to drag her into his arms and kiss those lips was so strong that only stubbornness saved him.

"What do you do for pleasure, Adam?"

He wondered what had prompted the change in tactics, but he wouldn't buy into her game. He'd already delineated the boundaries and wouldn't back down now just because his crotch throbbed and he wanted her to ease the ache she'd created.

She stood barely a foot away, and he noticed for the first time she wore sweatpants and a ribbed T-shirt that clung to her curves, leaving nothing to the imagination. She'd pulled her hair back in a ponytail, giving him a clean shot of her face.

She smiled, an invitation.

His pulse hammered harder.

Twisting her hand, she ran her fingers over his, drawing his attention to the way her skin still glistened with oil, reminding him of the way she'd touched him.

Adam was *definitely* in trouble here.

He hadn't been able to stop thinking about her. Now he could add the feel of her delicate hands on his skin, dipping between his thighs, toying with his toes. The room seemed to shrink to the size of a broom closet. Her breasts rose and fell with shallow breaths that suggested she felt their closeness as much as he did. His own reactions flared out of control, and he struggled even harder not to give her a reaction.

Except for the one raging between his thighs.

And that one pretty much said everything.

Had Adam been thinking clearly, he would have recognized his vulnerability with this woman so close, her expression challenging him to give in. But he wasn't thinking clearly. If he had been, he would have restrained both Tori's hands.

She made her move in the blink of an eye, her hand snaking out, oiled fingers zeroing in on his erection with lethal accuracy. His whole body shuddered with the power of impact and he choked on a hard breath as she glided those fingers upward with a silken stroke, smiling as he swelled in her hand, his greedy erection making a lie of his indifference.

"If I thought for one second that you didn't want me, Adam, I'd move on. But you not only want me, you need me."

"How's that?" He actually got the words out. Good for him.

Another light stroke.

Another shudder.

"You need me to help you lighten up and have a good time," she said matter-of-factly. "You're in the middle of one of the most unusual promotional campaigns ever and instead of enjoying yourself, you're so fixated on work that you're ignoring this amazing attraction we have."

"My choice." A growl.

"I know, but why? Life's way too short. Do you know I've never seen you smile? Not once. Isn't your Naughty Nuptials all about having fun? That's what Laura told me. Sex is a wonderful way to have fun."

Some part of his brain—the part that wasn't caught up in the feel of her fingers stroking him—recognized Laura's name and the fact that Tori couldn't have pulled off this quick switch without help. *A lot* of help. He hadn't mistaken Sandra's voice earlier.

Catching her wrist, Adam forced her hand away. "I don't mix business with pleasure. And I don't indulge in casual affairs."

She stopped resisting his grip and extended her fingers in a gesture of truce. "Okay, now we're getting somewhere."

He wasn't sure where she thought they were getting, but he released her anyway and braced his hands on the edges of the table. He didn't trust her, but he didn't want her to know that. He needed control right now, even the illusion of it.

And he couldn't think when he touched her.

Backing away, Tori cocked a hand on her hip and stared at him as if seeing him suddenly in a new light. "Talk to me, Adam. Help me understand why you're so determined to blow off what we have here. Here we are in a hotel for lovers. A full slate of events for couples. I know you're not dating anyone—"

"How do you know that?"

She gave a haughty sniff. "Okay, I know you think I'm only interested in one thing from you, and while I'm definitely interested in *that*—" she let her words trail off and her gaze drop to his lap again "—I want to understand you, so I interrogated some of the staff. They were very informative."

Adam would just bet. He was well aware of some of the stunts his co-workers pulled to keep the inn living up to its name. They usually yielded a light touch with their guests. Subtle things like having housekeeping place complimentary sex toys in the suites. Menus of aphrodisiac-spiced foods to get couples thinking about all the sex they could be having in those romance-themed suites.

There were not-so-subtle stunts as well. Adam had seen one of his co-workers get downright Machiavellian. Just last week, Annabelle, the sales director, had point-blank lied to a guest, frightening the woman into near hysterics just to chase her off the property to bring Laura and the woman's abandoned date, the Wedding Wing's architect, together.

Given his co-workers' opinions of his type A qualities, which weren't far off from Tori's, Adam guessed they'd had a field day filling her in about his personal life, or lack thereof. If he hadn't known better, he'd have accused them of arranging the departure of the original reporter assigned to the Naughty Nuptials just so fun-loving Tori would have to fill in.

Now that he thought about it, Adam *didn't* know better.

"Just tell me you're not attracted to me, Adam, and I'll back off. No problem."

"We both know that would be a lie."

"Then give me something to work with here, something I can understand. Do you have a girlfriend in another city? I'll certainly respect that."

Here again he had a chance to make his life easier. One lie would end her pursuit. He didn't doubt that she meant what she'd said, and for some reason that surprised him. Why? Because he'd assumed her boldness implied a lack of character?

Adam didn't stop to contemplate the answer. Nor did he lie, not even to chase off this woman. "I don't usually serve up my personal life at work."

"Do you have a personal life? I haven't seen evidence of one."

"You've only been on the property a few days."

"Neither has anyone else. I told you, I've been talking to people. That's my job and I happen to be good at it. No one around here knows anything at all about your personal life, and you've been working here *ten months*. Consensus seems to be that all you do is work, work, work."

He didn't intend to explain himself, and Tori apparently recognized his silence as her answer.

"You're a mystery," she said with a wry laugh. "I'll give you that."

"Why? Because I haven't accepted your invitation?"

"That, and because you're really convinced that you're content working your life away." She smiled, a soft expression, almost wistful. "I'm sure you have a very compelling reason, but you choose not to share it. I just gave you the perfect opportunity to send me packing. Yet you chose not to. I think you have a noble streak."

A *stupid* streak more aptly described it.

"Just because I'm attracted to a woman doesn't mean I have to act on how I feel. I'm in control of my actions."

"Implying that the converse applies to me, I suppose."

He shrugged. If the shoe fits...not that he'd point that out. His job was to run interference here. The inn wanted good reviews, after all. Tori had generously backed away before he could catch another whiff of her hair, which smelled fresh and vaguely fruity today....

"I'm heading for the showers, Ms. Ford. My time here is up."

Sliding off the table, Adam forced her to take yet another step back when he reached for his robe. He could feel the heat of her gaze as he pulled it on, knew she'd be smiling. He didn't glance back as he made his way to the men's locker room.

Of course she followed.

"How does a man with such a stiff neck wind up in a position of power at an inn that specializes in sex?" she asked.

"Do I consider this my official interview?"

She caught up so he had no choice but to hold the door for her as he exited the massage therapy center.

"Thank you," she said. "I'm not going to interview you. No point. I'll just pick your brain when we're together."

Great. A two-week long interrogation so she could catch him off guard. "A romance resort is different than a hotel that specializes in sex."

"That's not what I heard from your bedding consultant."

"I suppose my bedding consultant is the one responsible for sharing my itinerary today?"

She smiled. "What do you have against having fun, Adam?"

"Nothing. But how I choose to have fun is my personal business, and I don't get personal at work."

Although he'd seen a couple combine home and work successfully, he was still reluctant. When two people shared life together 24/7, they'd better be on the same page because there was no place to hide. He'd already made the mistake. Once was enough.

"That philosophy seems a little out of line with the way the staff operates around here. Did you know that when you accepted your position?"

"Not entirely," he admitted, playing her game until he could shake her off in the locker room. "I researched the inn before interviewing for the position, of course, but I didn't fully appreciate the staff's mentality toward romance."

"Yet you accepted the position. Did that have anything to do with the possibility of becoming a stockholder in Falling Inn Properties? I've researched the financials of this hotel, and it's no secret that your managers are all stockholders."

"Yes, it did." A half truth, because getting out of Seattle with its daily reminders of his broken engagement had factored, too. "The possibility for advancement moves me one step closer to my career goals."

"Which are?"

"Becoming a property owner without assuming all the risk, Ms. Ford. And I also found the opportunity to work for Mary Johnson compelling. She's well respected in the industry."

"Given what you've learned about this place over the past ten months, have you found the job to be a good fit?"

Leave it to a reporter to zero in on the heart of matters. "My job performance has been satisfactory."

"That's not what I asked—"

"Well, here we are. I'm going to have to cut our unofficial interview short." He pushed open the door marked Men's Locker Room and smiled cordially. "You enjoy the rest of your day off, Ms. Ford. I'll be by to pick you up in the morning for our stint in the kitchen with Bruno."

"Chefs de Carnal Cuisine." She frowned. "I better not eat anything. I'd hate to explore aphrodisiacs in food preparation when I'm stuck with an escort who can't stand the sight of me."

Now it was Adam's turn to frown. Why couldn't he get through to this woman? He needed to, *before* he alienated her completely and earned Naughty Nuptials lousy reviews.

And he needed to get a move on because Laura's schedule had them hosting events designed to take guests behind the scenes of party planning. The days would be filled with the Tempting Tango, which would bring them together to explore ballroom dance instruction, and Appealing Performances that would transform a ballroom into an upscale nightclub with a stage for karaoke.

At midweek, they'd host a party to send off the featured bridal couple on their official honeymoon and make way for the Hottest Honeymoon couple to step into the spotlight.

"I'm sure we'll find some common ground." He *hoped.* "Now good day, Ms. Ford."

Then he escaped into the locker room.

Sucking in a breath of steamy air, Adam retrieved his locker key from his pocket and headed for the showers. He let the hot water pound away the last of the raw effects of Tori's latest stunt while he decided what his next move would be.

Talk to Laura, definitely. He didn't have to ask if she'd helped coordinate today's ambush. Or gotten Sandra involved.

"I'm with the press, guys," said a familiar voice.

Brushing aside the curtain, Adam found Tori strolling into the shower room, holding up a tape recorder. "No photos, but I need some feedback about this place for the record. Anyone interested?"

Rings slid across shower rods as curtains opened and heads popped out to find a beautiful redhead in clingy sweats, boldly standing exactly where she shouldn't have been.

Of course, every guy in the place clamored to be interviewed. They emerged from the stalls, showing the effects of hasty rinsing. Surrounded by wet men, Tori Ford looked like a kid in a candy shop. She caught his gaze and winked.

She was savoring the moment, he supposed.

Adam returned to his shower, but the hot water had lost its appeal now that he'd witnessed men tripping over themselves to impress her.

After drying off, he wrapped the towel around his waist and stepped into the scene of chaos. Tori raked her gaze over him, a slow, hungry perusal that made him appreciate the towel.

"Where are you off to, Adam?" she strode right up to him, holding her recorder out between them. "Guys, don't you think the assistant GM should give me a few words, too?"

A chorus of assent echoed through the tiled room, but when she came to a stop in front of him, Adam said, "No comment."

"Why won't you talk to me, Mr. Grant?"

"You're outrageous, Ms. Ford."

She flashed a smile that made him tighten his grip on his towel. "I'm just not afraid of putting forth the effort it takes to get what I want."

She didn't have to say another word because her implication came through loud and clear.

I want you.

4

TORI PEERED INSIDE the open doorway of Laura's office, surprised and relieved to have tracked her cousin down so easily. "I don't believe you're working at this time of night."

Laura sat behind her desk, and she glanced up from a stack of papers and motioned Tori to come in.

"So what happened to all work and no play making the bedding consultant a dull gal?" Tori asked with a casualness she wasn't remotely feeling.

"I've been playing *a lot* during this grand opening. I've got to work sometime."

Stepping inside, she decided the office-chic furniture would have been too professionally generic if not for the eye-catching artwork that lent the office personality. She glanced at the striking art above the sofa, dawn breaking over a river in sharp angles and violent color.

Not your run-of-the-mill office print. "That's a sunrise, right?"

Laura nodded. "The view from a guest room at my parents' house. The artist stays at their retreat every summer."

The Niagara River Artist Retreat. Tori knew all about the Grangers' art colony, a family business that epitomized the differences between Laura's avant-garde relations and her own ultra-conservative ones. A business that offered a glimpse into why the bedding consultant might have chosen hospitality as a career.

"I wanted to let you know that our plan didn't work and Adam's probably coming after you," she said. "He guessed that you helped smuggle me into the spa."

"Been there, done that." Laura lowered a stack of papers to the desk and sat back in her chair.

"You already talked to him?"

She nodded.

"Wow, he moved fast." Tori supposed that shouldn't surprise her. Just because he'd chosen not to move fast in her direction didn't mean he couldn't move fast. Suddenly feeling too antsy to sit, she ignored the chairs in front of the desk and checked out the étagère instead. "Did you weasel your way out of trouble?"

"Of course. He knows I'm committed to helping him enjoy the grand opening."

"Poor guy must feel like he's in hell."

"No doubt, but I haven't lost hope yet." Laura eyed her evenly. "I don't think you should, either."

"I was with him, remember? I didn't gain any ground today."

"I beg to differ. He paid me a visit, too, and from what I saw, I think you gained a lot."

"How do you figure?"

"He's struggling." Laura sounded decided. "My guess is he can barely control himself around you. That's a good thing."

"You're dreaming, Laura. He isn't struggling with anything except how to shake me and not ruin your chances for a decent review. Tight-assed man."

"A nice tight ass is a good thing."

"Ha, ha." Adam's ass might be nice and tight—and Tori

knew that for sure—but Laura's efforts to make her feel better were wasted. She didn't want to feel better. Not after she'd been so completely rebuffed by a man whose restraint was nothing short of superhuman. Pride demanded she stop chasing him, but pride didn't have much to do with her attraction to Adam.

She'd barely been able to look at his gorgeously naked self without getting weak in the knees—a humiliating reaction when he stubbornly resisted all attempts to get him to have fun.

"I'm serious, Tori."

"You're just trying to make me feel better so I'll help you with your family reunion plan."

Laura laughed. "Well, I do still want your help, but I'm being honest about Adam. I've worked on him for a while and I've never seen him so ruffled. He's on the edge."

Tori gave an exasperated huff, still unwilling to accept Laura's reassurances or get her hopes up. Instead, she distracted herself. "Where was this picture taken?" Reaching for a framed photograph, she inspected a younger Laura in a cap and gown, surrounded by a group of people.

"At my house after my high school graduation."

The sun-drenched forest created a lush backdrop, but what struck Tori the most was how ideally the photographer had captured the mood of the group, caught more than warm glances and laughing smiles on film. There was something carefree about the way these folks had banded together around Laura and her folks, as if everyone had simply been happy to be together.

"I recognize your parents, but who are the others?"

"Pseudofamily. Resident artists."

"Really? They look like close friends."

"Most of them are. We have artists who visit every year and have since my parents opened the retreat."

Glancing up, she found Laura smiling at her thoughtfully.

"I've got an idea, Tori."

"Another one? Maybe I'm in hell now."

Laura only leaned back in her chair and steepled her hands. "You need to up the stakes. Send Adam a gift, something that will show him you don't plan to back down."

"A gift? I don't think anything from your sex toy store will do the trick."

"Agreed. It needs to be personal. Something artsy. A photograph, or maybe a sculpture."

Tori set the frame back on the étagère. There was no missing this maneuver and she was impressed with Laura's ingenuity. "And just who do you have in mind to make this artsy gift?"

"My parents."

"Why am I not surprised?"

"They're perfect, trust me. All we do is tell them you're trying to catch a man and they'll drop everything to help."

Lifting a figurine off the shelf, she inspected the tiny winged fairy that seemed as whimsical as this conversation. "Your father's the sculptor, right? So how long does it take him to sculpt something?"

"Depends on the medium. Body casting can take months, but for something like you'll need he can work in clay and it will only take a day or two. You won't have to pose, either. We'll get my mom to photograph you, and he can whip up something from that. Something *sexy*."

Tori liked the idea of a sexy gift, but…visit her estranged aunt and uncle for the first time for a round of boudoir photography? Sounded like a bit much even for someone who'd made a career of pushing the limits. "And your parents won't think this is strange?"

"Please." Laura scoffed. "Think who you're talking about here. My parents think love rules the world."

She had a point. Laura's mother had abandoned her family and the security of wealth to run off with the man she loved. "This is a ploy to get me to meet your parents, and start up the family reunion thing. So now I know— ruthless manipulation is a genetic thing."

"Must be. Will you come?"

"I'll be evicted from *my* family if I cross enemy lines."

"I won't tell. And think about Adam. He's on the edge."

Tori wasn't so sure about that, but when she thought about their encounter in the spa earlier…the way his toned muscles felt beneath her hands, the way his body had re-acted to her touch, she wasn't ready to give up the fight just yet. Even if it meant enduring a little more humiliation.

Setting the fairy back on the shelf, she crossed the room and cocked a hip against the desk. "Strictly speaking, your parents raised the little romantic who conceptualized the Wedding Wing I just happen to be covering. I could jus-tify a visit as work."

How could she pass up the chance to push Adam over the edge?

RISQUÉ RECEPTIONS. In spite of the provocative title and his persistent escort for the event, Adam was more enthusiastic about week two of Naughty Nuptials than he'd been about week one. The blatantly sexual Sex Toy Shower and Bad Bachelor/ette Parties were over and, start-ing today, the grand opening would explore the world of careful party preparation. The first event on the agenda— *Chefs de Carnal Cuisine*—offered guests a rare glimpse into Bruno's kitchen to learn about aphrodisiacs in food preparation.

Adam glanced around the kitchen at the guests who had paired off at various prep tables. The bridal couple, their parents and many of their attendants had taken over half the kitchen, conveniently separating Laura and Dale from Tori's sister and brother-in-law.

"Hungry?"

That one word was laden with so much innuendo Adam wasn't surprised when he glanced down to find Tori smiling as she wrapped an apron round her waist.

"No." Not for anything he'd admit to, anyway.

He hadn't been able to stop replaying the memory of her hands on him, and as a result, his senses were heightened enough that just watching her tuck up stray wisps of hair became something of a performance.

"This is right up my alley," she said with an enthusiasm that gave *him* the urge to smile. "Some good hands-on fun. Do we know what's on the menu yet?"

"Not a clue," he said. "Bruno insisted on secrecy. To my knowledge Ms. J is the only person who knows what's happening today and only because he had to get approval."

Excitement lit up Tori's beautiful face as she glanced around the kitchen. Immaculate at the busiest of times, the kitchen had been buffed and polished until every piece of chrome shone beneath the overhead lights. Midday on a Monday wasn't the busiest of times, even in season during the grand opening, so the guests not participating in Bruno's lesson had been redirected to the spa café for the meal, where cooking assistants were altering the menu to accommodate both traditional and health-conscious diners.

Tori had picked a prep table in the middle of the kitchen for them, presumably so she could view the proceedings from all angles. Yet Adam couldn't help but notice that their table was clear across the room from her sister and brother-in-law.

He glanced at the dark-haired Miranda Knight and realized he hadn't seen these two interact much. Were they close? Adam couldn't say, and that lack of understanding made him consider that he might be handling the situation with Tori all wrong. She'd been making an effort to get to know him. Perhaps he should switch tactics, too. If he made an effort to understand what motivated her, he could figure out a way to deter her interest in him. It might be worth a shot.

"I hope you made the most of your day off," Dale said to him from a nearby table. "Laura hit the ground running this morning. She's going to kill us with these events before this grand opening is over."

While Adam's mood toward Laura was up in the air after her collusion with Tori, he genuinely liked Dale Emerson, who'd been on the property building the Wedding Wing when Adam had arrived.

"But erotic events, Dale? What a way to go." Tori gave a laugh before turning to her photographer to direct him to shots of the kitchen from various angles.

She wasn't the only one documenting the event on film, either. Tyler had positioned video cameras around the room. Tori's photographer continued to wander through the tables, aiming his camera at the door when Bruno swept inside.

"Welcome to *Chefs de Carnal Cuisine,* everyone," he said. "Good, most of you have paired off already. That's how we like to do things at Falling Inn Bed, in pairs."

"The best way," Tori whispered under her breath.

"We need everyone to share that sentiment to enjoy today's lesson on cooking to feed the libido."

Bruno detailed what the next few hours would bring and informed them all their preparations today would grace the menu as this evening's specials. This was a brave move as far as Adam was concerned, since it was Bruno's reputation on the line. Then again, the chef was another of the "savor life to the fullest" crowd. No doubt he operated under the no risk, no reward delusion that everyone else had adopted around here.

"We'll cook in shifts," he explained as he assigned recipes to the various couples. As two dozen guests were participating in this event, he split them into groups. "One of the essentials to preparing successful dishes is timing. While our bouillabaisse team prepares their broth at the range, our truffles group will prepare their chocolate, butter and nuts. Our sherbet team will work with the food processors to concoct cream of violets from my own grandmother's special recipe."

Bruno was nothing if not melodramatic, and while sometimes his drama in the kitchen during a dinner rush could lean toward mania, it suited today's event to a *T*. He engaged his guests in the unusual activity and caught them up in the excitement.

Tori, too, jumped in feetfirst. They'd been assigned violet sherbet, a dish to cleanse the palate between the bouillabaisse entrée and the chocolate truffle dessert.

She sidled up close, her hip brushing against him, her fingers grazing his as she helped him handle his flower petals.

"Bruno said to bruise them, to release their essence, like this." Her fingers slipped over his and she guided him with a light touch, a soft pulsing motion that didn't seem so innocent with skin touching skin. "You've got strong, masculine hands, so it's easy for you to crush them, but you want to be gentle."

Her whisper was both full-bodied and low, a sexual sound that made him imagine how he might touch her, despite the couples working around them and the man who walked between the prep tables supervising the preparations.

Adam had known it was coming. He hadn't known what Tori had planned for him today, but he'd known without a doubt that she would pick up where she'd left off yesterday, tempting and teasing him until she got another reaction.

"But not too gentle." She breathed those words in a soft burst of sound that rippled through him like the hot afternoon sun. "You want to handle these petals like you might touch a woman. You want to feel her respond."

He was responding, and an erection suddenly loomed in his immediate future. Gratefully, the apron covered him to the knees but proved no help at all for figuring out some way to get her to knock off this game.

Her pursuit had symmetry; he'd give her that. She'd greeted him in a transparent robe to give him an image that would haunt him. She'd pretended to be his massage therapist so he'd remember the feel of her hands on his skin. Now she talked suggestively in that warm silky voice, making him imagine the ways she'd respond to his touch.

And he had no one to blame but himself. He'd had a chance to end her pursuit, yet he'd chosen integrity above self-preservation. Perhaps he'd overestimated its importance. Especially when faced with a dilemma that was proving to be even bigger than him—his desire for this woman.

"Cooking with aphrodisiacs isn't a new fad by any stretch," Bruno said when he stopped by their table to inspect their work.

Tori still worked his hand with that suggestive pulsing motion, leaving Adam to uncomfortably disengage beneath Bruno's knowing smile.

"Many foods throughout history have been touted as enhancing the libido. Take chocolate, for example." He motioned to where Laura and Dale currently chopped nuts for their chocolate mixture. "It was Casanova's aphrodisiac of choice, and Louis XIV's mistress routinely fed it to her lovers."

"So they could keep up with her, no doubt." Laura shot Dale a suggestive glance.

"To get those boys to show life signs," Tori said. "Have you ever seen Louis XIV's mistress?"

Laura laughed, and Bruno stood there, arms folded across his chest, smiling indulgently as if he couldn't be more pleased his guests were getting into the spirit of things.

"Chocolate will do the trick, my friends," he said. "Chronicles document that Montezuma used to drink up to fifty cups of a cocoa concoction every day to keep his harem satisfied."

"Fifty?" Dale asked. "How big was his harem?"

"History says six hundred women give or take a few."

History must have grown in the telling, because if Montezuma had even one woman in his harem like the redhead standing by Adam's side, he'd have needed more than chocolate to handle her.

"Even more recent are findings from research chemists who report that the caffeine, phenebromine and phenyline in chocolate act as chemical stimulants in the brain."

"Laura, Dale." Tori tossed a cup of sugar into a bowl and eyed them accusingly. "What were you two thinking when you designed this Wedding Wing? You've got condom dispensers in every room, but I haven't seen one vending machine. What are your guests supposed to do when they need a chocolate bar?"

Laura laughed and pointed to a wall phone. "Dial 1-5 for room service."

"You got that, Adam?" Tori asked.

Life signs weren't Adam's problem, especially when Bruno moved on and Tori sidled close again to mix her bruised violets with sugar syrup and grape juice.

"Will you pour the rest of those flowers in here?" she asked, caressing the concoction. "This is another important motion. I've got to knead apart these little clusters—"

"Ms. Ford, am I to assume you plan to get more and more outrageous until you get a response from me?"

"My determination rises with every attempt to thwart me."

"And provoking me brings you pleasure?"

That dainty chin lifted a notch. "Your response gives me pleasure. It means there's a living, feeling man inside there."

Feeling? He would have laughed, but she chose that exact moment to lash out and grab a handful of his crotch.

Tori got her response. Blood surged so hard to the point of contact that the erection fading back to his comfort zone reawakened almost painfully. Luckily, between his apron and the table no one could witness the event.

"You've got to remember, Adam. After yesterday in the spa, I know what's inside." She gave a stroke for good measure. "And I'm still interested. Most men would be flattered."

He stepped back, *not* flattered and determined not to give her anything else to taunt him about. She'd had enough fun at his expense today.

"I'm taking this to the freezer." Grabbing the bowl, he headed across the kitchen, willing his body to relax, grateful when he yanked the pressure-sealed door open and got blasted with the below-freezing temperature.

Damn woman. He hadn't once questioned who would win their power struggle, but his rejection had challenged Tori, and she was making it loud and clear that she would keep pushing until she got what she wanted.

Him.

He needed a new game plan quick because he didn't see her backing down any time soon. He refused to accept that he couldn't handle one predatory reporter, even though there was no denying that he was out of his league.

When he left the freezer to find Laura watching him, stifling laughter behind her hand, Adam came face-to-face with just how far out of his league he was. It took Dale rolling his eyes and glancing pointedly at his crotch to get him to look down at his white apron, where he found Tori Ford's handprint immortalized in grape juice.

Seriously out of his league.

"WHAT MAKES YOU think the sculpture will turn out as good as the pictures your mother took?" Tori asked Laura while driving them toward the Niagara River Artist Retreat for her second visit in as many days.

"Aside from the fact that my dad's an artist who knows what he's doing, you heard what he said. You were a great model."

"He was just being nice."

"He wasn't just being nice. He's honest about his work. *Brutally* honest sometimes."

"Oh, please. How brutal could he be? Are you saying he'd admit to using every drop of his talent to make me look good?"

"Probably not." Laura hitched a knee on the car seat and smiled. "Why are you so worried?"

Tori had to think about that answer. She *was* worried,

about how the sculpture would look, and about the effect it would have on Adam. Not to mention she was pumped up about meeting her aunt and uncle again. "A bunch of reasons, I guess. I wasn't sure what to expect from your parents, but whatever it was, they weren't it."

"They never are," Laura said dryly. "I warned you."

"They don't need a warning. They just weren't what I expected."

Although she wasn't sure what a couple who had blown off family, wealth and privilege to live their dream together should be like. So she'd visited with an open mind, and Suzanne and Russ Granger had turned out to be perfectly friendly people, who'd chatted with her as if they'd been catching up on a few weeks rather than a lifetime.

Aunt Suzanne had made the boudoir photography session a comfortable experience and Uncle Russ had indeed promised he could do justice to her likeness with his eyes closed.

Tori still hadn't figured out what to make of the whole situation, or what to expect from this second visit, but as the sky hadn't opened up and rained fire since she'd crossed the great family divide, she shouldn't be quite so nerved up.

"Trust my parents to do their jobs," Laura said. "My mom took great photos and Dad will do his thing, too. They'll have Adam on his knees."

"The stubborn man is barely talking to me. It was all I could do to get him to dance with me at the Tempting Tango today. All that wonderful ballroom dance instruction wasted."

"I'm sure your gift will bring him around. How can he possibly resist a sexy sculpture?"

"You're such an optimist, Laura. Or just plain crazy. I haven't decided which yet."

"I'm the bedding consultant. Trust me, I know what I'm talking about."

Tori frowned at the highway unfolding before her, the late afternoon sun bleaching the landscape and throwing a glare on her windshield so she almost missed her turn. Wheeling sharply onto the dirt road that led to the artist retreat, she maneuvered toward the farmhouse where Laura had grown up, feeling that same sense of the unknown, that thrill of the forbidden she'd felt on her first visit.

"Well," she said. "I hope you're right. I've never worked this hard to catch a guy before. Wouldn't it be ironic if I finally get him in bed only to find out he wasn't worth the effort?"

"Hey, I saw the infamous purple handprint. You tell me—will he be worth the effort?"

"Just because he's got the equipment doesn't mean he knows how to use it."

One glance was all it took to make them burst into laughter, a light-hearted feeling that chased away her nerves.

"All right, Laura," Tori said. "How is it that I can laugh harder with you than I can with some of my friends I've had for years? This isn't normal."

"Do you think we've got some sort of *thing* happening because we're family?" She pulled a ridiculous face that made Tori laugh again.

"Could be."

But the more she thought about it, the family theory didn't hold water. She had a sister she never laughed with. Miranda didn't do much in the amusement department, preferring to steer clear of anything that messed with her appearance of dignified perfection.

"Maybe all those rumors I heard about you are true,"

Tori said. "You're weird, which would explain the effect you're having on me."

"You're chasing my assistant GM when you're not sure he's even worth the effort, but *I'm* the weird one."

Okay. Most women would have probably given up on Adam Grant by now. But she wasn't most women. There was something about the man that made him impossible to resist.

Damn chemistry!

Pulling to a stop before a sign that read *Niagara River Artist Retreat, circa 1981,* Tori slipped out of the car and glanced at a life-size bronze sculpture of a naked woman—art that seemed symbolic since the Grangers' Retreat sat on land that had once belonged to the erotic artist who'd painted the *Falling Woman* now gracing Laura's Wedding Wing lobby.

"So when are you going to tell me how your family managed to buy this place or do I have to set up an official interview with your parents?" she asked.

Laura motioned her up the front stairs. "No mystery. Mireille Marceaux purchased the property just before she died, so it went into probate. My parents waited until it became available and made the best offer."

"But there is a mystery, girls," a voice said from the opening doorway. "The mystery of why the artist had acquired property around here in the first place."

"Hello again, Aunt Suzanne." She liked the feel of the name on her lips, and the smile her aunt gave in reply. As her father was an only child, Tori didn't have any aunts or uncles on the Ford side of the family. The experience felt new, special.

"Welcome back. For the record, buying this place was pure design. Your uncle and I capitalized on the local mystery to jump start our business."

"Like mother like daughter, hm?" Tori appreciated business acumen and ambition when she saw it. "Another Granger who understands the importance of spin. I've been impressed with the way Laura uses the media to benefit the inn."

"Acquiring *The Falling Woman* for her lobby was clever, wasn't it?" Aunt Suzanne gazed with approval at her daughter.

"She's brought me luck so far," Laura agreed.

"Laura also told me you're to thank for managing the loan."

"I had connections." Aunt Suzanne clearly referred to her job as CFO of Westfalls Academy while Laura had been in school there. "That's what mothers are for."

The accomplishment wasn't as casual as she made it sound. As a reporter with the local press, Tori knew all the stories about Mireille Marceaux. A French artist from the middle of the last century, she'd been known for her erotic paintings and had bequeathed the bulk of her estate to Westfalls after her death. No one had known of any previous connection to Niagara Falls, so that connection had become a source of much speculation. Tori had heard everything from a tryst with a married lover—which would *not* have been politically correct back then—to visiting an illegitimate child from said lover.

It was indeed a local mystery.

One thing that was common knowledge was how Westfalls Academy had hidden away the erotic paintings to keep them from students. That Aunt Suzanne had managed to get one released spoke highly of her connections.

"Come on." Her aunt motioned them through the door. "Your uncle is in his studio, and I know he's eager for you to see what he's whipped up."

"Can't wait," Tori said.

They entered the sculpting studio to find her uncle standing over a worktable. A big man, tall and broad-shouldered, he looked crowded in the room, but his studio was a neat place, raw with the smell of liquid metals and dusty powders, oddly macabre with bronze body parts littering the surfaces of worktables and shelves.

"Hi, Dad." Laura crossed the room to find herself the recipient of a hug that Uncle Russ extended to include his wife.

This family was so different from hers that the differences were no less striking than they'd been on her first visit.

"Hello again, Tori girl." He strode toward her, and for a second she thought he might hug her, too. But he only took her hand and brought it to her lips in a gallant gesture that made her feel welcome.

"Hello again, Uncle Russ." She wondered what it was about these people that made her go all soft and mushy inside. "I can't believe you finished it so quickly."

"I've been working since I saw you last. She's made from clay, so once I was satisfied, the glazing and firing didn't take long."

"I appreciate the rush job."

"It's the first chance I've had in over thirty years to impress anyone in your family. I didn't want to blow it. You never know if I'll get another."

"Dad," Laura said, but Tori laughed.

She liked how her newly acquired aunt and uncle played straight with her. She appreciated that about people. Especially in a situation as strange as this one.

"Russ, go get her," Aunt Suzanne said. "Tori must be dying to see her, and I'm dying to see what she thinks."

Her uncle retreated to cabinets at the far side of the studio, and Tori waited, trying to appear calm when she felt breathless. Her first glimpse of the sculpture convinced her that while the process might not have taken much effort, it had taken a tremendous amount of talent.

The figure rested on a blue velvet display board, a rendition of the photo she'd chosen to have the most impact on Adam. Maybe ten or twelve inches in length, she lay on her side with an elbow propping her up. Her chin rested on her hand, and her hair flowed around her shoulders and spilled over her arm. She wore a drape of fabric that artfully covered everything of importance.

While Tori had posed for the piece, she barely recognized the figure on display, with her mysterious expression, her pose that was both sensual and inviting.

"Well, what do you think?" Aunt Suzanne asked.

"She's…gorgeous." Tori wanted the right words to gift her uncle with praise the way he'd gifted her with this awesome sculpture. "I can't believe she's me."

"She's you, all right," he said. "An artist's vision of you, anyway."

"You're so talented."

Laura elbowed her. "Now who's sucking up? The way to Dad's heart is through his ego."

"Tell her what you've decided to name her, Russ," Aunt Suzanne prompted.

"The *Precious Gift*."

For a moment Tori didn't know what to say and speechless wasn't a place she knew very well. These people were so open with their emotions and honest with their feelings that she didn't have a clue how to respond.

She was the precious gift.

But instinct took over, and Tori didn't stop to think as she leaned up and kissed her uncle's cheek. "Thank you."

His smile assured her she'd done just the right thing. "Now you tell that man who'd rather work than make love

I'll be personally helping him sort out his priorities if he doesn't give the *Precious Gift* a good home."

Tori smiled. These people were acting like concerned family, and she didn't doubt that concern was real. The Grangers were just that sincere and open and honest. They were warm and welcoming, and it came as no surprise that Laura had grown up to work in hospitality.

But even this new insight into her bedding consultant didn't prepare Tori for these people sharing and caring for *her*.

She'd lived her whole life without acknowledging the Grangers, yet here they were trying to help her catch a man and worrying about whether or not he was good enough for her.

She found that…well, *touching*.

5

"THIS PARTY IS nose-diving," Laura said in real despair as she gazed around a ballroom that had been decorated like the set of the old TV favorite *American Bandstand*.

Tori hesitated to agree with her, but Appealing Performances certainly wasn't turning into the karaoke fun night Laura had touted in her press. Part of the trouble was the featured couples. Delia, the new bride, came from a conservative military bunch that didn't look as if they'd ever heard of karaoke, much less ever performed it. The groom's family possessed a few that showed promise, but as the bride's family looked so flummoxed, no one participated out of respect.

The Hottest Honeymoon couple wasn't any better. Tori's sister would no more have gotten on stage to sing pop tunes than pierce her nose. She made sure her husband didn't participate, either.

The rest of the trouble lay with the idiot deejay. The man, all decked out as a Dick Clark look-alike without a shred of the talent, managed to be more successful at drawing attention to the guests who weren't performing than at coaxing them onto the stage.

Fortunately for Laura, she had a guest who happened to have a Ph.D. in karaoke, someone who happened to owe her a favor.

"We need a few more people to get this party back on course," Tori said. "Who can we get on that stage?"

"Not me." Laura looked mortified. "I don't sing."

"Why on earth did you schedule a karaoke event if you don't like karaoke? And why on earth did you hire this guy?"

"I didn't hire this guy. I would have never hired *this* guy. *My* guy got sick at the last minute, and the entertainment company sent this one as a replacement. And I picked karaoke because it's supposed to be fun."

"It *is* fun. We just have to get a few people up there."

"I'm not getting on that stage, Tori."

"You don't have to sing, just be a back up dancer. Even with all the money my parents spent on voice lessons, I'll never get a crowd this size moving by myself. I know you can dance, so help me find some more dancers, unless you'd rather keep listening to your replacement deejay draw attention to all the guests *not* onstage."

Laura rose to the occasion, corralling Dale, Annabelle, the sales director, and Dougray, the maintenance supervisor, to perform. Tori never even bothered making a play for Adam. The man had barely danced with her during Tempting Tangos. He might spontaneously combust at the thought of getting onstage.

She flagged the deejay as he spun a pop tune she knew no one over the age of eighteen had ever heard before. And as no one *under* eighteen could get near Falling Inn Bed...

"We'll do Motown," she told Deejay Dick. "Everyone loves Motown. What have you got by Diana Ross?"

He rattled off a few titles, and she picked one guaranteed to get people moving.

"Everyone knows 'Ain't No Mountain High Enough.'" And with luck maybe one stubborn assistant GM would accept that no mountain would be high enough to keep her away from him.

Snatching the sunglasses off Deejay Dick's nose, Tori detailed the plan. "This is supposed to be *American Bandstand* so let's get people dancing first."

The man obviously recognized that someone had to start bailing out this sinking ship. Tori glanced at Adam to find him watching her and blew him a kiss. Then she shimmied out onto the dance floor with her posse in tow.

With luck, she'd get people moving, which would draw their attention away from the stage and their self-consciousness about getting up there. Or so she hoped. It always seemed to work at the Road Hog, her favorite weekend haunt.

The familiar strains of the well-known hit swelled in the ballroom, and Dale moved Laura impressively through a lambada they'd learned during Tempting Tangos, leaving her with Annabelle and Dougray, who both proved to be more than eager to cut the rug.

"Oh, I am so impressed," she said, watching these two older folks doing their thing.

When she saw the groom waltz his bride onto the floor followed by his brother and one of the bridesmaids, Tori decided this gig stood a shot. A few more couples flitted onto the dance floor and when Ms. J steered Adam out there, Tori knew her time had come.

"Come on," she hissed to Laura and grabbed Annabelle's hand to lead them onto the stage.

Through her new cool shades, she cued the deejay, then picked up her microphone and did her thing.

ADAM COULDN'T tear his gaze from the woman in action onstage. Between her smooth dance moves, the slinky skirt clinging to her shapely legs and the sound of her powerful voice, Tori Ford had presence in spades.

He'd called her outrageous, and she was. She made a prop of her bad girl shades and worked her audience until just about everyone in the place either danced or sang or helped choose what song they wanted to hear next. Before one tune had a chance to end, she launched into her next performance.

Ms. J wouldn't let him get away until the guests had extended the boundaries of the dance floor between the tables. "I'd say Laura is rethinking her position on our new reporter right about now, wouldn't you?"

"Undoubtedly," he said. "But you'd think the entertainment company she hired would have had a competent backup deejay on the schedule. She's used them before, hasn't she?"

Ms. J nodded. "With very good results, to my knowledge."

The only good results right now were compliments of Tori Ford. The way she'd stepped into the situation…well, it wasn't what Adam had expected from her. "Our reporter isn't turning out to be what any of us expected, is she?"

Ms. J watched Tori sidle up to Laura onstage where they danced a few steps together to the delight of the crowd. "I'm glad for Laura. For us, too. Tori's not only being fair in her coverage, she's sharp. We should make out well."

A no-nonsense businesswoman, Mary Johnson, fondly known of as Ms. J, had been in the hospitality business a long time. Adam had heard about her early in his career—she was a woman who'd taken on a predominately male industry and paved the way for women behind her. Working with her these past ten months had only proven her reputation had been well-earned despite the unusual theme of her newest property.

"I think you might be right," he agreed. "Tori Ford is very intelligent and a talented performer."

"Lucky for us." She eyed him curiously. "But I detect surprise in there, Adam."

"I am surprised," he admitted. "After Laura's concern about family bias affecting our coverage, I wasn't sure what to expect from our reporter. But it's been interesting watching her and Laura come to terms with their past."

"I agree. And I'm glad Tori has risen to the occasion for Laura's sake. The situation couldn't have been pleasant growing up. And who knows? Maybe the Naughty Nuptials will help them move in a new direction. We've been known to work miracles around here on occasion."

He didn't get a chance to comment when Tori chose that moment to change the ranks. With the party well under way, she turned the microphone over to an enthusiastic brunette from the groom's family.

She sauntered off the stage looking winded and flushed, and he flagged a passing waiter. "Ask Clyde to make something special for Tori Ford," he told the man. "And bring along a bottled water, too."

"You're taking good care of her it seems." Ms. J observed.

"'We aim to please.' Isn't that our mission statement?"

"Actually, I recall the word pleasure in there somewhere." She gave a soft laugh. "Which reminds me…I want you to factor some in during this event."

He glanced down at her in surprise. "Factor what in?"

"*Pleasure*. I distinctly recall instructing my management staff to enjoy themselves during our grand opening."

Adam opened his mouth to reassure her that he was enjoying himself, but the words died before making it past his lips. A waste of effort. Ms. J wouldn't have reminded him if she hadn't thought he'd needed a reminder.

"You're one of us now, Adam," she said. "And you've worked just as hard since you arrived to make this Wedding Wing happen. I'd like to see you enjoy that accomplishment."

She'd like to see him fit in. She didn't have to say it aloud because her implication came through loud and clear.

He'd be up for his yearly performance review soon, and with it an evaluation about whether he should be offered stock options in Falling Inn Properties.

"I understand," was all he said when the waiter returned. "Now if you'll excuse me, I'll catch up with Ms. Ford."

"Have fun." Ms. J waved him off with a smile.

Adam opted not to mull over the exchange, not when he was facing another one with Tori. He was well aware that his review approached, equally well aware that his insertion into the management team hadn't been seamless. These were all hard-working, strong people that he'd come to respect, but they operated on an entirely different level than he did. Their vision for the inn did indeed include pleasure and their fun-on-the-job attitude made him stand out like a sore thumb.

Adam pushed the thoughts from his head as he wove around a table to find Tori talking with her sister. He'd have to carefully evaluate his work situation soon enough, but not until after the grand opening. Right now, his reporter ranked front and center on his agenda. He didn't need any distractions that would leave him vulnerable to her maneuvers.

But vulnerability was exactly what he heard in Tori's voice when she said, "What is the big deal, Miranda? People are having a good time. That's what people are supposed to do at parties."

"Are you even capable of attending a function without making a spectacle of yourself?"

Upon first meeting Miranda Knight, Adam had been

thoroughly impressed with her poise and charm. Like her sister, she was a very beautiful woman. Unlike her sister, she handled herself with perfect composure and skilled grace. But now as he watched her frowning at the stage, he wasn't as struck by her impeccable manners as he was by her disapproval.

He hadn't been meant to overhear this conversation, but retreat wasn't an option, not without drawing attention to the fact that he'd been eavesdropping, however inadvertently.

And there was that vulnerability in Tori's voice, that... *something* on her face that suggested her sister's disapproval stung despite the defiant tilt of her chin.

"Good evening, Mr. and Mrs. Knight." Adam announced his presence. "Ms. Ford. Please accept this as thanks on behalf of the management staff." He handed her the champagne flute. "Clyde said he's taking you south tonight. I assumed you'd know what that meant."

She flashed him a smile and accepted the glass. "It means I'm about to be treated to a little sparkling mojito." Shifting her gaze at her sister over the rim of the flute, she took a sip. "Someone actually appreciates me. How refreshing. Come on, Adam. I know we've got work to do. We'll catch up with you kids later. *Try* to have a good time, Miranda. It won't hurt, I promise."

Adam followed her lead, inclined his head at the unsmiling Knights and escorted her away. They were barely out of earshot before Tori said, "Thanks for rescuing me."

"I suspect your sister didn't fully understand the kindness you just paid us." But he was beginning to understand why Tori placed such importance on having fun. He got the impression that her sister had some very clear ideas about what constituted a good time, and when he added that to what Laura had told him about the Prescott family disowning her mother, he thought it no wonder that Tori had become preoccupied with making the most of what life had to offer.

She looked so relieved as she exhaled a sound that was a half laugh, a half groan of frustration. "Not understand? That's putting it mildly. You'd think she'd be happy being the perfect sister. But noooo," Tori issued the word on a long breath. "She's not happy unless she reminds me I'm not."

There was such a wealth of emotion in those words that Adam was unsure of what to say. She'd crossed way over the line into personal, and he supposed he'd issued the invitation by interfering in her conversation.

The only thing to do was listen, and that seemed to be all Tori needed to launch into a breathless account of how Miranda purposely misinterpreted everything because she didn't have a clue what was really important in life, how she'd climbed so far onto the perfect pedestal that she couldn't hobnob with mere mortals anymore.

As one of the people who misinterpreted Tori's actions himself, Adam couldn't judge Miranda's motives, but he did recognize that Tori was hurt by her sister's lack of approval. Outrageous antics that left her open to be misinterpreted aside, Tori Ford had proven herself a big-hearted woman, a woman generous and open-minded enough to overlook a lifetime of family enmity to help out a cousin she barely knew.

He wasn't entirely sure what all this perfect sister business was about and said so. "If you're not perfect, Ms. Ford, then you're in good company."

She came to a stop between two tables before backing up a step so she wasn't within earshot of the seated couples. "Are you trying to make me feel better, Adam?"

He had to think about that for a second and to his surprise, he realized he had been. "Yes."

"Because I made myself a spectacle on Laura's behalf?"

He nodded. "Taking action to help someone out is a good thing. With regard to spectacles, you seemed to be having a good time and encouraged others to do the same. Your performance was spectacular."

"Well, well, well." Those pouty lips pursed, and Tori eyed him as if she wasn't quite sure what to make of this exchange.

Neither was Adam, and he didn't get a chance to figure it out because the bridal couple arrived.

"Adam, we need your opinion on something before we go to Ms. J," Delia Marsh said.

"Let's move over hear where we can talk." Adam directed the newlyweds into an alcove near a massive jukebox decoration that almost reached the ballroom ceiling. Of course, Tori worked proximity to her advantage. Suddenly, she stood pressed so close their thighs brushed and he was hard-pressed to ignore the awareness that rushed through him.

"What's up?" he asked Jackson and Delia.

"Tomorrow night is our farewell party and we want to share it with Dale and Laura. We can't go away without celebrating their engagement. When we—"

"Engagement?" Tori burst out. "What engagement?"

Delia and Jackson exchanged uncomfortable glances. "You didn't know?"

Tori shook her head and glanced up at Adam. "Did you know?"

"No."

"Well, the cat's out of the bag now." She looked delighted by the prospect. "So what's up with engagement celebrations?"

"I hope we didn't make a mistake by saying anything," Delia said. "We just assumed that since Laura was wearing a ring their engagement was common knowledge."

"Some reporter I am. I never even noticed." Tori shook her head, sending a tumble of red waves around her shoulders.

"If you don't mind my saying so, you looked a little busy on that stage," Jackson said with a smile..

"Nice try, but I don't feel any better. I was on stage with Laura and Dale." Though she sounded genuinely disgusted, Adam didn't miss the laughter in her deep blue eyes.

"So what can I do for you?"

"After we get back from our honeymoon, Jackson and I will be starting work on a restoration team," Delia explained. "We're not sure when we'll work with Dale again, and we're hoping to turn our send-off tomorrow night into a combination farewell/engagement celebration. We wanted to know what you thought before we went to Ms. J."

"I think it's a great idea," Tori said. "And wonderful of you to share your spotlight."

Jackson laughed. "We've had our fair share of attention lately. Sharing isn't a problem."

"I'm not convinced Laura will want her personal life up for public consumption with the grand opening," Adam said. He certainly wouldn't, but he was the anomaly at this inn. "If she's comfortable, I don't see a problem."

"Great," Delia said. "Then we'll go talk to Ms. J. If we have you all on our side, then Laura is sure to go along."

The newlyweds disappeared into the crowd and Tori rounded on him, eyes flashing midnight fire. "I don't believe you just gave them your blessing. Mr. I-don't-mix-business-with-pleasure. What has gotten into you, Adam? Is *moi* having an effect or are you finally succumbing to Falling Inn Bed and its magic?"

Damned if he knew. But Tori was right. Here he was assigning all sorts of noble motives to her escapades tonight, looking beneath the surface when he should be running in the opposite direction.

What had gotten into him?

One glance at this beautiful redhead, sipping her designer champagne cocktail as she eyed him boldly, answered that question loud and clear.

6

TORI SLID open the shower door and reached for a towel, feeling drowsy after a long stint under the hot water. After *Appealing Performances*, she'd holed up to write her column, then e-mailed it to her editor with barely five minutes to spare. Between the adrenaline rush of a large-scale karaoke gig, the surprise of Laura and Dale's engagement and the aftertaste of Miranda's criticism, her head had been spinning. Sleep hadn't been anywhere in sight without drastic action.

She'd stood beneath the jets so that the pulsing spray could pelt away every last ounce of mania from tonight's events, and, gratefully, the shower had done the trick.

Wrapping her hair up in a towel, Tori pulled another from the warmer and dried off, finally able to focus her thoughts.

Curiosity about Adam's reaction to her gift, her *scantily clad* gift.

She'd instructed housekeeping to leave the foil-wrapped package on his dining room table so he wouldn't miss it when he walked in. Had he opened it immediately? Or had he taken one look at the package and suspected she'd been the sender? If so, he might have waited. She had no trouble imagining Adam Grant as the kind of man who could keep wrapped gifts under his Christmas tree without the slightest urge to open them.

She, on the other hand, could never resist. As she did now, she wanted to know immediately what he thought of her unusual gift, but until he responded, she had no choice but to wait and hope anticipation didn't kill her.

After moisturizing with her favorite citrus body lotion, she ignored the robe hanging on the door and wrapped a towel around herself. She dragged a comb through her hair before heading into her bedroom, ready for bed. If this drowsy sense of contentment got away, she'd spend another night tossing, turning and obsessing about the reluctant object of her affections.

With thoughts of Laura and Dale's engagement filling her head, she sighed at her own sad state of affairs. Falling Inn Bed seemed to be working its magic on everyone around here—except her, which meant her coverage of the Naughty Nuptials would continue to be a factual account rather than the inspired, heartfelt piece she'd wanted to wow her editor with.

Why did she have to feel sparks for a tight-assed, intractable man who didn't know the first thing about how to relax and have fun? She wouldn't have had nearly this much trouble getting Tyler under the covers.

But no, she had to be attracted to Adam Grant, so this lavishly decorated suite with its velvet-draped state bed and Gothic fan vaulted ceilings wouldn't be inaugurated by her.

What a *tragic* waste.

Shaking her head, Tori headed to the kitchen for her vitamins, taking in her unusual surroundings along the way. This suite had been designed for lovers. With its frescoes depicting a *Kama Sutra* of love play, the main suite was as visually striking as the bedroom. A skylight with panels of stained glass created a cathedral-like ceiling. Stained glass also adorned the windows in the octagonal tower, depicting a chivalrous tale about a knight and lady who—natu-rally—wound up naked in the forest beside a waterfall.

When sun flooded the suite with jeweled light, the ef-fect was nothing short of visual artistry. By night, the ef-fect was no less dramatic. Moonlight bathed the room in fractured shadows and made Tori imagine what it would be like to be abandoned in some wild forest with one of the Round Table knights.

Unfortunately, no knights were here to share her sexy Dark Ages dungeon—or at least, what looked like a sexy Dark Ages dungeon. Inside the tower, a rack hung from the wall like a provocative version of a wall bed with padded restraints. A leather sex swing hung from chains on the ceiling. A faux-fur bear rug lay on the floor in front of a huge stone fireplace.

Tori honestly didn't know how historically accurate this suite might be, but there was no missing that this tower had been designed to play out sexual fantasies in style.

She didn't bother with lights as she made her way to-ward the kitchen, but when she caught a movement in her periphery, an eerie sensation stopped her cold. Suddenly, she could sense another presence, and apprehension skated through her as she made out the silhouette of a man in the shadows.

Sucking in an audible breath, she unintentionally alerted the intruder to her presence because he turned, revealing broad shoulders as he stepped into a sliver of moonlight.

Adam.

Her throat had closed around a breath, and her heartbeat throbbed in her ears. She'd locked her door. She'd have never taken a shower with an unlocked door. Yet here he was. In her suite. Unannounced.

He'd almost given her a heart attack, and her knee-jerk

response was to tell him about it. But before she could rally
and find her voice, common sense kicked in and made her
swallow the admonishment whole.

Adam was here in the Wedding Knight Suite, and hope
sprang eternal that she might not have to spend another
night alone in a room built for two.

"How did you get in here?" she asked.

"I have the master." His deep, oh-so-polished voice
sounded raw in the darkness, and she shook her head to
clear away the effects of his sudden appearance. His answer would have been a no-brainer had she been thinking
clearly.

"To what do I owe this honor?" she asked.

"I want to know you better."

She wasn't sure what she'd expected him to say, but until
that very moment Tori hadn't realized how little hope she'd
had of winning Adam over. Despite her *outrageous* moves.
Despite her unusual gift. "What changed your mind?"

"You did."

"How's that?"

"You keep surprising me."

His admission was simple, but somehow it filtered
through the darkness, an unfamiliar sound that was both
honest and promising. She found his calm flustering. He
was in command of himself, but she could barely catch her
breath.

"My gift?"

"That. Among other things. Laura's father was the artist, wasn't he?"

She nodded, surprised he'd asked. "Did you like her?"

"Yes."

That one word held such power Tori knew that she had
gotten to him. After all, he was here now, wasn't he?

"You posed for Laura's father to have that sculpture made?"

"Her mother actually. Her father sculpted it from a photo. Why do you ask?"

"Laura explained the situation about your families. I was surprised you'd gotten together with them."

"I needed a gift and it seemed like the perfect time to meet them." She wasn't sure what difference any of this made. "My uncle's very talented, don't you think?"

"The sculpture's beautiful. Like the woman who modeled for it." His voice was a low, sexy sound in the shadows, but before she had a chance to fully appreciate his admission, Adam said, "I don't generally mix business with pleasure. It's something that has to be done with a great deal of care between two people who understand the challenges that come along with the territory. It's not something I'd ever consider if I didn't know a woman very well."

"You don't know me very well."

"That's the problem. One I need to solve fast since we're on a time limit."

"A *serious* time limit," she agreed. "The Naughty Nuptials will be over at the end of next week."

He chuckled, a rough sound that made her stare into the darkness, wishing she could see his face. Tori had never heard him laugh before. Just as she'd never seen him smile.

"Ms. Ford, it's not the length of the Naughty Nuptials that concerns me. It's the time constraints of your interest in me. You want us to enjoy ourselves while you're on the property. But I've decided I want to get to know you better. Do you see the problem?" The rich sound of his voice trailed away in the silence, a sensual sound that made it difficult to concentrate.

"Why does it have to be a problem?" she asked.

"I've got barely ten days to overcome my concerns about mixing business with pleasure, get to know you and conduct an entire relationship. That's an abbreviated time frame for someone who doesn't do casual."

"I thought I could change your mind about that, Adam." She couldn't face his honesty with anything less than her own. "Casual can be fun. I think you'll like having fun."

"I think I'll like spending personal time together so I can get to know you."

For some reason, he made spending time together sound like more than fun. She'd wanted to challenge this man. She'd wanted to help him explore all that dark passion simmering under his skin. That was it. "You don't need to rationalize having fun. We're responsible adults. What's wrong with having a good time?"

"I told you, Ms. Ford. I don't generally do casual."

"Then what are you going to do, Adam? It is a pickle. Are you willing to give casual a shot?"

"I'm willing to compromise."

"Really?" She caught the sheen of moonlight on his hair as he nodded.

"I'm going to play your game by my rules."

"Really?" She liked the way that sounded, all dark and mysterious and perfectly in the spirit of a Dark Ages fetish suite. She'd sensed all sorts of passion simmering in this man. It had positively called to her.

"I brought you a gift. It's on the table."

Exactly where she'd asked housekeeping to leave his. How nicely symbolic. Heading into the dining room, Tori found a gift bag perched on the table. She loved gift bags. They cut the opening time in half.

Slipping her hand inside, Tori pulled away the tissue

paper to find a book, the title of which she couldn't make out in the dark. Rather than turn on a light, she sidestepped the sofa and joined Adam near the moon-soaked windows.

"*Sexcapades—Games for Energetic Lovers?*" she read. "I'm astonished, Adam. What's gotten into you?"

"Frieda from the Toy Shoppe said it was the thing for someone like me who didn't know how to have fun."

So he'd discussed her with a co-worker. Promising. Tori flipped through the pages, curious and very pleased. "So you want to have fun? Well, you've come to the right place."

And at exactly the right time. Here she stood in a towel with her hair hanging in damp strands around her shoulders, while he wore his custom-tailored suit and made her all the more aware of just how undressed she was.

Did it get any better than this?

Deciding there was a little too much distance between them, she set the book on the windowsill and moved close. "Thank you for the gift. I'm looking forward to playing games with you."

He nodded, the moonlight spilling across his face to let her see an expression that was far too serious.

Lifting her hands to his face, she fingered the line of his jaw, explored the velvet-stubbled feel of his skin. "I've wanted to see you smile since we met. You do smile, don't you?"

"Not enough, apparently."

She laughed, liking their nearness, the way his powerful body radiated a tension that shimmered just below the surface. She traced the curve of his mouth with her thumb, was rewarded when the corners tucked in slightly, definitely not a smile, or even a grin, but a start.

Rising up on tiptoes, she allowed herself to melt against him, experienced that coiled tension gathering in his body. Her breasts pressed against his chest, tested the grip of the towel.

He caught an arm around her waist and just as she tipped her face for a kiss, she was caught firmly against him, scooped into his arms.

"We're going to do this my way, Ms. Ford. By my rules."

Instinctively, she slid her arms around his neck and hung on, a move that called immediate attention to how entirely male he was. How undressed she was. At such close range, Tori could examine his beautifully sculpted mouth that looked perfect for smiling and kissing. She might not have been treated to either yet, but somehow she knew she would be. That zippy little feeling in the pit of her stomach promised as much.

With a luxuriant sigh, she rested her cheek against his shoulder. But to her surprise, he didn't take her into the bedroom, but turned and headed back into the tower.

"You got what you wanted, Ms. Ford. I'm in your suite ready to play. Now let's see how well you can take turns."

"Oh, I can take turns just fine. I'm very fair, but don't you think you might call me Tori?"

"Well, then, Tori," he said her name carefully, as if tasting the sound on his tongue. "Let's see."

Loosening his hold on her, he let her slide down the length of his body. The move put her in contact with all his hard places and ruched the towel enough so that for a breathless instant she thought she might lose it.

Yet that tuck of fabric held firm. Disappointment might have been part of the equation except that she could feel the powerful lines of his body despite the towel, and the utter thrill of the moment took her off guard.

His way. *His* rules.

Finally, she would get a glimpse of the Adam beneath all that polished self-control, the Adam whose desires were simmering beneath all that careful indifference.

Her stint as his massage therapist had given her a glimpse of how the man kept physically fit. His *real* massage therapist had told her he practiced some form of the martial arts, but Tori hadn't fully appreciated how the sport translated into smoothly powerful moves and lightning-quick motion.

Not until now, when he grabbed her hand and pinned her against the rack. Before she could figure out what he was about, he'd trapped her wrist in the padded restraint and was headed for the other.

"Wow," she said. "These are some rules."

"Still ready to play fair?"

He challenged her, reminded her of how often she'd done the same to him. But if he wanted to call her bluff, the man would be in for a surprise.

"Of course."

Snap. The restraint fitted into place around her other wrist, spreading her arms wide against the padded rack. Her shoulders drew upward, nudging the towel down a little farther.

Adam didn't seem to notice. He just knelt in front of her, treating her to a view of his dark head as he guided one foot and then the other into the restraints. She had to step up onto the platforms, which made the towel creep higher up her thighs as her legs spread wide. But Adam still didn't say a word, and she savored the warm caress of his fingers against her ankles.

Snap, snap. The restraints locked into place.

She supposed her current position would have been uncomfortable for some, spread-eagled before a man she barely knew, but the powerful vulnerability she felt right now had nothing to do with apprehension and everything to do with erotic fantasy. Here she stood like a visual feast for this man, subject to the power of his fantasy, his control.

She felt daring, and only then did she fully appreciate her cousin's genius at spinning fantasies. This tower, with its rack and sexy goodies, epitomized Falling Inn Bed's belief that sexual fantasy was a natural part of romance, a combination that let imaginations run wild with sensual possibilities.

And she couldn't resist fantasizing. Not when clouds drifted beyond the windows and moonlight suddenly illuminated the tower, casting Adam into a surreal glow as he rose before her, all tall and broad and male.

And in control.

She wanted to see his expression, but the glowing light at his back cast his features into shadow, heightening her anticipation and rising sense of unreality about the moment.

Inhaling deeply, Tori savored the rush of excitement instead, tasted the danger of not knowing his mood. This wild sense of tantalizing uncertainty pulsed through her, unfamiliar, a sense that prompted her to suck in another deep breath, this one making the towel slip another inch.

There was such power to the moment, such promise.

Adam had the next move in their game, and she waited, anticipation tightening her chest around each breath, stretching each moment as her mind raced with the possibilities of what he might do next.

He moved closer. The rack lifted her higher so that she faced him almost eye to eye, and proximity only heightened the awareness between them, distracted her so she missed the hand he lashed out. Catching the hem of her towel, he gave one good tug and that stubborn tuck of cotton finally gave way.

The moonlight spilling through the windows, a solid glow through clear glass and muted glimmers between decorative lead, gave him all the advantage. The light illuminated her as it shadowed him, leaving her exposed in detail.

Such calculated boldness wasn't what she'd expected from this man. Somehow, his determination to make work the end-all of his existence had fostered the image of equally conservative views about sex.

This power play came at her sideways. She'd looked forward to introducing him to the pleasures of *casual*. She'd imagined seducing her way into his pants, luring him step by sexy step into her suite and then into the bed, where she would delight in corrupting him until his impressive body vibrated with arousal and he couldn't keep his hands off her.

Surprise, surprise. She couldn't do much seducing with her hands and feet restrained.

"So why do you feel the need to restrain me?" she asked, pure bravado. "Is this your fantasy or do you not want me to touch you?"

He stared down at her, the shadows slicing his face into an interesting study of strong parts. The stern brow that so often wore a frown. The deep-set eyes that gleamed darker than midnight in the fractured light. The sculpted mouth she wanted so much to see smile.

"Both. I want to get to know you. If I leave you free to touch me, you won't give me the chance. You'll be too busy acquainting yourself with me."

She almost laughed. "I can't exactly argue. Do you always like the upper hand, or just while you're getting to know me?"

Those clouds shifted again, dimming the light. The only thing she could see now was the glint in his eyes as he raked his gaze slowly down her body, a visual caress reflected in the tightening clench of his jaw, the sudden, almost unnatural stillness of his body that hinted at some serious self-control.

That, at least, had promise.

"I generally like things to go my way," he admitted, and she saw a quick flash touch his mouth, suggesting her questions amused him.

After all, *most* people liked things to go their way.

"When I'm dealing with you, Tori, I've found that not having the upper hand can be dangerous."

She did laugh this time, thoroughly amused at his wariness.

Outrageous, he'd called her.

At the moment the same could be said of him. Perhaps she wasn't such a bad influence after all.

"So here we are, Adam. What's next?"

"There's a game inside your book called *Truthful Touches*. That's what I want to play tonight."

"Explain the rules."

"I touch. You tell me what you like or dislike."

Simple enough. And she did like the touching part. Or she would. "Sounds like the perfect game for a man who wants to get to know me."

"Yes."

That one word hinted at all his careful restraint, convinced her he felt the moment as strongly as she. He might not have touched her yet, or abandoned himself to the sight of skin as so many men would have, but having her spread naked before him was definitely having an effect.

She'd wanted a reaction from this man forever.

Wouldn't it just figure when he finally gave her one, she couldn't react? All she could do was melt against her bonds, let her body sink into the padded surface in silent invitation.

"Then let's play, Adam. I'm game." *Anything* to get the ball rolling. This anticipation was excruciating.

"You're comfortable?"

"I'm aroused."

This man was a gentleman through and through and he wanted her to know that while he wielded all the power at the moment, she wasn't helpless. But Tori had known that. She didn't doubt for a second that if she changed her mind along the way, she'd only have to say a word and this man would set her free.

And feel disappointed, she hoped.

Adam shrugged out of his jacket with the calm deliberation of someone settling in for the long haul. He tossed it over a nearby chair, his white shirt allowing her to see him in the darkness. She followed his movements, smooth and efficient as he loosened his tie, opened his collar. His tie went the same way as the jacket, and each piece of disappearing clothing upped her excitement until she could feel her pulse beat as an aching throb through her body.

He unbuttoned his cuffs, shoved up his sleeves and turned toward her, ending his striptease long before Tori wanted it to end. The memory of his naked body only added to her excitement as he raked his gaze over her, a lingering glance that took in everything.

"You're so beautiful."

Such simple words, but issued with such conviction that she realized she'd been waiting to hear them. Why? Was it this power game they played or simply that Adam touched her in places she hadn't known could be touched?

He'd challenged her in a way she'd never been challenged before. He dared her to make him come out and play. He dared her to make him smile and laugh. Adam Grant with his too-conservative views of the world, of *her*, a man she wouldn't normally have given a second glance, had made her respond to him.

Since the moment she'd first seen him, there'd been nothing normal about their rapid-fire chemistry. There was nothing normal about the thrill of forbidden pleasure she felt at being so exposed to him. Her heart sped up when he moved toward her. Her breath caught and held when he raised his hand. She shivered when he fitted his fingers around her jaw and tipped her face up for that first kiss...

7

ADAM'S simmering-beneath-the-surface passion had called to Tori and geared her up for an explosion, but his mouth parted over hers almost softly, as if he were poised on the edge of a breath and hadn't quite committed to the course.

Had Tori's hands been free, she would have slipped them around his neck and drawn him into a real kiss, convinced him with her mouth and tongue that he wanted nothing more at this moment than to kiss her.

But her hands weren't free.

Adam held the cards right now. They were playing this game by his rules, so she could only keep her face tipped toward his as he brushed his mouth across hers again, tempting her with the moist silk of his lips and the taste of his warm breath.

Then he swept his tongue inside.

It was a thorough kiss, one that gave her time to savor the wild thrust of heat inside. His strong hands held her face anchored as he explored her mouth, and a strange feeling of being possessed took hold of her, an exciting, out-of-control feeling that made her toes curl.

She wanted to wrap her arms around him and press her body close, but she could only return his kiss. She wanted fast and furious, but he championed a slow introduction that flustered her, tantalized her until her hands tested the restraints.

Was he teasing her as payback for teasing him?

Tori didn't know, but if that was Adam's game, it worked. By the time he let his fingers drift down the curve of her neck, her tension had mounted so much that she could feel his touch everywhere, a liquid heat that sank deep.

With each stroke of his tongue, her whole body felt alive, as if every nerve burst like the fizz in good champagne. He slanted his head to deepen their kiss, and she tangled their tongues together, encouraging him the only way she could. She was half-tempted to tell him his payback worked, but she couldn't talk and kiss at the same time.

And there was no contest between talking and kissing... Her breasts grew heavy. Her nipples tingled. Every muscle in her body felt aroused and tight as the air circulated freely between her thighs.

He caressed her throat in a steady motion, and she grew breathless, her chest rising and falling so her nipples almost grazed his shirt. *Almost.*

This was torture.

Which, Tori supposed, was the whole point. She'd urged him to grab life by both hands, but he was forcing her to slow down and savor the anticipation of the moment. She could only focus on how she felt when his hands slipped down her neck and rounded her shoulders, zeroed in on her breasts. His fingers cupped her in a smooth move, an erotic touch that made her gasp.

Adam caught the sound with his mouth, a throaty chuckle that became part of their kiss. He toyed with her, *goaded* her. If not for the restraints, she wouldn't have been able to keep her hands off him, and through the daze of arousal, Tori understood his game.

The very same game she'd played with him.

He wanted to tease her and tempt her until she insisted he satisfy this ache inside.

He wanted a reaction.

But Adam hadn't given her what she'd wanted. The man had sat on a massage table buck naked while she copped some serious feels of him and *still* resisted. She'd wanted to shred his composure until he couldn't resist her, and even though he'd finally given in, there was nothing out of control about him now.

If he thought she'd give in after one kiss—even a devastatingly delicious kiss—Adam Grant had another think coming. He wasn't the only one making up the rules to this game.

Restraints or no restraints.

Tori gave a melting sigh and swirled her tongue over his lips, a promise. While he might have all the control right now, he wouldn't always be the one in charge...

He thumbed her nipple and sparks shot through her, making her suddenly grateful for the restraints. All her bravado would go for nothing if Adam knew one kiss had her legs too rubbery to support her.

Breaking their kiss, he dragged his mouth away, leaving Tori to draw in a stuttering breath of surprise, to stare into his shadowed face, trying to make out his expression.

The darned man still looked too cool.

"I like it," she said, and though her voice held an edge of breathlessness, she sounded in control and assured. "I like the way you kiss me. Isn't that what you want to know?"

He inclined his head and stared into her face with those glittering eyes. "That's the game. I want to know what you like. And I want to know *you*. What makes you gasp..." He thumbed her nipple idly, shot that curling heat through her again. She dragged in another stuttering breath, not quite a gasp. "I want to know how your skin feels...and how it tastes."

He bent his head low. Tori held her breath, but instead of lashing his tongue across her, Adam sucked the tight peak into his mouth.

She did gasp this time, and his fingertips sank into her breast, firmly enough to make her squirm. He drew on her nipple, teasing her with easy swirls of his tongue, tasting her, making her moan. A low, needy sound that vibrated in the darkness, that seemed to amplify in the shadows crowding this tower room.

Tori suddenly felt the power Adam wielded over her as if it were a tangible force. Since the beginning this man had held a power over her that she didn't understand.

Wanting this man had obsessed her. Awake, asleep. Reality, fantasy. She'd wanted Adam Grant any way she could get him, and she found that intensity somewhat daunting, even though she was a woman who didn't find herself easily daunted.

But with Adam sampling her breast with those hot, sucking pulls, Tori found herself unnerved by the unfamiliar urge to arch against her restraints and offer herself up like some sort of erotic sacrifice to his pleasure.

He lifted his gaze, and she could see the glint in his eyes as he flicked his tongue across the sensitive tip. "What about that?"

"Yes." The word slid out on a wispy sigh that gave him so much more than she'd wanted to give. "I had no idea you had such a dark side, Adam."

It was a show of bravado, a chance to regain some of her control over the moment, but when he dragged his hands down her ribs, a powerful stroke that made her tremble, Tori knew her restraint was only an illusion.

"You've challenged me," he said, mouth still poised against her nipple, reminding her who had the control. "I either meet your challenge or disappoint you."

That startled her, but when she thought about it, she supposed he was right. She'd teased him mercilessly, and here he'd risen to her challenge, he played her game on his terms.

What surprised her was that she'd been so obvious. He'd known exactly what she was about—even when she hadn't fully understood herself. She'd only been thinking about getting this man to admit he wanted her. She hadn't thought about the effect of her pursuit on him, or the pressure he might feel to live up to expectations.

But she'd had a lot of expectations about this chemistry and all that wonderful passion Adam held so tightly restrained.

Such *dark* passion…

"Was this rack for me or for you?"

"Both." He flicked his tongue across her nipple again, earning another shiver. "I admit to being inspired by our surroundings. You've challenged me. You've made me want things I'd never thought about before."

"Like restraining me?"

"Like taming you."

Tori wasn't at all sure she liked the sound of that. She rather liked the thought of herself as a free spirit that couldn't be tamed. Let Miranda get gray hairs worrying about living up to everyone's expectations. She had a lot more fun worrying about living up to her own.

And Adam living up to the potential of his.

Who knew their passion could be so exciting? Tori hadn't, but there was no denying the urgency she felt right now, the way her whole body gathered tightly, awaiting his next move.

It was a very dark, very intense game they played, one that inspired a rush of feeling so potent that she tipped her face forward to brush a kiss against his silky hair, to make contact.

Adam responded by dragging his hands down her waist, over her hips, not a gentle touch but one that hinted at the power in his hands, the self-control he exercised in those long fingers.

Bending his head lower, he trailed his mouth beneath the sensitive curve of her breast, down her ribs. He circled her navel with a shower of openmouthed kisses that skidded along her skin and made her body tremble in reply to each one.

He dipped his tongue inside her navel, an almost playful stroke that made her realize that she'd never appreciated the sexy potential of belly buttons before.

But what potential. His warm tongue pressed inside in a sultry move that made her think of other places he might explore, other body parts he might use that would only heighten the caress of his skin against hers, the intimate promise of their bodies together.

But Adam only lavished attention there long enough to make her squirm some more, before he trailed his mouth along her hip, down into that oh-so-sensitive valley that rode along her hipbone to that juncture between her thighs.

Her stomach quivered with his touch, made her yearn for free hands to push his head even lower.

And then as if he'd read her mind, his lips trailed toward that juncture, making her heartbeat stall in her chest as he traced the neatly trimmed line of hair there and whispered, "I want to know what makes you climax."

His words had barely registered before he speared his tongue between her thighs, a slow lingering stroke that raked over the core of nerve endings. Tori rocked against her restraints, a full-bodied motion that was matched only by the moan that slid from her lips.

And suddenly his hand was there, fingers pressing into her thighs as he prized her legs wider to accommodate him, his faintly stubbled cheeks brushing her sensitive skin, his tongue swirling out for another heated stroke. And at this better vantage, he could draw that tiny nub between his lips enough to turn her body into a mass of conflicting impulses.

Muscles gathered and tightened as she rode her restraints. She rubbed that pleasure point against his mouth to feed the wild rush of sensations.

She wanted to wrap her legs around him to give him better access, but could only manage these pseudothrusts…so she exhaled a shuddering breath and closed her eyes. He drew on her with small pulls, his tongue laving to create a satin friction that mounted the heat inside her, lifted her faster and harder toward arousal than she'd ever been taken before.

And when he speared his tongue back into her moist folds, she bucked hard against her restraints, an undignified motion that made a total lie of her bravado. She was reacting to him big-time. Especially when his tongue lavished attention in places she'd had no idea were so sensitive, places that made her thighs vibrate and her sex clench.

Then he was gone, rising before her, his mouth sampling her skin as he worked his way up her stomach, the curve beneath her breast, the tight peak of a nipple, that sensitive hollow along her throat. He tormented her with those openmouthed kisses that tasted and teased and hinted that her reactions pleased him.

And only when he stood fully upright again, when she

wanted him to press against her so she could feel every inch of his hard strength full against her, did his hand slide between her thighs to join the game. Curling his fingers into her folds, he eased her apart, gliding along in her body's wetness.

"Do you like when I touch you here?" he asked, his voice a rough whisper.

Opening her eyes, she found him close, looking shadowy and different from this unfamiliar vantage point.

"Yes." She lifted her face to kiss the word onto his mouth, so tantalized by the intensity of the moment that she forgot to breathe, forgot everything but the way he held his mouth poised against hers, barely close enough to kiss.

He eyed her with a gaze that saw straight inside as he thrust a finger into her heat, a deliberate stroke that made her melt with the possessiveness of his touch.

"What about now, Tori?"

Nibbling his lower lip, she breathed another *yes* against his mouth, tried to catch him for a proper kiss. But he held himself so still, leaving her to wonder if he sensed her urgency in the way she teased his lips with those almost kisses.

"What about this?" he whispered as he skidded his wet finger backward, questioning the sensitive bud with a gentle thoroughness that dropped the bottom out of her stomach.

He probed inside just the tiniest bit, but she found herself riding that unfamiliar pressure; the only answer she could give was the almost kisses that broke as silken moans against his lips.

She could taste the smile on his mouth, and some barely functioning part of her brain protested because she couldn't *see* it, only *taste* his pleasure. And she'd been waiting so long to see it...

And then he withdrew, a lingering stroke that made her body arch greedily before he pressed back a little farther, this time the heel of his palm catching her in just the right places and massaging her with deliberate pressure.

Tori's moans echoed in the darkness as that friction made her burn, made her ache and yearn, made her strain against her bonds, wanting him to satisfy this need. She'd never blazed so hot before, and she strained to reach him, needing a *real* kiss, something more than this intimate probing to connect her to this man, to let her know that he was feeling something while she was on the verge of coming apart.

And Adam obliged. He brought his mouth down on hers hard, his tongue plunging inside, taking what she offered, proving that the moment affected him, too. And while he made love to her mouth with his kisses, he made love to her body with hot caresses of his wet fingers. He explored her as if memorizing the way she responded to his every touch, until she rode his hand trying to coax her orgasm into breaking.

And then there it was…a rush of heat that shimmered through her like a wave, radiating everywhere until she was barely aware of her throaty low moans, or the way Adam's kiss yielded to a lighter brush of his mouth against hers, tender caresses that took her breaths and gave them back when she forgot to breathe.

"You liked that," he whispered, only it wasn't a question.

"I did." Resting her head back, she forced her eyes open to face his look of male triumph, to prove she still had some control left when she sagged boneless against the restraints.

But she found no triumph, only a slow smile spreading across his mouth, a smile that softened the sculpted lines of his face and gleamed white in the darkness.

It was a breathtaking smile, worth the wait. Pleasure

glimmered in his eyes and transformed his expression, and she was grateful her eyes had adjusted to the shadows so she didn't miss out on the sight.

This was Adam *very* pleased, and more relaxed than she'd ever seen him before. Somehow, that smile felt like an accomplishment, and it struck her that she liked seeing him this way, liked it more than she'd ever imagined.

It was a wildly romantic thought for someone not inclined to wildly romantic thoughts, but Adam looked absolutely bold as he stood with his hand wedged between her thighs while she was restrained and utterly powerless to do anything but smile back.

Conservative, indeed.

"I'm so glad I didn't let you scare me off," she said, a tone that was pure bravado. "This was fun."

His smile melted back into that familiar expression she never knew quite what to make of, but he didn't say a word as he slid his hand from between her legs. Tori tried to look dignified and in control as she hung there limp. He circled around to the other side of the rack and reached for a crank she hadn't realized was there.

She hadn't been far off in her comparison to a wall bed. Adam cranked an arm that smoothly eased the rack from its place against the wall down into the horizontal position of a bed.

"Going for a ride, am I?" The sound of her voice masked the wild heartbeats as she wondered what Adam had planned next.

"We've still got a lot of ground to cover."

"More Truthful Touches?"

He nodded and brought the bed to a stop. "I've still got a lot of places to touch. You're not asking me to stop after one little orgasm, are you?"

"Not in this lifetime." Although that orgasm hadn't been nearly as little as he seemed to think. Not that Tori would let him know. Not while lying here bound and naked.

"Good, because I'm having fun."

"I knew you would."

He chuckled again, a warm sound that made her feel drowsily content, aware of the way the heat slowly receded and goose bumps brushed along her skin. Or maybe this was just excitement. When he sat down next to her, his hip was only inches away, and he swept his gaze over her, a promise of so much more to come.

He brushed stray hairs from her cheek, a gesture that told her so much about the man. Adam might not smile often, might present a professional mien to the world, but inside, he was a very honorable, very solid man. And he wanted to get to know her. Somehow that felt like another accomplishment.

"Still comfortable?" he asked and she nodded, turning her face until she could kiss his palm.

Something about the gesture seemed to surprise him, and she took advantage of the moment, nuzzling her cheek against his hand, pressing another kiss there.

"Do you like that?" she asked and was gifted with another smile.

"Trying to turn the tables, are you?"

"Not really." She gave a laugh, giving a tug on her restraints. "There's no place to go."

"I know where I want to go."

"Where?"

"I want to hear you moan again."

If Tori had been the kind of woman who blushed, she might have just then. His words were potent, and her anticipation grew as he moved through the shadows and kneeled on the rack between her legs. He skimmed his hands over her feet where he could reach beneath the padded restraints.

"Do you have a thing for feet, Tori?"

"What makes you ask?"

"When you were playing massage therapist, you spent a of time on mine. Made me wonder."

There was something almost disappointing about the silence, and Tori couldn't have that, not when he was putting forth so much effort to live up to her expectations. "You have *really* nice feet, Adam. Did you like when I touched you there?"

"Yes."

"I'm glad." And she was. Pleasing Adam seemed to inspire reciprocal treatment.

He trailed a finger into the restraint around her ankle, testing. "Still comfortable?"

"Excited. I can't imagine what you'll do for an encore."

"Can't you?" he asked, and there was something about his questions that sounded almost...*playful*.

"Well, I'm thinking you're not done exploring yet."

"Any objections?"

She was lying here naked and spread wide before this man, her body still languid from his *little* orgasm. "None at all. You go ahead and have a good time. Don't you give it another thought."

She earned a full-fledged laugh that time. The moonlit windows cast his face in shadow, and her heart thudded hard as he settled between her legs, repositioning himself until he lay full on his stomach with his face aiming *there*.

Oh, my.

Wedging his broad shoulders between her thighs, he lowered his face to her most intimate places. Tori relaxed against her restraints, closed her eyes and reminded herself to breathe as he tried to make her moan again.

Sinking his fingers into her bottom, he lifted her against his mouth, then dragged that devilish tongue from back to front and then back again, making her tremble with one of those full-bodied shivers that forced a sound past her lips. Not exactly a moan…

Oh, my, my, my, my, my, my.

She'd *so* underestimated this man. Here she'd been thinking she would tease and torment him into mindless passion, and here he was making a joke of all her intentions.

Irony at its finest, Tori decided, as he explored her with the thorough deliberation she suspected was simply a part of this man. But that was her last coherent thought as he swirled his wicked tongue around the bundle of nerve endings that shouldn't have reawakened so quickly, but suddenly seemed eager for another go at Adam's attention.

And did he pay attention.

With his hands maneuvering her bottom and his mouth exploring her most private places, he tasted, tested and teased until his lightest stroke made her lift off the rack and give a moan the front desk staff could probably hear five floors down.

Then he speared his tongue inside while his hands slithered up her to her breasts. Tori had never burned so hot, had never needed so intensely, had simply never known desire the way she knew it with Adam, whether she wore clothes or not.

She wasn't the least bit shy about riding his face and arching her breasts into his hands, so he knew he had her permission to tug on her nipples a little harder, and when he did the most amazing sensations spiraled through her.

And they hadn't even had sex yet.

That thought alone would have been enough to give her a heart attack had she been thinking clearly. But thinking had gone the way of her muscle control—lost somewhere between the brush of those stubbled cheeks against her thighs and his mouth making her vibrate until she was a quivering mass of nerve endings. Sighs slipped from her lips only to be met by Adam's throaty growls as he lifted her higher and higher, and her pleasure mounted, somehow even more powerful this time around.

Little orgasm?

This man's little orgasms might just kill her. Her whole body felt flushed and out of control, and she thrashed her head against the soft padding, her hips lifting to meet Adam's thrusts. Then she was coming apart again, just dissolving, and the only sounds in the moonlit room were her pleasured moans and Adam's laughter echoing a reminder...

They hadn't even had sex yet.

8

TORI WATCHED drowsily as Adam unfastened the restraints. The night had worn on, the moon rising to cast him in a silvery glow as he moved around in silence, slipping her foot from a restraint, massaging her ankle and calf with solid strokes.

Though Tori suffered no discomfort, she didn't tell Adam that. Not when he so thoughtfully soothed away all her imagined aches and made her feel so delicious in the process.

"How do you feel?" he asked, before moving to her arms to perform the same service.

"Perfect. As long as you tell me you're not done having fun."

"You convinced me to give casual a try, Tori. Now it's my turn to convince you of the merits of good old-fashioned lovemaking in a bed."

"Be still my heart."

He surprised her by pressing a kiss to her wrist, a tender, openmouthed kiss that spoke more loudly than words how pleased he was with her and their game. It was such a romantic gesture, one she hadn't expected from the strait-laced Adam.

One she hadn't realized would charm her so much.

Wasn't Adam just full of surprises?

And it just so happened that Tori liked surprises, which left her feeling warm and wonderful and oh-so-willing when he scooped her off the rack into his arms. And relieved. She wouldn't have been able to stand right now if she'd tried. Adam had annihilated her—her body felt like a jumbled mass of nerves.

Wrapping her arms around his neck, she rested her cheek on his shoulder and inhaled his masculine scent. She felt protected and right in his arms. It was a singular feeling, one that made her content with the silence, with the way her heart upped its beat as he strode into her bedroom and that huge bed appeared, so regal and unusual, so promising.

He deposited her into the middle, and she stretched out, giving Adam an eyeful. But he didn't join her. He backed away from the bed to unbutton his shirt, still silent, still contemplative, still so incredibly desirable in the moonlight.

Despite her drowsiness, Tori wanted nothing more in that moment than the privilege of undressing this man for herself, and rolling to the side, she took a leap of faith and trusted her legs to support her.

She moved to stand in front of him, gratified when his gaze raked over her and his chest rose and fell sharply. She liked his reactions, liked that he wanted her, liked that the world was right again and she was at eye level with his throat, a position that leant to that unfamiliar sense of being sheltered by his big body, by the power of his desire.

Brushing his hands away, she gazed up into his face and asked, "May I?"

He watched her with those serious eyes, as if assessing what type of stunt she'd try to pull this time.

"I just want to touch you," she said, and somehow her admission sounded intimate and needy in the moon-soaked night, a wish she wanted him to grant.

Adam inclined his head and, feeling strangely fluttery, she bent her head to her task and unbuttoned the first button.

She'd carried the image of this man in her head since playing his massage therapist; she'd reveled in the sight and texture of his deep golden skin, in the hard sculpted muscles that proved Adam was as disciplined with his body as he was with his emotions.

There'd been something forbidden about touching him then, about knowing any moment he'd catch on to her game and bust her, but now she had his permission. And there was something equally enticing this time, as if she'd been given a precious gift and full license to savor it as long as she wanted.

All these feelings were so new, almost unreasonable in their intensity. Tori had made it her life's calling *not* to need permission to do whatever she wanted, yet here she was ridiculously eager to simply touch this man.

She tugged the hem of the shirt from his pants with a smile. There was powerful magic at work here at Falling Inn Bed and it had her good. Powerful *dark* magic, because her fingers trembled with excitement as she loosed his buttons and slid the sleeves down his arms.

All the dreamy satiation of only a few moments past melted away in the face of this powerful desire she felt as she carefully smoothed the wrinkles from the fabric before spreading his shirt over the back of a chair.

She thought he'd appreciate neatness rather than having her throw his clothes into a heap on the floor, which is exactly what she would have done had she not wanted to please him.

But that's what she wanted to do right now.

Please Adam.

It was only fair, after all, since he'd pleased her, and

there was something so tantalizing about the way she felt, so eager. The white undershirt clung silkily to the ridges and hollows of his chest. Fanning her hands over it, she explored the firm muscle below, the way his chest swelled on a breath as she dragged out each stroke, savoring the moment.

She slipped her hands underneath and splayed her fingers against his waist. His skin was warm to the touch, and she followed the waistband of his pants, touched his tight tummy with a freedom she hadn't dared during her massage.

Trailing her hands upward, she forced the undershirt up as she did, liberating more skin. She skimmed her fingertips along the broad vee of his ribs, over the light covering of hair on his chest, across pebbled nipples.

All the while Adam stood calmly, the only signs of his arousal in the flare of his nostrils as he drew a sharp breath and the growing bulge at his crotch, which had grown so much that it smoothed the pleats in his slacks.

Completely inspired, Tori motioned him to lift his arms as she dragged the undershirt over his head. She went about the ritual of folding it neatly before depositing it beside his shirt on the chair, determined not to rush things, even if it killed her. Adam had gone to great lengths to play his game, to protect himself from the temptation of rushing. She would prove to him that she didn't have to be impatient, that she could savor the moment as well as he could.

Glancing into his face, she pressed her mouth to that curve connecting shoulder and neck. She swept an open-mouthed kiss there, and was rewarded when he shivered.

"Do you like that?" she asked, deciding that Truthful Touches could work both ways.

Playing his game was the perfect way to keep herself focused on his pleasure when her own pulse had started throbbing languidly again, distracting her with all the sensitive places he'd aroused and satisfied.

"Yes."

One word that said everything and gave Tori what she needed to keep going. Rising on tiptoe, she brushed a kiss to that stern mouth, pressing her body full against his. Her breasts molded his chest, bare skin against bare skin, and that first contact made her gasp with pleasure, made him make a deep-throated rumbly sound that issued from low in his chest.

Slipping her fingers into his hair, she coaxed his head lower, brushed kisses up his neck toward his ear. He slid his arm around her waist. Sinking his hand into her bottom, he anchored her close, grinding that rock-hard erection into her tummy. Tori rode the stroke, nibbling his earlobe, enjoying the way he shivered.

She rolled her hips again to accommodate him, from side to side, massaging that hardness until he swelled more.

"How about that?" She traced the curl of his ear with her tongue, gusted a breath that earned another ripple through his powerful body.

"Yes."

His hand tightened on her bottom, pulling her impossibly closer, and she was surprised that he continued to indulge her, to let her keep the control. Perhaps this was payback for her good behavior. Or perhaps he was just as caught up in the moment. Tori didn't care as long as she could feel this man naked.

Kissing her way along his jaw, she dragged her tongue along his skin, learning him by touch. She slipped her fingers through his hair. She traced his neck, then his broad shoulders before skimming her palms down his back, exploring, memorizing, enjoying.

She didn't understand what it was about this man that made him so irresistible. She only knew that she'd waited forever for the freedom to roam her hands over his beautiful body by invitation.

And she wanted Adam to be pleased he'd issued the invitation, so she dragged her open mouth down his chest, continuing her exploration, determined to prove how much potential their chemistry had.

Spearing her tongue through those fine hairs on his chest, she nipped at his nipple, and he exhaled sharply, making her smile as she continued her downward trek. She savored every inch of this man, until she was finally forced to break contact to unfasten his belt.

She made short work of business and was suddenly levering that impressive erection free from the tangle of pants and briefs. Adam assisted, shifting his hips and leaving Tori to marvel once again at his control. Just these light touches had her body melting, her sex clenching with the memory of his hands and mouth on her skin.

"Sit." With her hands on his chest, she guided him back the few steps toward the bed.

With an awesome display of flexing muscle, he sank down, his thighs spread wide, erection jutting.

Dipping to her knees before him, she removed his shoes and socks. She was practically at eye level with his groin and could barely resist the urge to reach out. But he'd expect her to go for the gusto and he shouldn't be the only one full of surprises tonight… Lifting his foot into her lap, she began to massage his arches.

"How do you like this?" She liked it very much. There was something decadent about being poised on her knees before this man, both of them naked, *wanting,* but taking the time to savor the moment. After all, they'd waited so long.

"I can't decide if I like how I feel or the way you look more," he said.

There was no missing the hunger sharpening his expression, making his shadowed face seem stark and unfamiliar.

"I'm flattered."

And she was. His need struck an echoing chord inside her, made her want to satisfy him more than she'd wanted anything before, because only when she satisfied him could she satisfy her own hunger.

Working her fingers with deliberate motion, she explored his insteps, worked each toe before she started over with the other foot.

He braced back on his hands and closed his eyes, clearly enjoying her attention and graciously letting her have the lead while she worked her hands up his legs.

"I've got something I bet you'll like better than the way I look."

He opened his eyes and arched a dark brow. "Really?"

"Really."

She chuckled as he stared down at her with a look of pure bravado—she recognized that look because she'd been playing the same game ever since he'd trapped her in that first restraint.

Trailing her fingers along the insides of his thighs, she made his erection jump as if a live current had surged through him. "May I?"

He granted her wish with a regal nod, and she slipped her fingers beneath the delicately puckered skin, cupped him gently while bending forward to drag her open mouth along his length.

His whole body gathered on the edge of that stroke, his

erection swelling against her lips, his low groan sending a
thrill that skittered through her, touching every part of her
body and making her ache.

Who knew that pleasuring him could bring *her* such
power?

Tori hadn't known, not honestly, not until Adam. She
hadn't realized that her ability to make such a disciplined
man quiver with her slightest touches could make her pulse
race and her whole body yearn. She hadn't realized she
could want so much.

Kneeling before him like a sex slave, poised over his
erection with her hair spilling over his thighs, she slipped
her mouth down for another hot taste, swirled her tongue
against the smooth, perfect tip.

His gravelly moan made her slide her fingers around
him and give a tug. Adam's eyes shuttered closed again,
his chest heaving, and Tori drew on that hot erection again,
a long, sucking pull that made him shake.

Some reckless part of her wanted to bring him to com-
pletion just to prove he wasn't as in control as he seemed
to think, and that thought kick-started a rhythm that no man
on this planet could resist.

But as Tori was learning firsthand, Adam wasn't just any
man. He was the man who inspired her to greater impulsiveness, which was saying something. He was the man
she'd wanted to tempt enough to pose for an erotic sculpture with an estranged aunt and uncle who might bring her
grandfather's anger down on all their heads.

He was the man who'd made her submit to restraints in
a fantasy tower to suffer climax after climax at his skilled
touch. Only Adam had ever made her feel this way, and
each downstroke on his erection made *her* ache, made her
sex clench and her body weak with pleasure.

What was it about him?

This was a blow job, for goodness sake. She was pleasuring *him*. How was it that each of her lingering strokes had its counterpart between her thighs, made her sex clench greedily, made her rock her hips simply because she couldn't stop.

She wanted to be lying on the bed alongside of him, so she could spread her legs and ride his hard thigh to soothe this ache. Better still, she'd crawl on top of him, feel him stretch and fill her and then pound into her hard and fast until she exploded in yet another *little* orgasm.

All those thoughts spurred her to a frantic pace, one that lifted Adam to meet each thrust, made him grind out those pleasured sounds, but *still* he didn't lose control.

Finally, Tori was the one who broke, scrambling out from between his knees and grabbing a condom from the dispenser on the nearby night table.

With a few practiced moves, she cracked open the package, unrolled the protective covering. Adam didn't say a word as she hoisted herself onto the bed and straddled him until they fitted together just as she'd always known they would.

Divinely.

She didn't ask his permission this time. She didn't ask what he would like. She only concentrated on knowing that in one downward thrust, he'd finally be inside her. She'd ride him until she satisfied this ache. She'd bring him along with her.

But Adam clamped his hands on her bottom, hard enough to make her yelp. He lifted her in an inspired move that pitted his strength against hers to flip her over onto her back.

In that one move, her whole view changed.

His shoulders and chest suddenly blocked out the world, filled her gaze with his expression, a study of hungry lines.

He lowered his face to whisper in her ear, "My rules to-night, Tori."

Using his hips to lever her wider, he positioned himself to strike into her heat.

Tori couldn't argue, not with that thickness prodding her most sensitive places, dragging across through her skin to ease his entry. Not when he pressed in just enough to test their fit, to make her gasp out at the feeling of fullness as he pushed in a little more.

Hooking her ankles around his hips, she spread her thighs to invite him deeper. But Adam had meant what he'd said, and with arms bracing him, he sank inside with a slow, thorough motion that radiated through her body.

That one heated thrust became almost agonizing in its deliberation, made her body coil with an urgency to move that she'd never known before. But she couldn't. Not when Adam had stolen her breath. Not when he lifted out of her, a withdrawal that immobilized her with purposeful slow-ness, with an intensity of sensation that made coherent thoughts scatter.

"I like the way this feels," he told her almost conversa-tionally when she could barely manage, "I'm glad."

He laughed, then sank back inside her, slipping his arms under hers to cradle her against all the hard, hot hollows of his body. He caught her mouth in a kiss, and the instant her lips parted to kiss him back, he surged into motion. All that carefully restrained passion she'd sensed inside him from the moment they'd met, unleashed in an explosion of motion.

He took her hard on the side of the bed. Each thrust dragging him almost completely out before he plunged back. Each stroke rode her exactly where she needed fric-tion the most. Each smooth arch of his hips was so in tune with hers that she strained against him to meet his thrusts, so exhilarated and overwhelmed that her kisses became laughing gasps as the tension coiled tighter inside her, lifted her higher on a swell of sensation that made Adam's *little* climaxes seem genuinely small.

And still he held her and kissed her and made love to her. His breathing grew ragged, his kisses frenzied, his body taut in a scrumptious explosion of hard muscle. Her tension mounted until her legs grew weak, until she could only gasp and kiss him and marvel at the surrender she felt as he carried their pace with his forceful thrusts.

He came with a growl that rumbled through her, his driving thrusts taking her over with him. He rode her as she moaned out her orgasm against his mouth, her sex clenching in wild bursts, her body spinning beyond her control.

And then Tori couldn't move. She could only lie beneath him, sated and stunned and sapped of all strength while their hearts pounded. That he was breathing as shakily came as some consolation, but not when she realized that while he'd definitely come, his impressive erection wasn't nearly as depleted as she'd have thought.

"Wow," she ground out. One breathless word that barely penetrated the darkness. "Is sex always like this with you?" Another week and a half of this and there wouldn't be much left of her.

Adam laughed, a deep-throated, heartfelt sound that amazed her almost as much as the playful way he pulled her into his arms. Tangling his big body around hers, all warm muscle and long limbs, he rolled them together into the middle of the bed.

Peering down into her face with that breathtaking smile, he said, "Tori, sex like this is only this way with you."

9

WHEN THE climate-control system cycled on, Adam maneuvered the comforter from the side of the bed and pulled it over Tori. Now that the heat of the moment had cooled, goose bumps were sprayed along her bare skin. Not that she seemed to notice.

She'd stretched out on top of him with her arms thrust over their heads and her cheek on his shoulder. Her slim curves draped across him, breasts to chest, one leg pressed against his, the other hiked across his waist.

Then she'd promptly fallen asleep.

Adam was glad for a chance to run his hands over her smooth curves. She'd been as generous with her body as she was with everything else—her emotions, her help and her praise. Tori had proven herself a very generous woman, a surprising woman. And with each moment he spent in her company, he discovered new things that convinced him that he'd judged her too quickly. There was so much about her he needed to understand to have a clear picture of who she was.

Smoothing a hand along her spine, he marveled at how such a simple touch sent fire through him. By rights, he should be asleep now. Their game tonight had called on reserves of self-control Adam hadn't tested before, hadn't known he'd possessed. But Tori had gifted him with her trust, and in doing so, demanded he live up to the gift by playing fairly.

He hadn't entered this suite tonight lightly, and as he lay here with this neat bundle of naked female wrapped around him, he found himself pleased with the way events had progressed.

She touched him in ways Adam hadn't realized he could be touched—hadn't realized he'd wanted to be. He felt good. Physically sated. Emotionally content. Tori had accused him of never smiling, and while he hadn't thought about why that might be the case, he was smiling into the darkness right now. Here he was with this neat armful of sexy woman, a woman as wildly delightful in bed as he could have imagined. Not that he could have imagined the turns tonight had taken.

Truthful Touches? Restraints?

Adam knew intimately how Falling Inn Bed, and Breakfast catered to couples' fantasies, but he'd never guessed how much pleasure he'd find playing sexy games.

When he'd arrived in her suite armed with his book, he'd had no real clue about what would happen next. He wanted Tori, wanted to know the woman beneath. He'd figured that would lead them into bed.

But in their limited dealings, he'd learned a lot depended on her actions. She had a neat way of forcing him to react, of pushing buttons that caused him to reexamine his behavior.

When faced with Tori fresh from a shower, restraining her had seemed the only smart thing to do. With her determined moves, he wouldn't have withstood her for long any other way.

His co-workers had been haranguing him to get into the spirit of things ever since he'd arrived on this property. He'd dismissed their suggestions, believing their modus operandi had no place in his life. How wrong he'd been.

He liked the way he felt right now.

Satisfied. Content.

Tori sighed, her breath gusting across his skin in a soft burst, her hair tickling his mouth and nose as she nuzzled her face against him. He inhaled deeply of her clean fragrance, still amazed at how they'd come together. At how they'd responded to each other.

She'd played his game, carefree and eager and generously yielding the control simply because he'd asked. In return, he'd risen to her challenge and discovered they were combustible together. She'd been right about that.

And now that they'd taken this step…falling in bed with this woman meant taking a serious look at where he wanted to go with her.

She wanted sex.

He wanted a chance to figure out why the sex was so good. And his first step was getting to know her. He wanted to know what kind of woman made him think about winning her smiles when she looked hurt by an exchange with her sister. He wanted to know what kind of woman made him bend his beliefs about business and pleasure. Especially after his breakup with his ex-fiancée.

"How can you be awake?" Tori asked in a husky voice, shifting sleepily so her knee nudged his groin, still lingering hopefully in a semierect state. "And how is *this* possible?"

"It's been a while for me."

Tipping her head back, she peered into his face through heavy-lidded eyes. "I didn't think I was the only one who had a good time tonight. If I was, I'm going to be crushed."

Her frankness made him smile. "I had a very good time."

She slithered her hand down his chest, curled her fingers around his erection so that semierect took a giant step toward erect. "If that's true, then what's this?"

"Not much."

She shook her head, sending her silky waves tumbling around his neck and shoulders. "It's a perfectly respectable hard-on going to waste."

Slipping a knee over his hips, she gave a gigantic push until she rolled over and straddled him.

"Tori, what are you—"

He cut off abruptly when he realized exactly what she was about to do. Without touching him, she caught hold of his erection between her thighs and maneuvered it into position. There was just enough bend there to make him wince before she slid home.

She sighed. "You don't have to do anything. Just lie here. I got it under control."

And she did. Rocking her hips back and forth, she rode him in that unique way only a woman could. "Oh yeah. That's nice." She paused for a moment to realign herself, then nuzzled her face against his neck. "So it's been a while for you, Adam? Do tell. Inquiring minds want to know."

He took advantage of her position to familiarize himself with the smooth curves of her bottom. "I haven't dated since moving to Niagara Falls."

"You've been here what—ten months now?"

He wasn't surprised that Tori knew of his job history with the inn, even if he was surprised at how fast his body was heating up with that steady swaying of her hips. "Yes."

"That's a long time for a man to go without sex."

"Just made a career move."

"I know, I know," she said on an impatient breath as she shifted on top of him again, this time to anchor her knees against him for better leverage. "And in your spare time you practice martial arts and get massages. Laura and Sandra already told me. Tell me something I don't know."

She probably didn't know he was finding it difficult to concentrate on anything but the way she'd clamped her thighs around him with each rocking stroke. Or maybe this was nothing more than a clever way to catch him off guard to conduct an impromptu interview. But Adam couldn't resist sinking his hands into her backside and nudging her higher, his body caught up in her rhythm, in satisfying the need that made him have to think hard to answer her questions.

"Mmm." She smiled but didn't open her eyes. "I saw a game in your book called Truth or Dare, so 'fess up, Adam. I want to know all your sexy secrets."

"Truth or Dare is about secret fantasies." He'd read about that game, too.

"We can change the rules. You want to get to know me and I want to get to know you."

She didn't let up with that steady rocking motion, so he lifted his hips to ride each stroke. "Off the record?"

"Of course."

"Broken engagement before I accepted this position."

"Who broke it off? You or her?"

Leave it to Tori to zero in on the heart of the matter. "Her."

She cracked an eyelid and stared at him. "Really? Why would any woman forgo a walk down the aisle with you? Even if you don't smile much, you're marvelous in bed."

"Thank you." He drove inside hard enough to make her breath hitch, which made her body clench him hard enough to make his breath hitch.

"No, thank *you*, Adam, for finally giving in. I'm so impressed. And here I was thinking I was the only one who could pleasure myself and talk at the same time."

She almost was. He could barely focus with all his blood rushing to his crotch. But he recognized this as a test. One he intended to pass. "Is that what you're doing—pleasuring yourself?"

"Oh, yeah. You're catching me in just the right spot. Feels divine." Hitching her elbows over his shoulders, she kicked up her pace to ride him a little faster, pushing focus even farther from his reach.

If he wanted to pass this test, he had to resist meeting her thrusts and hope she didn't notice.

"So give," she said. "Tell me about her."

"We were a power couple until she decided I worked too much." He wouldn't mention that she hadn't decided this until *after* the wedding invitations had gone out.

"*You* work too much? I'm shocked. Define power couple."

"Two career people with a goal."

"The same goal?"

"We were learning the hospitality business so we could open a property."

"*We?* As in you worked together?"

She sounded so surprised that Adam guessed what was coming next. "It was different than mixing business with pleasure."

"How?"

"Common interest. Common goal. We worked toward it together."

Tori frowned, but she still didn't open her eyes. She nestled so close he could feel her heart beating. "She thought you worked too much?"

"Yes."

"Is this why you shut me out when you realized we had chemistry? Do I remind you of her?"

Adam hadn't made the connection until Tori pointed it out, but now that he thought about it, perhaps his determination to stick to business and steer clear of personal since making this move to Niagara Falls had been a result of dealing with his ex's sudden change of heart.

He'd always been focused on his career goals, but at least in Seattle he'd had a life outside of work—although, apparently, not enough of one in Vanessa's opinion. He'd known no one in this part of the country, and his new position had made it all too easy to immerse himself in work, despite his co-workers' efforts to get him into the spirit of things around here.

"You don't remind me of my ex-fiancée, Tori. Although she had a similar epiphany about her life—she wanted to stop working so much and enjoy herself."

"So what'd she want—more vacation time, a family, what?"

"More downtime than I'm apparently capable of."

"So you don't want a family?"

"One day. Right now, I'm focused on my career. I got a late start."

"Does this…have something to do with selling your family business?" She sounded breathless, as if the tables had turned and suddenly she was the one struggling to concentrate.

He gave a few slow thrusts to take advantage, ruthlessly controlling his own need to keep thrusting.

He *would* pass this test.

"So does it, Adam?" She gave another full-bodied shiver, all drowsiness fading as she stepped up her pace, looking close to the edge.

Adam could answer her question or push her even closer.

A few more thrusts was all it took to make her stop talking. Sliding her hands beneath his butt, she buried her face against his neck and rode him hard, the only sounds slipping from her lips were tiny purring noises that signaled the oncoming explosion. And with her body arching sleekly and her sex clenching greedily, she almost took him with her.

But with a grim effort of will, he struggled to contain himself, to enjoy the experience and further his advantage. He stepped up his pace until she tensed and gasped out those very appealing sighs she made when she came.

He barely managed to control himself as she strained against him, then finally she heaved a sigh, tipped her head back and started talking again. "You can answer my question now. I'm done."

He laughed, a broken sound. "You are, are you?"

"Mmm-hm. You should have come along for the ride. It was great." She gave him a smile that did incredible things to his ego, and his restraint. "I feel wonderful."

While he'd had his fair share of lovemaking experiences in the past, Adam had never had the pleasure of being used as the instrument of a woman's pleasure in quite this way before.

Sinking his hands into her backside, he took care of himself, lasting all of five glorious strokes. "Now I feel wonderful, too."

"Happy to oblige." She gave a laugh and stretched languorously against him.

Before he had a chance to respond, she rolled off him, making him grunt at the sudden absence of body warmth when she cleared the side of the bed.

"Now tell me about why you sold your family business while I grab something to drink." She stopped short by the edge of the bed, looking magnificent with the fading moonlight spilling over her creamy skin and that wavy hair tumbling over her shoulders. "Do you want something?"

"Water."

She nodded and swept from the room, unabashedly naked, heart-shaped backside swaying sexily as she faded into the darkness.

"I can't hear you," she called from the next room, prompting him to answer.

Getting to know Tori meant sharing himself, so Adam explained how he wasn't able to save what was left of the business after his grandparents' deaths.

His grandparents had been retired when his parents had died in a factory explosion. They'd stepped up to run the family manufacturing company until he could take over, but the changing economy had meant changes to the way they'd always run the business.

They'd done their best, and Adam had made every effort to pull things back onto stable footing after their deaths. He'd finally opted for a ground-up restructuring that would protect the jobs of employees who'd established their careers working for his family and left him reevaluating his own career goals. He'd taken a chance on a fresh start in a fast-paced business that had interested him.

He had no regrets and told Tori as much. Content with the direction his career had taken, he enjoyed learning the ropes in the hospitality industry, looked forward to investing his resources in a property of his own.

Falling Inn Bed, and Breakfast had seemed like a logical first step into the position of stockholder without sinking all his assets into a smaller property where he held all the risk. What he didn't tell Tori was that after nearly a year on this property, he wasn't convinced that making the leap to stockholder—should he pass his year-end review, which was a definite question mark at this point—would be his next step.

When she reappeared in the bedroom, she handed him a champagne glass.

"Water in style." She clinked the rim of her own with his, the tinkle of glass ringing out in the darkness. "I finally got you into bed, Adam. I want to celebrate."

After taking a sip, she set the glass on the night table and left again. This time when she returned, she was balancing a huge basket, which prompted him to leave his warm place under the covers to assist her.

"What's this?" he asked.

"My welcome gift from the inn. Laura's been sucking up to me ever since I got here."

He placed the heavy basket on the bed where she directed and sat next to it. "She was worried about your family history affecting our press."

"Can you blame her? If it was my neck down on the chopping block with her holding the ax, I'd have been worried, too." Tori sank down beside him. "I told Laura I'd play fair if she did."

Adam liked her honesty. At first, he'd found her frankness disconcerting, almost to the point of abrupt, but he liked knowing where he stood with her, found it refreshing.

"Oh, would you look at all this." She unfastened the ribbon and peeled away the decorative cellophane so that nuts and crackers and chocolates tumbled all over the bed. "I can't believe Laura sent me something this big. With all the events happening around here, when did she think I'd get hungry?"

Lifting her gaze to him, Tori smiled. "Maybe she was hoping I'd work up an appetite late at night. I'm sure that's why she moved me into this suite."

"She didn't say."

"She was a lot more optimistic than I was. At the rate I

was going with you, I didn't think I'd be doing anything in this suite but sleeping."

"Surprise."

She laughed as she rummaged through snack items, finally bypassing them all for an apple. "Good thing I opened this. I didn't realize there was fresh fruit inside."

Adam finished off his celebratory glass of water and attempted to repack the basket as Tori snuggled back against the pillows crunching contentedly on her apple.

"So tell me about the ex-fiancée," she said between bites. "Does your breakup answer the question of why Adam doesn't mix business with pleasure?"

"No."

"No?"

Tori had destroyed the cellophane so he couldn't repack the basket. He settled for replacing what he could and moving the rest onto the nearby dresser.

"Just because my relationship didn't succeed doesn't mean I don't think the right relationship can't. My grandparents worked together their entire marriage and were very happy. They made that happen by keeping their work lives and their home lives separate."

"That's nice to hear. Then how does your ex factor in?"

Adam bought himself some time to mull his answer by pulling aside the comforter and sliding between the sheets. He didn't intend to get into the gory details of calling a wedding off.

"Up until a few minutes ago, I didn't think she did, but I might have been mistaken. I haven't made any effort to settle in and build a new life since I got to town."

"Oh, my, my, Adam. What prompted this conclusion?"

"You did, when you asked if you reminded me of my ex." Reaching up, he touched her hair, liking the way the glossy waves curled around his finger, vibrant and alive, like the woman herself. "Got me thinking that maybe I've been determined not to get into the spirit of things around here because then I'd have had to look too closely at why my relationship failed. My ex never told me her goals were changing, but I was so wrapped up in work, I never recognized the signs of trouble. When I look back, I know they were there, and fairly obvious."

"I see," was all she said, and Adam knew she did.

He'd just confirmed everything she'd accused him of since they'd met, and yet, she was generous enough not to point that out. Her self-control made him smile.

"No, 'I told you so'?"

"Wouldn't dream of it." Tossing the apple core into a trash can, she sipped her water, then snuggled next to him.

He cradled her close, liked how she fitted against him. "Why?"

"Sounds like you got the point." She chuckled softly. "I like when you smile, Adam. You've got a great laugh."

He chuckled, and rested his cheek on the top of her head, an intimacy that somehow felt right.

"No man should go without sex for so long, either," she said. "Now that I've got you where I want you, I'll make sure you don't neglect *that*. A couple of hours a day, at the least."

"A couple of hours? You'll be a big distraction."

"Distraction?" she demanded. "I'm a good influence. We've known each other less than a week and already you're broadening your horizons. You've smiled and laughed and tortured me in a Dark Ages dungeon. You even had a bed picnic. Will wonders never cease?"

"I *tortured* you?"

"It was a good torture, trust me, and I'm not saying I didn't deserve it."

"You did deserve it. After that stunt in the spa—"

"You liked my massage. You said you liked my gift, too."

Adam heard a question mark in there, and something about her struck him as tentative. He couldn't decide if this was a sneak peek behind the face Tori showed the world. Had he been trying so hard to avoid her that he'd missed the obvious?

When he remembered her encounter with her sister at tonight's party, he decided that perhaps he had.

Yes, Tori was bold. And, yes, she was outrageous. But inside beat the heart of a feeling woman. One who wasn't always so confident, no matter how much she appeared to be.

"I did like your gift. It's what brought me here tonight." He repaid her honesty with his own. "It wasn't just a beautiful sculpture. I knew you'd had to cross some tough lines to connect with Laura's father and have it made. It helped me appreciate what a caring person you are."

"You're kidding?"

"I'm not." Rounding the curve of her shoulder, he ran his hand down her arm, liking the way she felt.

"It wasn't all that caring, Adam. Laura and I were killing two birds. I'm reporting on this grand opening, which means understanding the woman behind the Wedding Wing. Getting to the truth and all that."

"I see," Adam said, and he did.

Tori was doing exactly what Laura had feared she wouldn't—making the effort to look past their family history to give unbiased coverage of the Naughty Nuptials.

Adam also couldn't help but wonder if some of Tori's interest wasn't curiosity about her aunt and uncle and cousin. He understood how she needed to research the bedding consultant for her story, but there was a family connection that had been long denied. Tori was just bold enough, and caring enough, to want to make a judgment for herself.

In his mind, that spoke very highly of her, even if she found it hard to acknowledge.

There was so much more to this woman than he'd let himself see. As Adam held her close, the night faded beyond the windows, along with their last chance to claim any sleep.

"Adam," she said quietly.

"Hm?"

"You didn't tell me if you're heartbroken about your fiancée breaking up with you."

Heartbroken? Adam had to think about that. His professional life with Vanessa had been exceptional. They'd managed the demands of hotel management well. They were compatible, focused. That she'd been unfulfilled in their personal life had come at him sideways.

When he compared their sex to the way he felt right now…he knew something must have been lacking. He'd thought their sex life had been satisfactory, but they hadn't shared anything that came close to leaving him feeling the way he did right now. Had she discussed her discontent with him sooner, they might have addressed the problems. Maybe not.

He kept going back to the fact that he'd never felt this way with Vanessa. Adam had loved her, but he couldn't regret their breakup. Not when she'd been unhappy, and he simply hadn't stopped working long enough to notice.

"No, I'm not heartbroken," he finally said.

His admission echoed through the room, quiet, final, and yet somehow promising.

"Good." Tori snuggled closer sleepily. "I wouldn't want you thinking about another woman while you were making love to me."

The idea of thinking about any woman besides the one who'd participated so eagerly in tonight's sexy games made Adam laugh, and the sound felt good, a way he hadn't felt in too long.

I'm a good influence, Tori had said.

Perhaps she was right about that, too.

10

BETWEEN THE BLAST of her blow-dryer and the shower jets currently working their magic on Adam, Tori marveled that she heard the knocking from an entirely different room across the suite. But there it was, an insistent, almost impatient sound. Flipping off the blow-dryer, she left the bathroom.

"Who is it?" she asked through the unopened door, refusing to be caught in her robe with no makeup and a still-damp head for just anyone.

"Miranda," the familiar voice shot back, and Tori recognized the tone—*definitely* impatient.

Damn.

She could have ignored just about anyone, but her sister didn't pay visits without a reason. Unfortunately, Tori wasn't sure she'd want to know what that reason was.

Still smarting from the way Miranda had ragged on her at the karaoke party, she didn't want her sister raining on her parade right now. She'd made love to Adam all night long, and hadn't gotten much sleep before conducting interviews all day. She'd just emerged from the shower where they'd gotten pleasurably sidetracked in their preparations for the engagement/farewell party. She felt good and wanted to stay that way.

Heaving a sigh, she opened the door.

In a glance, Miranda took in her wet hair and robe as she swept inside. "Running a little late, aren't you?"

"It's been a long day." And getting longer.

Of course, Miranda had already dressed for the event—it would never do to be late—and looked remarkable in a ruby silk pantsuit that showcased her dark hair and Snow White coloring, ever ready for a camera lens to swing her way.

But her perfect sister didn't look quite so flawless when her mouth popped open and she said, "Ohmigosh!"

To Tori's amusement, Miranda seemed genuinely flabbergasted as her gaze traveled from the suite's vaulted ceilings and stained glass skylights that depicted a variety of positions from the *Kama Sutra,* to the tower room, where the rack had been neatly replaced after an earlier house-keeping visit.

"That's just sick."

"What have you got against sex, big sister?"

"Nothing, but if dungeon fetishes don't strike you as depraved, you're worse off than I thought."

"Now I'm scared to ask what you think of your suite. The Egyptian Pleasure Pyramid doesn't sound much less fetish-y than the Wedding Knight Suite. In fact, if I were choosing—"

"My suite's fine, thank you." Sweeping inside, she propped a hip against the kitchen counter and motioned around her. "Erotic and subtle—not trashy like this place."

Good for Laura, who'd apparently scored a hit. "My suite isn't trashy. It's just different. Falling Inn Bed isn't about fetishes, it's about fantasies and those happen to be unique."

"I do not want to hear about how you like to get tied up, Victoria Ford." Miranda frowned. "And since when have you become a proponent of this place? I've been reading your coverage and hadn't noticed you swinging either way."

"That's because I'm a good reporter. You're not supposed to read my personal feelings between the lines. But I'll tell you, the more time I spend around here, the more I like what I see."

"Oh, that's the kiss of death, isn't it? I suppose I should be grateful you didn't bring a date. Especially after meeting your last affair du jour."

Tori wouldn't bother correcting *that* misimpression. Not with her sister on such a roll. "I liked George. There wasn't a thing wrong with him."

"Not if you like sweaty construction workers with biceps bigger than their brains."

"Oh, I do." Tori remembered George's big biceps bulging on those tanned arms. And sweaty…well, she'd been partially responsible for *that*. She hadn't noticed he'd been brainless. Then again, she hadn't noticed he'd had a brain, either.

"Why are you here, Miranda? And speaking of, where's Troy? I though you two were permanently joined at the hip."

Something about her sister's expression made Tori regret the comment. She wasn't sure what it was. Maybe the surprise in Miranda's gaze maybe, the uncustomary flash of emotion from a woman who could face a tornado without blinking.

But it disappeared just as fast when Miranda said, "As much as we'd like to be, Troy and I can't always be together. Delia's father wanted to talk shop, and with the war going on, spouses aren't always privy to the details."

"Oh," was all Tori could think to say. She hadn't ever considered how the war might affect her sister's life, had never even thought to ask.

And even sadder was that she didn't feel comfortable asking now. Such a simple question, an *important* question, and she didn't feel close enough to her sister to ask without feeling as if she were prying.

Suddenly, Tori recalled Adam's admission in the dark of late night, how he'd let work blind him to what was happening in his relationship, and couldn't help but wonder if there wasn't a lesson for her in there somewhere.

"You warned me when Laura's mother was coming to the rehearsal dinner, so I wanted to reciprocate," Miranda said. "Somehow the bridal couple's farewell tonight has turned into Laura's engagement party, and unless I miss my guess, her parents will be there."

"Really?" Playing stupid was the only way to go here. Her sister wouldn't take kindly to learning that Tori had already known and hadn't warned her, a total oversight because she'd been so wrapped up in Adam.

Hm, there *was* a lesson in there.

"How'd you find out?" she asked.

"Tyler mentioned it on the helicopter ride over the falls this afternoon."

"Do you want to invite Mother and Dad? I'm sure Laura won't have a problem—"

"No, no." She waved her hand dismissively. "I've already talked to Mother. She and Dad have a ribbon-cutting with the mayor scheduled. They're going with Grandfather."

Tori knew their parents wouldn't renege on a deal with the senator. She also knew that Miranda would never ask. Her sister hadn't fallen far from the tree that way. She'd learned how to walk the path of a public servant from the best—their mother.

Tori hadn't been nearly as proficient and was reminded again of the irony there.

Aunt Suzanne hadn't learned the lesson, either.

"Are you going to be comfortable?" she asked, wanting

to help. "You can always beg off. I'll make your excuses. You deserve a night off to have fun with Troy."

"Don't I wish. I don't know what I was thinking letting Troy talk me into coming back here."

"You and Troy are still practically newlyweds. Three weeks alone at a romance resort *gratis* should be an adventure."

"Oh, it's been that all right—" Miranda broke off, pivoting around toward the bedroom, where Tori heard exactly what had caught her sister's attention.

The sound of the closet door sliding open.

Miranda scowled, and the easy moment between them slid away. "Who's in there?"

Unfortunately lack of sleep had dulled Tori's reaction time, and before she could produce a reasonable explanation, her sister had decided to answer the question for herself.

"Miranda, you don't—"

Her sister came to a skidding halt in the open doorway, and Tori didn't need to be a fly on the wall to know she'd just seen Adam—and hopefully not in all his buff glory.

"You don't want to know," she whispered into the silence.

Miranda didn't miss a beat. She spun on her heel and said, "You're sleeping with the manager."

"It's not what—"

"Technically, I'm the assistant general manager," Adam's voice issued as he appeared in the doorway....

Not naked.

This was exactly what Tori didn't need, and she wished Adam had stayed inside the bedroom so she could deal with her sister—this wouldn't be pretty. But he strode into the living room, looking all freshly scrubbed and scrumptious, and worried.

And he didn't stop there. Crossing the suite, he came to

stand beside her. He slipped his hand over her shoulder and that was when she recognized the show of force for what it was.

He didn't say anything. He didn't have to. She got the message loud and clear. He wanted her to know he was in this with her, that he'd stand by her side to face the consequences of taking their relationship public. Knowing Adam and how noble he was, he probably wanted her to feel reassured that she wasn't alone—even when facing her own sister.

And surprise, surprise, she didn't feel alone.

Hm. Tori wasn't sure what to make of *that*, but with Miranda glaring at them, she didn't have time to figure it out.

"This isn't what it looks like," she said.

An outright lie. This was exactly what it looked like, but she was just defiant enough to take a shot at an excuse— no matter how remote the chance of success.

Miranda obviously knew what to expect from her, and zeroed in on Adam instead. "Does all the staff at Falling Inn Bed share suites with their guests, Mr. Grant?"

Tori cut him off, taking a stab at reason. "If you're referring to Laura and Dale, you know they're engaged."

"Their engagement didn't happen until after they'd been in their suite through half this event," she corrected, her narrowed gaze traveling to Adam again. "Is that the game around here—management sets the example for guests?"

The implication of gross unprofessionalism came through loud and clear, and her cool delivery typically rattled people. Hell, Tori fell for it every time.

But Adam apparently didn't rattle so easily.

He inclined his head in that familiar gesture that was no less regal for his wet hair. "Not under normal circumstances, Mrs. Knight. But the Naughty Nuptials is a ground-breaking event. It's given our management staff a chance to interact with our guests and experience some of the magic that Falling Inn Bed, and Breakfast is known for."

Magic? Was Adam really buying into Laura's whole sales pitch about this place or was this simply his way of rationalizing their fling to her sister?

"Technically, Victoria isn't a guest, is she?" Miranda said, and Tori knew from that tone she wasn't buying it. "She's a reporter assigned to your grand opening. Are you using my sister to make sure your inn gets good reviews?"

"Miranda!" Tori really wanted to appreciate the defense on her behalf—a rare occurrence, as it was—but could manage nothing but mortification that she'd actually voiced that opinion. Not PC at all for a woman who would be PC in a coma.

"I appreciate your concern for your sister, Mrs. Knight." Adam clamped his hand a little tighter on her shoulder, clearly warning her not to interrupt. "But my interest in Tori has nothing to do with our coverage, and everything to do with finding something special in an unexpected place. No doubt she'll continue to review the events with the same integrity she's shown since before we became involved."

Special? Was this man for real?

Tori glanced up at him to find him wearing the totally unreadable expression that had frustrated the hell out of her on more than one occasion during the past week. He could have handled her sister's accusation in a variety of different ways, one of which would have been to simply tell her the truth—that Tori had relentlessly pursued *him*.

Miranda would have believed that.

But *special?*

She could tell that Miranda didn't know what to make of this and, to be honest, neither did she. But Tori had to give the man credit. He was good at what he did. No question. He'd charged in to rescue her, sidestepped Miranda's accusation without offending her and even supported Tori while he was at it. *Very* nicely done. A move like this would have impressed her father and grandfather, who both practiced their smooth moves in the tough political arena.

Had Tori not needed to assume control of this situation and fast, she would have laughed at the irony of *that*.

Slipping her hand over Adam's, she said to him, "I'll be fine. Go finish getting ready. I'd rather one of us makes it downstairs on time."

I'd rather you not witness the carnage.

And it was coming. Miranda's scowl broadcast that loud and clear. Adam's dark gaze held hers for a charged moment, and Tori forced a smile to reassure him.

He bowed his head and said, "Mrs. Knight," before disappearing back into the bedroom.

The door closed with a finality that seemed to echo through the suite.

"Can't we just leave it with you defending me to the black-hearted villain?" Tori suggested mildly. "I really liked you jumping to my defense."

Judging by Miranda's deepening scowl, clearly not. Big sisters were big sisters, and hers had less patience for fun than most. "I cannot believe you're sharing this suite with the assistant general manager of this hotel."

"This isn't exactly a single-occupancy room, and at least he's not sweaty with biceps bigger than his brains." Not that she had any complaints about Adam's biceps, or working up a good old-fashioned sweat, either.

"How can you make a joke out of this?"

"It makes me feel better." There was honesty. Folding her arms across her chest, Tori leaned against a table and met Miranda's gaze. "Been here, done this. You're going to criticize my behavior, so I'm gearing myself up for the lecture."

"That's unfair."

"Is it?"

They exchanged a glance that had a wealth of meaning. This was one of those "sister" moments, the kind when whatever they chose to say could affect their relationship forever. Only sisters had the sort of telepathy that signaled the arrival of these all-important moments, and the ability to divine what the other wanted to say, or chose not to.

"Victoria, how can you not understand that everything you do reflects on this family?"

Okay, Miranda chose to exercise impulse control instead of outright ragging on her. They were off to a good start. Tori would do the same.

"I do understand, and I honestly don't go out of my way to reflect poorly on you and the family. But try to understand that I'm not going to stop living my life so the press can't find something to sensationalize about me." She heaved an exasperated sigh. "I *am* the press, and trust me when I say it's a losing proposition. There'll always be something to dig up."

"All the more reason to keep your nose clean. You invite ridicule with your behavior."

"Like I did at the karaoke party last night?" Nothing like passing open wounds under the saltshaker. One day, Tori was *really* going to learn to keep her mouth shut.

Had Miranda inherited the same lack of impulse control, she'd have said, "Yes."

She wanted to. Tori could tell that Miranda wanted to call her on her embarrassing behavior of the night past. But when she opened her mouth she only said, "You do what you want, Victoria. You always do."

With that, she strode out the door without a backward glance, leaving Tori staring after her, feeling as if someone had rained all over her parade.

ADAM SLIPPED his hand around Tori's waist as he led her through the atrium and outside into the garden, where tonight's party proceeded beneath the sultry summer twilight. Guests mingled around tables and down brick walkways that wove through hedges and blooming flower beds. A band played a smooth jazz tune that melted into the warm night air.

Enjoying the break from the ballroom, Adam marveled yet again at Laura's ability to space out three weeks' worth of functions at the same inn, yet keep them new and inviting.

Tori didn't appear to notice. Dressed in a sarong-type bronze skirt and matching blouse, she looked stylish with her hair piled on top of her head and her toes peeping out of strappy sandals. And while she worked the crowd with her usual skill, sipping another variety of champagne cocktail, Adam could sense her distraction.

Their encounter with Miranda had upset her, whether she chose to acknowledge it or not. He wanted to understand what the problem was between her and her sister, because that same phenomenon that had gripped him at the karaoke party was gripping him again now.

He wanted to make her smile.

"Becoming involved with me will present a problem with your family," he said, not a question but a statement she could choose to discuss with him, or not, as she saw fit.

He hoped she'd open up to him.

"It's not you, Adam, trust me." She rolled her eyes. "My family has lit candles in church so I'd bring home someone like you."

"I didn't get that impression from your sister."

"It's the circumstances." She took a healthy sip of champagne as if trying to wipe her palate clean of a bad taste. "And just what is so wild about you sharing my suite anyway? It's not like you've publicized our fling on the lobby marquee. You're my escort for this affair, and we're enjoying ourselves. I don't understand the problem."

Adam thought he might, though. Just a guess, but he'd overheard most of Tori's exchange with Miranda, despite the closed door. Combined with what he'd learned last night about their relationship and what he knew about the whole family from Laura, he suspected there might be a lot more emotions at work here than simple disapproval. Both on Tori's part and that of her sister. Maybe even her family.

Until he got to know her better, he couldn't formulate opinions. But he would need some idea of what was going on because he'd meant what he'd said. The attraction they shared was special. Tori might not be willing to think beyond casual, but he wasn't ruling out something more solid, not after last night. If it looked as if they could have something lasting, Adam would pick up the pursuit where she'd left off.

An antagonistic family wouldn't make his job any easier.

"How do you suggest we handle the problem?"

She gave a huff of exasperation. "There isn't a problem, so don't worry about Miranda. She isn't going to approve of anything I do, no matter what it is, and her finding out about us is distracting her from a potentially larger problem."

"Which is?"

"She'll have an absolute cow if she finds out I went to visit Laura's parents."

Adam didn't understand why two families had drawn

such hard lines between themselves, but he recognized the potential trouble Tori faced by crossing those lines.

But he respected her stance on the situation. She'd been sent to cover Laura's grand opening and judging the woman and her event based on their family history would have been biased. He was learning firsthand how much Tori valued fair play.

She'd been fair with him as well, having given him ample warning that she intended to pursue him and wouldn't stop until she got what she'd wanted.

Him.

At first, he'd been uncomfortable with that kind of honesty, but he'd come to appreciate knowing where he stood with a woman. Had he known with his ex-fiancée, he'd have had a chance to address the problem. But by not sharing how she felt, Vanessa hadn't given him that chance. Had Adam been paying closer attention, he might have seen the warning signs. He hadn't.

But he had a chance to approach Tori differently, a chance he decided to take.

Scanning the crowds that meandered through the garden, Adam searched for the people who were causing that frown on her beautiful face. Some guests slow danced to the band's music in the piazza or gathered around the bar that had been set up for tonight's event. Others walked the brick paths in conversation.

He caught sight of Laura's parents, along with an elderly family friend, talking with Ms. J and Annabelle around one of the patio tables strung with twinkling white lights. Dale was with them, but not Laura. He guessed she'd be stemming some emerging crisis with the food or entertainment. Despite her status as guest of honor, she was still hosting this party, and he knew she wouldn't forget that. The bedding consultant had found her balance between business and pleasure.

And, sure enough, Laura turned up beside them in full management mode, not to deal with a crisis but to coordinate a photo shoot.

"What time do you want me to corral everyone for your photographer?" she asked Tori. "Before or after the buffet?"

"Before," Tori replied. "We'll get it over with so your guests of honor can relax. You included, Laura Granger. Last I heard, you were supposed to be celebrating your engagement, not working. I'd cancel the whole shoot, except that I want a picture of that rock on your finger for my article tomorrow."

"I'm still not sold on publicizing my engagement."

"Pshaw." Tori laughed. "What's not to be sold on? Don't tell me you're camera shy. You've got Tyler dogging your heels while he films a documentary about *you*. Surely you've gotten used to the attention by now." She waved a hand dismissively. "Just let me do my thing and everything will work out fine. Even Adam agrees. Don't you, Adam?"

She flashed that beguiling blue gaze, and he found himself smiling back, words popping out of his mouth before he'd even considered what to say. "I do, indeed."

"It's the perfect opportunity to tout all this magic you say is happening around here, Laura," she added. "You and Dale are that magic in action."

"You think this is a good idea, Adam?" Laura darted her gaze between him and Tori. Her broadening smile left him wondering if she'd figured out the change in their relationship status yet, and he squelched the familiar discomfort at having his personal life under scrutiny.

A *very* familiar feeling after calling off a wedding.

"Tori made a valid point about slanting the press in our

favor, since news of your engagement will eventually be publicized anyway."

"He even agreed to the party, Laura," Tori said, tipping her glass toward him in salute. "Delia and Jackson approached him first with the idea before they went to Ms. J."

"I'm shocked," Laura said. "So you've finally decided to get into the spirit of things, Adam? Should we thank our local reporter for that change?"

There was subtext in that question, but Adam wouldn't discuss the details of his choices with Laura. If she didn't already know, she'd find out soon enough that he'd visited the Wedding Knight Suite. That was all she needed to know as far as he was concerned.

"There's another benefit to publicizing your engagement that I only just considered," he said to swing this conversation away from his personal life. "Tori mentioned concern about her family's response to crossing boundaries. Her reporting on your engagement might help prepare whoever has objections, so it doesn't come as such a shock."

Tori eyed him over the rim of her glass with a hungrily assessing look that made him recall the way she felt underneath him last night. "There are *lots* of brains underneath those good looks. You're absolutely right."

Laura gave a laugh that hinted she had no more questions about the turn their relationship had taken. "And at this point anything will help."

"He is helping," Tori said. "You should have seen him handle Miranda earlier. Too smooth."

Laura's smile faded. "Is your sister okay? I was surprised she didn't invite your parents tonight. They'd have been welcome."

"Not for lack of trying. Previous engagement."

"What exactly do you need help with?" He kept getting the impression they were referring to something that he didn't understand and the thought of Tori and Laura colluding made him decidedly uneasy.

"We're trying to work a miracle," Laura said. "We're trying to spread some of Falling Inn Bed's magic on our parents."

"*Laura* is trying to work a miracle," Tori clarified. "I don't believe in miracles myself, so I'm just along for the ride, helping out when and where I can."

Adam eyed them both in surprise, not sure what they hoped to accomplish. "What are you planning, ladies?"

"To get our mothers back together."

"I'll be the first to admit that Laura's lost her mind thinking she can bridge that chasm," Tori said. "But I do agree that there's something special happening around this place."

"Of course there is," Laura said smugly. "*You* jumped the chasm between our families and it's gone very well."

"That's because I'm *me*. The official family pain-in-the-ass. And I did tell you I'd help. But just because I made the first move doesn't mean my sister will, or my mother." She shook her head. "Most likely, I'll get disowned, too, and then you'll be obligated to invite me to your house on holidays."

Both Tori and Laura laughed, but Adam didn't miss the very real concern beneath the laughter.

"You're trying to fix the problem with…*magic*?" Even the word sounded absurd. "I don't understand."

He wasn't sure he wanted to know. He had a lot on his plate already, dealing with Tori and the fallout from their relationship. He braced himself as Laura took a deep breath to wind up for her explanation.

"We're trying to find out exactly what caused the problems all those years ago and what's keeping our mothers apart now. Maybe there's some way to fix things. A lot of time has passed."

"Thirty years," Tori agreed. "That's a long time not to forgive and forget."

"And you think that dragging everyone together on this property will do...*what*, exactly?"

"Get them thinking about what happened, the good and the bad." Laura looked thoughtful. "Maybe we can get them to take a look at what they're missing out on and decide to talk. It's worth a shot, since it's the first time any of us have been together in years. And what better place than here?"

"You can't deny something special is happening around here, Adam." Tori hit him with a smile. "Look at Laura and Dale. Look at you and me."

That answered the question about whether Tori had told Laura about their relationship.

"I don't deny it," he admitted.

"Maybe you can help us." She shot a sidelong glance at Laura. "I'm telling you he was awesome with Miranda today. He can help us figure out how to smooth ruffled feathers."

"We're ruffling feathers already." Laura glanced across the garden to where Miranda stood watching them with a frown.

Tori set her glass on the tray of a passing waiter, looped her arm through Adam's, sidled close and asked, "Will you help?"

Adam nodded. And had he not been so busy ignoring the fresh citrus scent of her hair, he'd have been amused it hadn't taken Tori long to get him to agree to whatever she wanted.

11

TORI THOUGHT it said a lot about a couple when so many people cared about their happiness. That was obviously the case with Laura and Dale. Not only had the featured bridal couple wanted to share their honeymoon send-off, but Laura's family had braved the social functions they'd been known to disdain to celebrate their daughter's engagement.

Many of Laura's friends had arrived as well, despite the short notice, not the least of which was Ms. Cecilia, the indomitable headmistress of Westfalls Academy, where generation after generation of Prescotts had attended school.

The Falling Inn Bed staff also appeared fond of their bedding consultant and architect, which turned out to be a mixed blessing when Ms. J arrived with news about trouble with some of the outdoor lighting near the garden's perimeter.

She insisted Laura pay attention to her new fiancé and sent Adam to tackle Dougray and the lighting instead, leaving Tori temporarily without her escort.

She wasn't complaining, though. She'd have Adam all to herself again as soon as this function ended. That, combined with all the happy people milling through the garden, helped distract her from her earlier encounter with Miranda, who'd been shooting her daggers all night.

Tori suspected part of the problem for her sister's extreme lack of humor could be summed up in two words: Laura Granger.

Tonight was Laura's night.

Since their parents couldn't make the event, she might have hung out with Miranda to take the edge off, but they simply didn't interact on that level. They never had. It had been hard enough living in the shadow of her perfect sister. She'd always been so busy trying to keep up that she hadn't had any energy left to form a real sister relationship—whatever that might be.

Tori wouldn't know because she'd never managed to live up to anyone's expectations. With Miranda in the lead, there hadn't been much left to achieve, and she'd eventually stopped trying.

Let everyone in her family, and in this hick town, too, for that matter, have fun disapproving of her. She was living her life to the fullest and when she inevitably got booted from the family, she'd simply show up on Aunt Suzanne and Uncle Russ's doorstep for Thanksgiving dinner.

She suspected they'd welcome her—especially when they found out cooking was one of her favorite hobbies.

With that thought in mind, Tori beelined across the room, making her way to where her aunt and uncle were sitting. Dale had just dragged Westfalls's headmistress out onto the dance floor after being abandoned by Laura yet again. It was about time she said hello and she had just enough time before meeting with her photographer for the photo shoot before dinner.

Casting a surreptitious glance Miranda's way, she found her sister heading toward the bar with Troy. Perfect.

"Mission accomplished," she said, slipping into a seat beside her aunt.

Aunt Suzanne turned in her chair, her gaze welcoming. "Adam liked your gift, dear?"

"I'll say. It was the straw that broke the camel's back, so to speak."

"Then you're getting along with your young man." Uncle Russ's smile came just that easy, his approval rating in his warm voice. "Good for you."

"I had help. Thank you both."

Aunt Suzanne laughed, a happy sound that made her think of Laura. "Our pleasure. You were a delight to photograph..."

"And to sculpt," her uncle added. "And we wouldn't have missed this chance to visit with you. That's been an unexpected pleasure. I'm sure Suzanne will say the same."

"I do. You're always welcome at the house, dear, and you don't need Laura to come visit. Please remember that."

Tori had no doubt that her aunt meant what she said. And her uncle, too. Not only did they seem to have an uncanny knack of finishing each other's sentences, but they wore their emotions on their sleeves.

And they weren't afraid of reaching out to her.

That said a lot about them in Tori's mind.

"So, are you enjoying the party?" Aunt Suzanne leaned back against her husband, who'd scooted his chair close to partake more easily in the conversation. "It was clever of Laura to take advantage of this beautiful summer night. The grounds here are gorgeous."

"It's no wonder we can hardly get her to leave this place," Uncle Russ added.

My parents are the happiest couple I know, Laura had said during their interview. Tori could understand why she felt that way. Uncle Russ easily slid his arm around his wife, apparently having no qualms about public displays of affection.

She had an odd sense of unreality about the exchange as they chatted about how much success Dale would have getting Laura to work less and enjoy life more after their marriage. They even talked about Tori's plans to enjoy Adam's company for the duration of the grand opening events.

She hadn't discussed boyfriends at home since high school, when the conversations had always managed to degenerate into discussions about family occupations and college alumni. Then again, as Miranda had reminded her earlier, Tori simply hadn't brought home anyone worth discussing at the Ford dinner table in a very long time. She suspected that whoever came home to the Granger dinner table would be accepted with nothing more to vouch for him than Laura's word.

When she caught a glimpse of Miranda across the room, now back at a table with her husband, she couldn't help but notice the striking difference between this family and her own.

"You're worried about her," Aunt Suzanne said quietly.

Tori glanced at her, surprised. Despite their blood connection, they were strangers. Then she remembered that while her mother and aunt didn't speak, they were still sisters, even though choices had driven them apart.

"Russ, my love," Aunt Suzanne said, turning to her husband. "Would you get me a Virgin Bloody Mary…"

"Heavy on the Tabasco," he said. "Tori, how about you?"

"No, thanks, Uncle Russ." She watched him head away from the table, seeing right through her aunt's ploy to get her alone. "Something's not right, Aunt Suzanne. I thought she might be feeling uncomfortable because Laura is the guest of honor. No doubt she's holding her breath waiting for me to embarrass her."

Her aunt's expression softened, but she didn't reply.

"I'm not so sure that's all it is, though. Miranda hasn't been home in a while, so my mother's not really sure what's going on with her, which means neither am I."

"I see." Aunt Suzanne followed her gaze and watched Miranda thoughtfully. "If she's so uncomfortable around Laura, I wonder why she agreed to come to this grand opening."

"Who knows?" She hadn't felt comfortable enough with her own sister to ask. "I know that Troy had to talk her into getting married here. Maybe he wanted to be the Hottest Honeymoon couple. Miranda is so crazy about him, she'd come back if he asked."

"Anything you can do to help her out?"

It was a nice thought, but…Tori glanced at her aunt and decided to shoot straight. After all, she'd been the first to cross the line that two generations had established, so she really didn't have much to lose at this point. And if she was going to wind up descending on her aunt for the Fourth of July picnic with a big bowl of potato salad and her special American Flag cake, she might as well start off their relationship right. "More often than not, I make things worse where Miranda's concerned."

"I know that feeling."

Tori couldn't miss the wistfulness in Aunt Suzanne's expression, the sadness in her voice, and in that moment, she felt connected by more than blood, something deeper than family acceptance. They were bound by understanding, and it turned out to be a connection more powerful than Tori would have thought.

"How did you handle it?" she asked.

"Not as well as I could have, I'm afraid." Her aunt gave a wry smile. "I got tired of trying to live up to my father's expectations and walked away without a backward glance."

"Was that the right thing to do?"

"Yes, and no."

Tori laughed. "This isn't helping."

"If you're asking me if I'd do the same thing over again, I'd tell you I'd do it differently." Aunt Suzanne brushed her long hair back, a gesture that looked nonchalant, but one Tori recognized from her own mother as meaning she wanted to shrug the world off her shoulders.

Then she fixed Tori with a serious gaze. "At the time, it was important for me to stop trying to live up to everyone else's expectations and learn to live up to my own. Since I'm pleased with the life I'm living, it was the right choice. But the cost was high. I'm older now and see ways I might have kept the lines of communication open so the situation didn't become what it has. Who knows, something might have changed along the way. Maybe a chance to fix things."

"Do you think Grandfather would have let you?"

"Not at the time, but who's to say that if I hadn't gotten so frustrated and wiped my hands of the whole situation that he wouldn't have chilled out eventually. Sadly, dear, that's age and wisdom speaking. Back then, I was young and hurt and determined to prove I didn't need my family or my father's approval. I felt like he cared more about his constituents than he did about me and my happiness."

Tori appreciated her frankness, and the way she didn't cast blame, only addressed what she might have done differently. Tori recalled the memory of her mother's face in the documentary, and there was a question she very much wanted an answer for. "How come you and my mother never made an effort to fix things?"

Aunt Suzanne met her gaze and inside her beautiful eyes, Tori could see the striking similarity to her own mother, the remnants of that sorrow Laura had dragged her into Tyler's suite to see captured on film. Her own heart gave an aching beat.

"You know better than anyone that the senator's political career means there are a lot of expectations on the family," she said. "Those expectations were even more rigid when your mom and I were growing up. And you've got to remember that my grandparents were alive at that time and they had some pretty clear-cut ideas about what was acceptable behavior."

Tori could see this. She'd heard enough stories about the generations of venerable Prescotts, and her great-grandparents, to know that the apple hadn't fallen far from the tree.

Aunt Suzanne gave a mild shrug. "Had my father been willing to compromise and I been less rebellious, perhaps we might have come up with some middle ground. That didn't happen, and the more I veered off track, the more the responsibility to live up to family expectations fell on your mom's shoulders. That's a heavy load, as I'm sure you know."

Tori considered her words, knew in her heart they rang true. She'd grown to hate how her mother, and her sister, always kowtowed to satisfy the demanding old man who never seemed to appreciate their efforts. She'd felt the pressure, too, along with the feeling of never quite making the cut.

What had Aunt Suzanne said? *I was young and hurt and determined to prove I didn't need my family or my father's approval.*

Those words made their way straight through Tori, and she couldn't avoid the obvious question: Is this what she was doing, too?

She didn't have to look hard for the answer. Instead of working harder to meet expectations as her mother and sister did, she'd decided not to waste her time. She was living her life to the fullest and proving she didn't need anyone's approval along the way.

She hadn't ever considered the effect of her choice on

her mother or sister. But Aunt Suzanne was right—she'd made their burdens heavier in the process. Miranda likely felt even more pressure to be perfect, which could explain her growing frustration and impatience with Tori's behavior. Her mother expended even more energy running interference for her with her grandfather so she didn't wind up cut off like Aunt Suzanne.

As she gazed into her aunt's wistful face, felt the warm hand cover hers, Tori knew her aunt understood.

And didn't judge her for being so wrapped up in her own needs that she didn't consider anyone else's.

"Just don't close the door," she said.

"Is it possible to keep it open?"

"My mother used to say that all things were possible."

"Would things have turned out this way if she hadn't died?"

The pain on her aunt's face made Tori wish she hadn't asked. But instead of hiding from that pain, her aunt met Tori's gaze and shook her head. "I don't think so. My mom raised us to love each other no matter what, the way she loved us. I think that's why it hurt so much when she died."

She gave Tori's hand a reassuring squeeze. "You have the ability to make things better. You're flexible and adaptable, and not so burdened by living up to expectations."

"Yeah, but is that a blessing or a curse?"

Her aunt laughed, and it was a happy sound that put the past in the past and gave her hope for the future. "I like you, dear. No matter where life takes us from here, I'm glad you came with Laura to the house."

"You haven't answered my question."

"That's because I don't have an answer. I haven't decided yet. Maybe you'll help me figure it out."

For the first time since Laura had suggested her crazy

idea to share some magic with their families, Tori felt as if believing in miracles might not be so crazy after all.

ADAM MADE HIS way across the garden to where Troy Knight stood, abandoned by his wife for Tori's photo shoot. He circled the piazza, where couples were dancing to a slow jazz tune.

"Your sister-in-law has your wife working." Adam glanced in the direction of the atrium to see Tori lining up the women for her photographer. "This shoot shouldn't take too long."

"No problem," Troy said. "It's a small price to pay for an all-expenses-paid vacation to the most romantic getaway."

"We haven't been working you too hard, have we?"

Troy shook his head. "Not yet. We'll see what happens when the new bride and groom go off duty."

"Laura informs me the whole focus of the campaign will shift after Risqué Receptions ends."

"I know. According to Laura, honeymoons are supposed to be a two's-company-three's-a-crowd deal. I have to admit I'm not sorry. Miranda and I are about partied out at this point."

"It's been an eventful few weeks."

Troy nodded. "For the management around here, too. I've seen you at every party."

"Comes with the territory," Adam said. "After the grand opening, life will get back to normal. Or as normal as we get."

Troy laughed.

Adam nodded to Ms. J as she walked by with Laura's parents, and decided to get to his point before they were interrupted. "Listen, Troy. I don't know if your wife mentioned our meeting in your sister-in-law's room earlier—"

"Heard all about it."

Adam had suspected as much and could only guess by Troy's frown that what he'd heard hadn't been good. Adam felt the need to address the situation. "My decision to become involved with Tori didn't go over very well."

Troy raised his beer mug in salute. "That would be an understatement, but if it's any consolation, the problem isn't about you. It's between my wife and her sister."

Adam nodded. Tori had said as much. "Your wife expressed some concerns, so I wanted to let you know what my intentions are. I can't promise that Tori will give me the time of day after she leaves the inn, but I plan to convince her to keep seeing me. I thought you both should know."

Troy eyed him curiously, a look that didn't judge but made Adam feel the weight of the task ahead. "Good luck, and I will let Miranda know. She worries about her sister. *A lot.* Unfortunately the situation doesn't make it easy for her."

"Why is that?" Adam asked. The more he understood, the better prepared he'd be.

"My wife's father and grandfather are politicians, so the family is pretty visible around here. That translates into every decision they make having the potential to come back and haunt them, so the family plays things pretty straight." Troy shrugged. "Or at least, most of them do."

"Tori doesn't."

"Nothing against my sister-in-law, Adam. She's a doll, but she marches to her own beat. I've seen it get awkward for the rest of them, and she doesn't seem to care."

Adam had heard Tori's references to not living up to her family's expectations. She'd told him about trying to prove herself to her managing editor. He'd also heard her tell Miranda she wasn't going to stop living her life to please people who would never be pleased.

Did Tori *not* care, or did she care *too much*?

He couldn't help but wonder if the family expectations were so high that she'd simply given up trying to prove herself. And could that also explain why she'd be willing to risk getting involved with Laura's family?

Was she looking for a place where she would be accepted unconditionally?

Adam couldn't answer that question, but he was surprised by how much he wanted to. A lot more than he would have thought, given that they'd just become involved under tenuous circumstances.

But it appeared to him that too many people in Tori's life were overlooking all her good qualities. He had, too, and those qualities were ultimately what had prompted him to mix business with pleasure. Tori was an open-minded woman who'd been willing to cover the Wedding Wing's grand opening without letting her family problems bias her coverage.

A very honest woman, who hadn't minced words about capitalizing on the local angle to win her editor's approval.

A generous, caring woman, who'd headed out onto a stage with a microphone in hand to get a stalled party started and help her estranged cousin.

A determined woman, who'd wanted to help him enjoy himself and hadn't given up until she'd accomplished her goal.

Tori had pushed him past his first impressions of her to make him appreciate the warm, wonderful woman she was.

Adam wanted her, and he couldn't help but wonder what she would do when she discovered how much. He intended to convince her to continue letting their relationship evolve after the Naughty Nuptials ended.

"Let me ask you something, Troy," he said. "You've stood where I'm standing now. How'd you make the cut?"

"You're that serious about pursuing Victoria?"

"Yes." And he meant it. They had something special together, and he wanted Tori to give him a fair shake to see where it led.

"You've got a job."

"So I gather."

Troy laughed and gave him a companionable clap on the back. "You know, Adam, you're in upper management with a decent haircut and no visible piercings or tattoos. You've got a head start already."

"I'm a good influence on your sister-in-law."

"That'll work in your favor with this family, trust me."

"I'll hold you to that," Adam said, because it was turning out that this influence thing worked both ways—he and Tori were good influences on each other.

12

"I AM SO out of here," Tori said, eyeing Adam, who wore bun-hugging jeans that clung to his trim hips and gave her a clear shot of his butt. "This is the first night since Sunday we haven't had something going on. It felt good to send my column in without crushing to make deadline."

He thanked the valet, slicing that dark gaze her way as he opened the car door. The hungry look in his eyes reminded her of their second night spent tangled in each other's arms. After consulting his sexcapades game book, Adam had drawn the bed curtains and cocooned them in total blackness as they played a very sexy version of Blind Man's Bluff. Just the memory of this man seducing her with random touches sent a tingle through her.

Sliding into the passenger seat, Tori felt suddenly flushed, although she wore only jeans and a sleeveless blouse, and the early evening sun still hung low in the sky.

"Your article on the farewell/engagement party seemed to be well-received today." Adam slipped into his SUV beside her and shifted into gear.

"Even my editor approved my angle. So far, he's impressed with the work I've been turning in on this assignment."

"Why does he doubt you'll do impressive work?"

"He *always* has doubts." Tori scooted around in her seat

as far as she could in her seat belt and took in Adam's strong profile backlighted by the fading sun. "I'd have never stepped foot on your property during this grand opening if not for the other reporter leaving town unexpectedly."

"I'm surprised your editor didn't want to capitalize on your connections to Laura and Miranda."

"Don't be. He's buried me on the municipal beat where I can benefit him with all my political connections."

"So you have something to prove with this assignment."

"I'm determined to rise above the blessing/curse of my family. I'm good for a lot more than riding the political spin in this town."

"If you're being typecast because of your family, why are you still in town? For them?"

She nodded. "Although that's not quite what it sounds like. I tried to get away from here, believe me. I had five— count them—*five* full rides to some very impressive colleges around the country, but I made everyone happy by continuing the illustrious family tradition of attending Westfalls Academy and Hawthorne College."

"Why didn't you leave after graduation?"

"And miss out on the job of a lifetime with my grandfather's best friend's newspaper?" She chuckled dryly. "Seriously, Adam, the only acceptable way to leave the family fold is the way Miranda did—on her husband's arm."

"I see."

And something about that deep-throated admission told her he did. "So what else do you want to know about me?"

He slanted his gaze her way as he slowed for traffic. "You know I'm fishing."

"I'm the interview queen, remember? But if you want to know something about me just ask. I'm forthcoming."

"You are that."

He made forthcoming sound like a good thing, and it was exactly what Tori needed to hear right now. Her talk with Aunt Suzanne had thrown her into some serious self-analysis. She'd been second-guessing her motives about her behavior ever since, which might explain why one simple comment from Adam had the ability to influence her mood right now.

Reaching for his hand, she brushed her lips across his knuckles, enjoyed the feel of warm skin against skin.

"What's that for?" he asked, a throaty sound above the steady hum of the SUV's engine.

"For making forthcoming sound like a compliment."

"It was a compliment. Forthcoming is a good quality."

Before he'd shown up in her suite, Tori would have bet money he hadn't felt that way. Amazing how much their opinions about each other had changed. "Not everyone thinks so. I've been called brusque, thoughtless and downright blunt."

"Were you brusque, thoughtless and downright blunt when you were called these things?"

"You know, you're so damned reasonable it's scary."

Twisting his hand in hers, he brought it to his lips, where he pressed a soft kiss to her knuckles. "Why scary?"

"Because it challenges me to get a reaction from you, and *I'm* scary when I start obsessing about something. Or someone."

"I'm glad you made me react."

"I am, too." She sounded breathless. "Otherwise I might have never seen you smile."

He gifted her with one now, and she couldn't help feeling amazed at how one smile could lift her mood even more. He had the most amazing effect on her. So powerful, she was finding *him* scary.

"All right, we're on the highway heading north," he said. "Now where am I going?"

Tori directed him to a favorite place of hers on the outskirts of town. A place where she'd been hiding out whenever she needed to escape the somber quiet in the mansion she'd grown up in, or the restrictive halls of her prestigious schools.

She needed to escape the thoughts roiling around inside her head right now.

They fell silent as Adam maneuvered his big SUV through the early evening traffic, and Tori enjoyed the companionable quiet after so many days of interviews and nonstop socializing. She needed some down time to clear her head, and getting away from the property for a few hours would do the trick.

"I want to discuss where our relationship's going," Adam said, not letting her enjoy the peaceful silence for long.

Slipping her hand from his, she gazed out the window to the familiar road with the sun glowing over the trees. "I did invite you to ask, didn't I?"

"You did."

Figures he'd pick a topic she had no answers for. She had enough questions about her own behavior to answer yet. Well, what would it hurt to add a few more to the list? "Shoot."

"I don't want a time limit, Tori. I want to see where our relationship can go after the Naughty Nuptials ends."

"How far past sex do you think we can go?"

He shifted his gaze off the road and surprised her with a smile. "I don't know. I want to find out."

The promise in his words prompted her to smile back, another of those wild mood swings she hadn't figured out yet.

She'd obviously lost her mind around this man.

"All right, Adam, you say you appreciate forthright, so here it comes."

He cast her a sidelong glance, and she leaned back against the headrest, turning to watch the shadowy forest zoom by so fast that trees blurred together in a way that seemed to symbolize how fast life could rush by.

"I don't have a clue where we can go beyond sex," she admitted. "But I do know I don't need to rationalize having a fling with you. You're good in bed and we're attracted to each other. That's enough for me. I don't understand why you're looking for more."

"You think I'm rationalizing making love to you?"

"Aren't you?"

"I'm going to be equally forthright, Tori, even though I suspect you're not going to want to hear what I have to say."

Brave man!

"I did have to do some rationalizing at first, but once I realized we can have more than casual together, I stopped."

"*More* than casual? How much more?"

Had Tori been thinking clearly, she might not have asked. Adam was right—she didn't really want to hear this. Not at the moment, when she was questioning her motives in other areas of her life and not entirely pleased with what she'd been finding.

Her determination to enjoy life was smacking of an immature need to prove to her family that she didn't need their approval.

And if this thought alone weren't hard enough to swallow, even more difficult was questioning her dating criteria.

Was she really attracted to dark, dangerous men who only wanted casual or was she simply dating these types so she wouldn't be compared to her sister and all the perfectly suitable men she'd brought home through the years?

Tori didn't think she'd like this answer, either.

Not when she realized she had nothing against commitment per se. In fact, the thought of a whole life filled with casual struck her as…*lonely*.

"I think we can have a lot more," Adam said.

"Really? We only got into bed a few days ago. I didn't think you were the kind of man who jumped into things feetfirst. That's what you've been telling me since we met, anyway."

"Generally, I'm not," he said, so damn rationally he really was starting to freak her out. "I know how I feel, though."

"Isn't it a little soon to be having this conversation?"

He shook his head. "You should know where I stand. Tell me what's making you uncomfortable talking about our relationship?"

Uncomfortable? Niagara Falls' resident wild child?

She wanted to deny his assertion, but to Tori's surprise, she couldn't. Not without lying. "You're asking me all these little questions that should be easy, but they're not."

"Why?" he asked with a smile that convinced her he thought he already knew the answer.

Why had she ever been so determined to see this man smile?

"In all honesty, I guess I'm just not a big one for thinking about what comes next."

"I think I might enjoy convincing you otherwise."

"Honestly, Adam." She gave a huff of pure bravado to cover up the way her stomach flip-flopped crazily. "We're polar opposites in every way that counts—"

"I don't think we're polar opposites."

"Oh, please. You're in management working your way into property ownership."

"How's that different from a reporter working her way off the municipal beat? We're both focused career people."

"I operate on an entirely different speed than you do—fast. I'm a spontaneous live-for-the-moment type of gal."

Or so she'd been telling herself. Even that was suspect at the moment.

"So we each bring different strengths to the relationship. We also bring a lot of similarities, Tori. We're both career-focused, ambitious, determined, honorable people."

"Honorable? That might work for you, Mr. Let-me-politely-ask-if-I-can-restrain-you, but how do you ascribe that quality to me? I doggedly pursued you against your will."

"You told me what you wanted from the start. You were up front and well-intentioned. I think that's honorable."

"Hmph." Well, she supposed that could be true.

"Maybe what's so different here is your expectations for me. I suspect I'm not the kind of man you're normally involved with. I got the impression from your sister that you usually date men who are only interested in casual."

How much worse could this get? She was a captive audience in this car and short of jumping out the window…

"You heard about George," she said flatly.

"I heard about George. So what have you got against noncasual relationships? Inquiring minds want to know."

She might have laughed, except none of this felt very funny. They were analyzing *her* actions and on the heels of her conversation with her aunt last night, Tori faced some hard truths. Not the least of them was admitting that a lot of her choices had everything to do with proving to her family—and herself?—that she could be happy without being perfect and not so much with what she really wanted.

This was a question Tori would have to answer. Not only didn't she like the thought of taking left turns just because everyone wanted her to take rights, but it explained so much about how she felt about Adam. Her determination to help him loosen up. Her instant attraction when she shouldn't have given a second glance.

She'd felt something for him from the moment they'd met, and although she hadn't analyzed it, she'd known it was special.

And when Tori thought about it, she really didn't have any objections to a relationship, no opposition to marriage, or even babies, in the future. She'd just dismissed them out of hand because her family had expected her to graduate from college and find the perfect man to become the perfect wife.

Like Miranda. And their mother.

But Tori had resisted by pursuing her career and making sure she dated only the most unsuitable of men.

Until Adam.

"Turn!" She blurted, waking up from her thoughts to notice that Adam had already steered off the highway and merged onto the county roadway. "Turn right here."

He made the sharp turn with an impressive reaction time and wheeled into the parking lot of a low-slung building that looked like a hunting lodge nestled in the edge of the forest.

"The Road Hog?" Adam asked, glancing at the sign over the porch depicting a rustic wooden image of a pig riding a chopper.

Tori nodded as he slid his big gas-guzzler into an empty space. She didn't need to tell him the Road Hog was a biker bar, not with the impressive array of motorcycles around. From well-maintained classics to newer bikes, the parking lot could have doubled as a Harley-Davidson showroom. To Adam's credit, he just parked and opened his door.

"I'll get it," he said when Tori went to open hers.

Honorable this man definitely was. But he wasn't a pushover, because when he emerged on her side and assisted her out, he didn't let her get away. Crowding her against the open door with his big body, he stared down at her with those intense eyes and said, "You haven't answered my question. So what do you have against noncasual relationships? I can't convince you to try one if I don't know what your objections are."

Tori might have appreciated the irony except that Adam chose that moment to trail his thumb along her cheek. Combined with his thoughtful expression, the touch became intimate, reinforcing just how serious he was about convincing her.

As serious as she'd been about getting him to smile.

And something about that made her all fluttery inside, made it difficult to face the intensity in his eyes when he asked, "So?"

"So, nothing specific's coming to mind. I just haven't met anyone who made me think about having one. Sort of put marriage out of my mind when I chose to break from family tradition and go to work."

His smile softened his sculpted features. "That's what I was hoping."

Again, the fact that he'd read her so closely surprised her. Not that he gave her a second to deal with his little revelation. No, Adam proved that some of her spontaneity had rubbed off on him by lowering his face to kiss her, a kiss so potent, and so tender, that her insides went wild.

Threading her arms around his neck, she couldn't resist taking advantage of the moment. And Adam rose to the occasion by plunging his tongue inside her mouth, transforming their kiss into a demand of hushed breaths and warm bodies that left no question in Tori's mind about just how pleased this man was.

"Get a room," a familiar female voice called out, forcing an end to their scrumptious kiss.

Tori was more than a little breathless when she replied, "You've got terrible timing. Did anyone ever tell you that?"

Their intruder was the Road Hog's owner. A five-foot-three dynamo of attractive female in blue jeans and cowboy boots, Diana stepped off the porch toward them. "I could see someone making out on my doorstep. I should have known it'd be you."

Tori laughed. "Howdy, stranger."

"Since I don't ever leave this place, who's been the stranger?" Crossing the lot with her heels crunching over the gravel, she gave Tori a hug. "So who's the man of the hour?"

"Adam Grant." He didn't give her a chance to reply, but turned on his hospitality management charm.

Diana shook his hand while inspecting Adam with a sultry, dark-eyed gaze. "Well, well, well, Adam Grant. Diana's my name and any friend of Tori's is a friend of mine."

"If you don't let him go, you're going to force me to get your dad's shotgun. You know I hate you drooling over my men."

"Oh, touchy today, aren't we?" Diana said earnestly, swinging her gaze Tori's way. "Honey, you've got to admit this delicious hunk isn't your usual dinner special."

She wondered what gave Adam away—the fifty-thousand-dollar SUV or the neatly trimmed hair.

"Yeah, yeah, so everyone keeps telling me." She meant to sound light, but came across cranky instead, which appeared to amuse her friend and her atypical "dinner special." She obviously had too much on her mind today.

"So you brought me by to introduce me to your friend?" he asked, with a hint of a smile playing around his mouth.

"Come on, handsome." Diana looped her arm through his and guided him back toward the porch, leaving Tori to follow. "Welcome to my place."

Since the weekly pool leagues filled the Road Hog tonight, Tori couldn't get through the door without a lot of bear hugs and greetings from the various team members.

"You should be glad this isn't karaoke night," Tori heard Diana tell Adam. "You'd never get her back again."

Adam just smiled as Diana led him to the bar. Tori greeted friends and acquaintances and begged off shooting a game, while the familiar rustic surroundings helped balance her equilibrium and squelch all the analytical thoughts swirling around in her head.

"Jet-fuel latte?" Diana called out from behind the bar. "Or should I break open some bubbly to celebrate your new man?"

"Jet-fuel, please." She stepped onto the foot rail and scooted close to Adam. "So what do you think?"

"I can see the appeal." Adam glanced up at the antlered stag head mounted on a wall in a spot of prominence, which Diana's late father had shot on some long-ago hunting trip. "Big fireplace to warm you up during a blizzard. Lots of friends to shovel your bike out. I'm assuming you have one."

"Of course not. She just helps herself to everyone else's." Diana gave Adam a wry smile, then turned to Tori. "So tell me why you haven't been by lately. I bought that karaoke machine for you, and you're letting rank amateurs kill me with it. What kind of thanks is that?"

"I've been dead busy with work."

"So I've been reading," she said. "Your articles are the hot topic with the daytime elbow benders."

"Glad to hear it." She nudged Adam's foot beneath the bar. "See, it's working already. Happy readers mean better circulation, which means I'll get a shot out of the courthouse."

"I wouldn't hold your breath," Diana said. "Your grandpa isn't going to let anyone move you off the municipal beat. Now, no caffeine until you tell me exactly who Adam Grant is."

"I'm Tori's latest man." Adam obliged. "The one who plans to be around for a long time."

Diana's face split into a fast grin. "You get to drink on the house tonight. Any man brave enough to declare open war on this one is someone I want to know."

"Yeah, yeah," Tori said, not a little surprised. Who knew Mr. Never-Stop-Long-Enough-To-Have-Fun would do such a good job at fitting in at the Road Hog? "Diana's just full of threats."

"So how does a senator's granddaughter wind up in the Road Hog?" Adam asked.

"Tori's a troublemaker, if you haven't figured that out yet," Diana offered.

Leaning toward her, Adam pressed a kiss to her ear and sent a tingle through her when he said, "I have."

"This place has been my salvation, if you must know," she admitted, surprised by Adam's public display of affection, pleased by it.

"She's been coming here since long before she was legal to drink." Diana pushed herself away from the bar and headed toward the espresso machine.

"Diana's dad built this place long before either of us were born," Tori explained to Adam. "And I'm only a troublemaker. She's a horrible influence."

"Don't blame *me*." Diana scoffed. "If you're planning to

be around a while, Adam, you need to know not to believe a word Tori says. She's been a horrible influence on *me*."

"Right. And *I* talked *you* into stealing your dad's chopper to go moose hunting when you weren't old enough to drive."

Diana waved her off and told Adam, "Like I would have messed with my dad's bike. I wound up on my hands and knees scrubbing every bathroom in this place with a damned toothbrush while Ms. Only-The-Best-Schools-In-Town got off scot-free."

"Oh, please. Your dad threatened to call the police just so he could see my face plastered all over the front page."

"But he didn't, did he?"

"That's because he liked me." Tori winked at Adam. "And he didn't give me a toothbrush, either."

"Make it two jet-fuels, Diana," Adam said with a laugh. They stood at the bar and chatted with Diana as she took care of her guests.

Adam seemed at ease, not at all out of place with his polished good looks in the earthy surroundings, and very, very interested in finding out all he could about her.

"So where did you two meet?" he asked Diana.

"At an arcade in town while we were in school," Diana informed him. "Different schools. I went to the local public middle school, while Ms. Good Influence over here went to *Westfalls Academy*." She made a ridiculous woo-woo sound that made Tori roll her eyes. "She sneaked out of her dorm for midnight game night and lost her ride. I met her in the parking lot scoping out rides back to the campus."

"I had to get back before the room monitor found the pillows I put under my blankets."

Adam reached for his mug. "A very good influence."

Tori laughed. She'd discovered an escape with Diana, her dad and their patrons and had indulged in an escape from life ever since. Miranda had nearly fainted after meeting George; she'd have gone straight to their parents and demanded a seventy-two-hour lockup for her little sister if she ever saw the Road Hog.

Yet Diana, and her father before he'd died, had been an important part of Tori's life. She could let her hair down with them, have fun and simply be accepted for who she was. It was a feeling she'd come to rely upon.

And it was also too much analysis for one night. Accepting the multishot latte that Diana plunked down in front of her, she sighed with gratitude when that first hot sip went down.

Adam tried his beside her and to his credit, he didn't flinch at the first swallow of a drink that had so much caffeine it would have blown the top off of most people's heads.

He seemed entirely comfortable for being inside a bar where the overwhelming majority of patrons wore T-shirts, black leather and boots. He'd said he wanted to be around for a while, and he'd gone a long way toward proving it as he easily chatted with Diana about the inn's grand opening.

Not that she'd questioned him, of course. Tori had known from the start that Adam wasn't a man to make idle comments, or commitments. If he intended to convince her of the merits of a "real" relationship, then he would do everything in his power to accomplish exactly that.

He was an honorable man.

And she was thinking again.

"Diana, I need your keys," she said.

"Only if you leave this gorgeous man at the bar to entertain me." Sweeping her shiny hair behind her shoulders, she flashed Adam a high-beam smile.

Tori bit back a laugh, instantly recognizing this old game for what it was—a test they'd designed long ago to verify a guy's integrity before he could be considered worthy to date. Make a flirty pass at a friend's date, and if the guy flirted back, he was sent packing.

"So what do you say, Adam?" Diana asked. "Will you sit here and visit with me while Tori runs her errand?"

"I appreciate the offer," Adam said politely before turning to her. "But Tori won't shake me so easily. And I've got to ask—keys for what? Is she helping herself to your bike?"

Tori laughed as he graciously and neatly deflected Diana's advance and earned a real smile from her friend.

"She wants the keys to my brand spanking new Low Rider." She gave Adam a conspiratorial wink. "But she'd not getting them. You're planning to be around a long time, so I need a lot more information before I can approve you."

"Chat fast, then," Tori said. "Because I'm taking him for a ride. We've been working way too hard lately."

Diana tipped her nose in the air and leaned on her elbows on the bar in front of Adam. "So tell me, what does a man like you want with my karaoke-singing, dart-throwing friend?"

"She's a good influence," Adam said, and while he and Diana chatted, Tori circled the bar and headed through the swinging doors to the kitchen.

She snagged Diana's keys from a wooden rack on the wall and reemerged to find her friend blocking her path. "You little sneak. Hand them over."

Tori tried to step around her in what quickly became a game of chicken, before she ducked under Diana's arm and made a laughing getaway.

"Come on," she yelled to Adam as she bolted toward the door. "I'll be back before close."

Tori swept out onto the porch, half expecting Diana to raise the alarm and send her patrons out to confiscate the keys, but when the door opened, only Adam stepped outside, his disapproving expression making her laugh harder. She didn't bother to reassure him, just headed to Diana's bike and slid onto the leather saddle.

"You do realize this is technically grand theft," he said.

"Only if she calls the police." Slipping the key into the ignition, she cranked the bike, thrilled to the grumbling purr of the powerful engine.

Escape called to her right now. She had too much on her mind and needed to chew up the road as the full moon rose high in the sky, feel the wind whipping against her as they traveled the dark back roads she'd learned to ride on.

She wanted a wild ride where she wouldn't have any time to think—about work, about her need to prove herself, about the effects on her family, about Adam and his plans for the future, and if she could live up to his expectations.

And why she cared so much whether she could. She'd wanted this man with a single-minded focus that she'd never known before. And now that she had him, she only wanted him more. Enough to bring him to the Road Hog, when he thought there might be something more than casual between them.

I'm the one who plans to be around for a long time, he'd told Diana.

And he'd meant it.

That much she knew. She wasn't sure what she thought about it, and she wouldn't. Not until she could clear her head and make sense of everything going on inside her.

"Hop on, Adam. A ride is just what the doctor ordered."

13

ADAM EYED the bike, its two-tone gold-and-black body gleaming in the lot lighting. Aside from his concern about grand theft—however acceptable the occurrence might appear—there was something inherently wrong with him climbing on the back to let Tori drive him.

When he didn't move, she pulled a grimace of utter disgust. "Oh, please don't pull this macho-man crap on me."

"Are you telling me that George would let you drive him around?"

She scowled harder. "No."

"Then what makes you think I should climb on the back of this bike?"

She reached out and slid her fingers along his crotch, hard enough to elicit a response. "Because I'm asking nicely."

Now here was an opportunity to distinguish himself from other men she'd dated, men he didn't want to think about anymore. Tori was testing him, perhaps trying to shock him by bringing him to a biker bar set out on a lone country road. When he got down to the crux of the issue, it was the macho-man crap that was making him hesitate.

He'd claimed they weren't polar opposites, which meant they could each bring something to the table in this relationship, and that they could learn to compromise when they needed to.

Time to put his money where his mouth was.

"Take me for a ride, Tori."

It wasn't as if she hadn't been doing just that since the day they'd met.

She shot him a blinding smile and pointed to a helmet hanging on a nearby bike. "Grab that helmet. Sol won't mind. He never leaves before closing."

Here again was more familiarity and presumption than Adam comfortably operated with, but he unstrapped the black helmet and slipped it on. He'd agreed to trust Tori tonight, so he would let her chart their course to see where she led.

Sliding onto the seat behind her, he brought his knees up so she nestled neatly between them. Then she shifted the bike from side to side to test her balance before wheeling out of the parking lot onto the moonlit road.

Adam had ridden before. His neighbors in the home he'd grown up in had been mountain bike enthusiasts. A nice family, they'd recognized the restrictions of being reared with elderly grandparents and had invited Adam along for many weekends to their cabin in the mountains.

But no ride he'd ever been on over those rough mountain trails had ever prepared him for this experience as Tori steered him down isolated county roads, their headlight slicing through the falling darkness and throwing everything into gloomy relief. Only an occasional car would streak past with a blinding jolt, a reassuring connection to humanity, when the surreal isolation for mile after mile made him feel as if they were the only two people on the planet.

Tori obviously knew the roads and was in control of the powerful bike. The engine purred beneath them, a constant growl that kept his blood humming. Long strands of hair flew out from the edges of her helmet, catching him across the chest and throat as the night air whipped them, cool even in summer.

This place has been my salvation, if you must know, she'd told him, and Adam could envision her slipping away from Niagara Falls, with all its pressures, expectations, surprises and disappointments, to head to the Road Hog and find acceptance with friends or escape on the open road on someone's bike.

That her friend let her take off with her clearly valued vehicle was yet another piece of the Tori Ford puzzle that was falling into place.

People who cared about her were loyal to her.

The Tori he'd seen interacting with her friends tonight had been relaxed, at ease in a way he hadn't seen her before. Adam liked the change. So much, in fact, that he didn't mind riding on the back of this bike.

He'd take her for a ride one day, too. *If* he could get her to hang around long enough. But he wasn't letting her get away because he was too wrapped up in work to pay attention. He wanted a chance to figure out what they had together, and he intended to get it.

"Hold on," Tori yelled over the wind as she slowed the bike for a turn that took them onto a hard-packed dirt road.

Adam leaned into the turn with her. Their ride grew rougher, but she handled the terrain skillfully, winding them down the black stretch, where only the rising full moon penetrated the thick cover of forest.

She pulled them to a stop when the road ended, balancing the bike while Adam dismounted before shutting off the engine. The steady roar in his ears faded, yielding to the night sounds of the forest.

"I'm going to owe Diana a detailing," she said, lifting off her helmet and shaking out her hair.

"Where are we?" Adam took her helmet while she set the bike on the kickstand.

"Diana's property. She inherited this acreage when her dad died. It has one hell of a view."

"We're near the Road Hog?" He hadn't realized they'd circled back.

Shaking her head, she motioned for him to put the helmets on the bike. "She owns the land around the Road Hog, too. Her dad built a cabin not far from the bar." Slipping her hand through his, she led him off the road into a stand of trees. "Her dad had wanted to build her a cabin on the ridge here, but he died unexpectedly before he could."

Adam recognized her wistful tone and wondered if the death of a man she had obviously cared about had added to her determination to make the most of her life. He didn't ask. She looked too thoughtful to start up the interrogation again.

Her hand felt like ice, so he caught it between his as they walked, massaging warmth back into her fingers. She glanced up at him with a smile, and he kissed her palm, enjoying the sudden silence, the glint in her eyes.

She stopped where the trees suddenly parted and didn't have to tell him they'd reached the view.

The full moon rode high in the clear sky, illuminating a sweeping vista of black treetops that descended into the dark valley. There was no light except for the liquid moon and the stars bright enough to penetrate that silvery-gold glow.

"What do you think?" she asked, and Adam drew her close, sharing his body heat while they stood together admiring the spectacular view.

"I bet it's something during the day."

"Oh, yeah. And it changes with the seasons. Right now, the valley is so green you'd think you were looking at a lawn. But in the fall, the trees turn color, and after a snowfall, it's so quiet you feel like you're the only person on the planet."

Such poetic descriptions reminded him why Tori wrote for a living and struck him with his own similar thoughts about the dark road earlier. "What's your favorite season?"

She took a moment to consider. "The winter. Only then, we'd ride a snowmobile to get here. Diana and I come often."

"Hunting moose?"

She grimaced, but Adam could easily see her out here, racing snowmobiles through the trees, escaping all the pressures and expectations of her life. The wild terrain suited her.

Having been reared clear across the country, whenever he'd thought about Niagara Falls, he never thought about the seasons or the terrain that made up western New York, but the Falls specifically. He liked that Tori had brought him to her special place. He wondered how much her family knew about the Road Hog. Had Miranda ever met Diana?

He'd guess she hadn't. There was just something private about Tori's mood, about the way she stared out over the moon-washed valley as though the ever-changing landscape were an anchor to cling to. He was glad she'd shared it with him and he tucked her closer, enjoying the way she fitted against him, the way she snuggled close to keep warm, awakening a heat inside him that he could use to ease her chill.

One-handed, he tugged the shirt from his waist and guided her hands underneath, shivering when her cold fingers touched his skin.

"Mmm, that feels good." She kept her face pressed to his shoulder as she swept her hands along his ribs, his waist, warming in tantalizing degrees, almost in pace with the way the blood soared to his crotch and changed his thoughtful mood into so much more.

Adam didn't know what it was about the night, or about holding Tori in this special place, but he suddenly needed to feel her against him, needed to test what it was about her that made him feel so urgent.

Nudging her face upward, he captured her mouth, tasted her lips when they parted. He needed to prove that what they shared tonight was more than what they'd shared before.

His tongue swept inside, tangling with hers, and he grew breathless at the way she dragged her fingers along his skin, touching him the way he longed to touch her. Her hands lingered over his back, pressed firmly along his ribs, ignited an ache inside that he needed to satisfy, and not after a long drive back to the Road Hog and then into town.

Now.

Adam wasn't sure if it was the night, or the wind whipping up from the ridge, but he needed this woman in a way he'd never needed before, not with his ex-fiancée, not with *any* woman.

Bracing his legs apart, he leaned back, forcing her to hang on to him for balance. He pressed his erection against her stomach, and Tori welcomed him, her kiss growing eager, her sleek body riding against him as if her need was as great.

He didn't know what it was about Tori that fueled him to such recklessness, but he enjoyed letting his guard down to share this moment, to savor the excitement of making out on a windy ridge at night.

She'd helped him see what he was missing when he hadn't realized he'd been missing anything at all.

Threading his fingers into her hair, Adam coaxed her head back to deepen their kiss. She gave a breathless sigh that melted against his lips, and he dragged a hand down her throat, parting the tiny buttons that held her blouse together. Her laughter burst against his mouth as she arched her back to aid his cause, her breasts swelling over the bra, her skin pale in the moonlight.

He freed her breasts, thrilling when the pebbled hardness of a nipple brushed his palm, and he caught one of those pebbled peaks between his fingers and squeezed, his own ache sharpening. He could taste that her need spiked in her kiss, liked the way she didn't hold back. She showed him how much she yearned by arching her back, inviting him to touch her.

Breaking their kiss, Adam dragged his mouth down her throat. He filled his hands with warm satin skin, tugged at her nipples, aroused by the way her fingers slipped around his neck to urge him closer. Pressing kisses to her sweet-tasting skin, he felt her pulse flutter beneath his mouth and swirled his tongue around a nipple, flicking the tight peak, before he drew her inside with a slow, wet pull. She trembled, so caught up in the moment she went boneless against him.

Adam chuckled and scooped her into his arms.

But where? Back to the bike? Impulsiveness did have some negatives. They were standing on a ridge far from shelter, without even a backseat to make out in.

Then he spotted a moonlit place where the ridge ascended up a forested slope.

Perfect.

He didn't ask if any of Diana's other friends took late-night rides to view this valley. He honestly didn't care if anyone happened across them right now as long as he wasn't interrupted from kissing her.

Only this woman could make him ache to hear the sounds of her pleasure, to feel her collapse against him.

And when she lifted her gaze to his, the excitement he saw there answered every question Adam had about what he'd found with her, made him grateful she'd pursued him, that she'd instinctively recognized what he'd been too blind at first to see.

That what they had was special.

Now it was up to him to convince her that something this special could last beyond casual, and to do that he would have to be as determined as she'd been, perhaps as *outrageous*…

And that feeling surged through him again, more powerful this time. Maybe it was the long ride on the motorcycle with Tori between his legs, or maybe it was finally accepting that this woman did things to him he hadn't realized could be done, but Adam wanted her. Here and now. He wanted to touch her everywhere, settled for letting her glide down the length of his body as he stood her upright, feeling every inch of her firm curves and those long legs on the ride down.

She looped her arms around his neck, still unsteady, and with a gut-deep certainty he'd never known before, Adam reached for her waistband and unfastened the buttons and dragged her jeans down her beautiful legs.

"Oh my, Adam." Her whisper filtered through him, a provocative sound. "First you restrained me and now you're undressing me in the moonlight. What if we're caught *in flagrante delicto*?"

"If I pleasure you properly, my dear Ms. Ford, you'll make those delicious moaning sounds that'll warn off anyone who might be out strolling the ridge tonight."

"I've created a monster."

He could hear the smile in her voice while he worked the triangle of fabric from between her thighs, and he laughed, more excited than he could ever remember feeling, with the breeze whipping around them and his face pressed to Tori's bare skin. Unable to resist, he rained light kisses down her legs, then tugged her shoes off. He peeled away her pants until she stood before him tantalizingly naked from the waist down.

Running his hands along her smooth skin, he sank his fingers into her firm bottom, drank in the feel of her, the scent of her, feeling a blast of pure male satisfaction when she trembled and leaned back against the ledge for support.

He slipped his hands behind her, protecting her from the stone, and the position elevated her hips enough so he could sink to his knees and bury his face against that neatly trimmed brush of downy hairs. Her hips arched higher to accommodate him and he obliged her with pleasure.

Kneeling before her, he buried his face between her thighs until she overwhelmed his senses…the ripple of pale skin whenever her thighs trembled…the feel of her sex gathering with every glide of his tongue…the scent of her skin mingled with the taste of her desire.

He held her anchored against him so he could knead her orgasm into breaking. And when she rode against him, her throaty moans tumbling from her lips as she climaxed, Adam knew he wouldn't be content until he'd made this woman his.

"You really think I'm noisy?" she gasped out on broken breaths.

Adam couldn't tell if she was amused or embarrassed, so he gazed up to find her looking tousled and satisfied and amused.

"I wouldn't exactly say noisy." Pushing himself to his feet, he unzipped his jeans and freed himself. "You make these erotic sounds that turn me on."

She gave a laugh that chimed through the night, a breathless and sultry sound. "Be still, my heart."

Retrieving her pants to bundle on the ledge, he hiked her onto the makeshift seat and guided her legs around his waist. Nature had obviously made this ledge to fit them perfectly, because by pulling her into his arms he could slide inside her.

"Nothing's going to be still right now." He withdrew, then sank back again, a hot silk stroke that made his body tense. "Especially not your heart."

If Tori recognized the underlying threat in his words, she didn't comment, or resist. She just locked her ankles around his waist as he rode her with strong thrusts, gasping and laughing and kissing him with breathless kisses.

As his body rocked against hers, his tension mounting in pace with hers, as their bodies worked together in perfect sync and they reached orgasm at the same moment, Adam knew he'd found the woman he was meant to be with. No matter how much life circumstance or personality might indicate otherwise.

He'd been waiting for this woman, waiting to know this sense of excitement. Their hearts racing, their pulses rushing, their climax trailing away on fading bursts, he knew he'd do whatever it took to convince Tori of the same.

Because when he saw her with her friends, he understood. The Road Hog and its people accepted her with no questions asked. They didn't care about her family or that she didn't walk the same straight line as her sister.

They cared for her *because* of who she was, not in spite of.

While Adam didn't fully understand the situation with her family, he'd guessed from her dealings with Miranda that she expected disapproval and generally got it. Whether by design or because her family held unrealistic expectations, he couldn't say. But he knew he didn't need to know Tori as long as her Road Hog friends to realize she was a woman who deserved to be loved and accepted for who she was.

For a man who normally didn't make snap judgments, this one came from the gut. And he knew why—Tori was a woman who dared to push him past his boundaries, a woman whose vulnerability and bravado touched him in places that made him feel eager and protective and excited in a way he'd never imagined he could.

Not even for his ex-fiancée, and he'd loved Vanessa, no question. But as he willed his legs to hold them, after Tori had inspired him to get outrageous, Adam knew while he'd loved before, he'd never been in love.

Not until now. Until Tori.

And even if she wasn't clear on what she wanted from him yet, Adam had the facts on his side. *She'd* pursued him even though he wasn't the type of man she normally dated. She'd seen that they were special together.

Now, he just needed to prove to her she was perfect exactly the way she was—the *right* woman for him.

14

TORI HAD BEEN having a perfectly wonderful morning. Her tryst with Adam and the visit with Diana last night had been the cure-all for her mood. She was thinking more clearly, looking at her own actions more objectively.

But to Tori's surprise, she didn't mind all this self-analysis. Watching Adam open up and have fun made her realize that perhaps that's all she had to do, too. Reevaluate some of her choices and grow in a new direction.

Feeling much more positive than she had the previous day, she'd conducted a breakfast interview with the maintenance supervisor and had found herself not only with marvelous insights into the management staff, and the general manager in particular, but starting her day with lots of laughter. Who knew sharing a meal with one wiry Scotsman could be so much fun?

She'd still be laughing were it not for the hostess who'd arrived at her table with a message that her mother had shown up in the main lobby for an unscheduled visit.

Tori thanked Dougray for his time and headed out of the restaurant to find her mother in conversation with Adam. She'd known from the start that Adam was a perfectly respectable man who'd have been welcomed with open arms in the Prescott family mansion, but never so much as when she saw him with her mother. Both of them wore custom-tailored business suits while they stood in front of the lushly decorated fireplace, conducting a perfectly polite conversation.

As she approached, she shot Adam a relieved smile that he'd had the presence of mind to warn her with the message rather than just sandbagging her inside the restaurant.

"Hello, Mother." Tori kissed her cheek. "Nice to see you. So you've met Adam Grant, the inn's assistant general manager."

"Adam and I have just been getting acquainted. Miranda mentioned he'd been very attentive to both of my daughters so I wanted to thank him personally."

Uh-oh. Though her mother wore a gracious smile on her face, the subtext in that statement was enough to make the back of Tori's neck prickle. Had her sister narced on them about their fling? One glance at Adam told her he was wondering the same thing.

"So what brings you around here this morning?" She grabbed the reins on this conversation fast, feeling refreshingly upbeat about handling a situation that seemed marked for a downhill run. "Don't you have your advocacy meetings on Friday mornings?" She referred to the group of Niagara Falls's lawyers, her mother included, who volunteered their services.

"I rearranged my schedule to visit you."

Her mother's volunteer endeavors were sacred, and she never rearranged her schedule without a compelling reason. The fact that she was standing in Falling Inn Bed's main lobby instead of downtown said everything.

Miranda had *definitely* narced on them, the witch.

"Is there someplace we can go to talk, Victoria?"

"Coffee in the restaurant?" she suggested, knowing her mother would have eaten breakfast already—after her morning stint on the treadmill and before she'd left the house for work.

"I was hoping for someplace private. How about your suite?"

An image of the rack adorning the tower snatched the reply right out of her mouth.

"Housekeeping will be working on your floor now, but you're welcome to use my office," Adam said, a knight in shining armor when she needed one most. "I'm sorry for the inconvenience, but at least you won't have to trek across the hotel."

Carolyn Prescott Ford was nothing if not socially grace-ful, and she couldn't turn down Adam's offer graciously.

Tori shot him a grateful smile as he escorted them back to the offices. His expression gave nothing away, but his dark gaze caught and held hers as he swung the door wide, a look that told her he'd be here for her no matter what; she only had to ask.

No, this man was nothing like George.

And what she felt for him was like nothing she'd ever felt before. As she glanced around his neat office, the or-ganized stacks of files on his desk, the photos propped stra-tegically on the étagère, Tori decided that she was glad. She liked Adam just the way he was.

"Would you like me to have coffee sent in, ladies?" he asked, and when her mother declined, he said, "Then please make yourselves at home. It was a pleasure meet-ing you, Mrs. Ford."

Her mother watched him go, and when the door finally closed, she said, "He seems like a very nice man."

"He is," Tori said, having already decided on the up-front approach. Her mother didn't have patience for game-playing on a good day, and Tori had already had too many hints that today wasn't shaping up to be a good one. "So what's up? Must be big to get you to blow off an advocacy meeting."

Tori knew the continued silence didn't bode well for her, so she followed her mother's lead and sat in a winged chair in front of Adam's desk.

"Victoria, I've heard some rather disturbing news, and before I form my opinions, I wanted to talk with you."

"Shoot."

"Miranda mentioned her concerns that you're conducting yourself in a questionable manner while on assignment here. I want to understand why."

Tori had always liked that about her mother—she didn't mince words. What she didn't like was the way her mother never questioned Miranda's view of the situation, whether she claimed she hadn't formed an opinion or not.

"By questionable, I assume you mean my relationship with Adam and my interactions with the Grangers."

Her mother nodded.

"I've got a job to do. As the woman who conceived the Wedding Wing, Laura's a big part of it."

"And her mother?"

Not *my sister*, but *Laura's mother*. Tori couldn't help but remember Tyler's documentary footage and that look on her mother's face when she'd looked at *Laura's mother*.

"Please listen to me. At first, I was trying to figure out Laura. I've never met anyone so in love with being in love, and that was the slant I needed for my coverage. You know as well as I do that my editor has me buried on the municipal beat because of my connection to Dad and Grandfather, and I have an opportunity to prove to him I can be more. I needed to understand Laura and where all her romantic idealism comes from. Her parents are a part of that."

"You said 'at first.' What changed?"

Tori met her mother's gaze, refused to spare herself the reaction to her admission—an admission she feared might hurt. "Laura didn't handle me the way I expected. Given everything between our families, I expected her to be guarded or defensive, but she wasn't. She put her concerns on the table, and we moved on from there. After I got to know her a little, I was surprised. Her parents seemed nice, too, so I decided to formulate my own opinion about who they were."

"And you like them."

Not a question, and Miranda couldn't have divined that from witnessing one conversation with Aunt Suzanne at the engagement party. "How'd you know?"

"I've been reading your articles."

Tori sank back in the chair. "Tell me you haven't read my personal feelings in them." If she'd had a regular column of her own that would have been fine, but not on this assignment, not when she'd been trying to portray herself as a competent professional.

Her mother shook her head. "I'm your mother, Victoria. I know what you're saying even when you don't come right out and say it."

Okay, no arguing that point. "How are you with that?"

"I don't have a problem in principle. I've always tried to rear you girls to think for yourselves. Your grandfather, however, is of another opinion altogether."

He usually was. "He's been reading my articles, too?"

"Everyone in town has been reading them, which I assumed was the whole point of your slant."

Busted. Tori forced a smile. "It was, as a matter of fact. Local interest. Good for circulation."

Her mother shook her head, looked troubled. "I'd like

to know what the point is. I spend a lot of time explaining your actions to the rest of this family, and you're walking on thin ice now. I need to know what you're hoping to accomplish so I can do damage control."

Her admission and her frustration hurt, and Tori was struck again with just how true Aunt Suzanne's statements had been the other night, just how much they applied to her own situation.

Hearing her mother now only drove home how busy she'd been worrying about proving she didn't need anyone. And along with that came the renewed sense that she hadn't given one thought to the effect on the people she was proving herself to. How much they cared about her or how much she might hurt them.

She took her mother's hands. "I'm really sorry for making things difficult for you and Dad with Grandfather. But please try to understand that I'm tired of trying to live up to everyone's expectations. I'm not Miranda. I'm never going to be Miranda. Everyone needs to accept that."

Her mother could barely contain her surprise. She squeezed her daughter's hands reassuringly, gave a wan smile. "I don't want you to be Miranda, and I'm sorry for whatever I've done that has made you feel that way. I know we're not always the easiest family to belong to, but we all love you. You know that, don't you?"

Any reply Tori may have had was lodged in her throat at her mother's heartache. She recognized this look and could only nod.

"Then you've got to meet me halfway on this, Victoria. Your grandfather's not rational on the subject, and you've already got enough strikes against you."

"How?" she managed to get out.

"I won't ask you to stop seeing the Grangers. I know that would only challenge you."

Ouch!

"But, Victoria, do not flaunt what you're doing."

"Are you asking me to hide?"

"Of course not. But if you throw this in your grandfather's face, you're setting yourself up for consequences that you need to be very certain you're willing to live with. I'm not."

"Aunt Suzanne—" she broke off when she saw her mother flinch at her use of the name. "She said nearly the same thing. She said what happened was all about choices. What happened between you all? I'm having a hard time believing this is about her marrying Laura's father. He seems nice enough. A bit strange, I'll grant you, but he's crazy about his family."

"What did...*your aunt* tell you?"

Tori recognized an opportunity here. Her mother hadn't cut her down and demanded she stop seeing the Grangers, as Tori had expected. They were discussing the situation instead. A first. She had an opportunity here to show that she'd decided to handle things differently. Making her mother believe wouldn't be easy, but it was a first step.

Launching into everything that Aunt Suzanne had said the other night, Tori tried to take a step back and watch her mother's reactions. And behind the composed expression, Tori thought she saw surprise when she explained her aunt's spin about choices and rebellion and handling things differently.

"I'm sure she wasn't telling me a tenth of everything," she admitted. "I think she was beating around the bush about the specifics, but it was more than I'd ever heard before."

"No, that wasn't everything."

And, to Tori's amazement, there was a hint of a smile playing around her mother's mouth. "I think your aunt wouldn't want to color your opinion of your grandfather."

"About what?"

"The final blowout had to do with an old argument between her and your grandfather about our mother's paintings."

"Your mother was a painter, like Aunt Suzanne?"

The wistfulness that crossed her mother's face stole Tori's breath. In her whole life, she'd never heard anyone mention that about her grandmother. Was that why her grandfather had been so opposed to Aunt Suzanne becoming an artist?

"Not like your aunt," her mother finally said. "She painted as a hobby, but she had a studio in the house—"

"That room grandfather doesn't use on the third floor?"

Her mother nodded. "That was her studio while I was growing up. She used to spend hours there when your grandfather was in Albany. He was only a congressman then."

"Didn't Grandfather approve of her painting?"

"I can't answer that, Victoria. He never speaks about her. Not since she died. It was too painful."

Given her mother's expression, Tori could only guess that speaking about her mother was painful for her, too. She hadn't ever thought of her stern grandfather as a man who could be hurt, but maybe that was because he'd already been hurt.

"What did she paint?"

"Mostly portraits of me and your aunt. She'd tell us stories about how her father would paint her while she'd been growing up."

"Wait a second." Tori spread her hands in a gesture of entreaty. "Your grandfather was an artist, too?"

Her mother nodded.

"I've never once heard a thing about this and I was the busybody. Does Miranda know?"

"I've never mentioned it, but it's no secret. As I said, your grandfather doesn't like anyone to discuss the subject."

"And you don't see anything wrong with this?" Tori was beginning to get an idea about why Aunt Suzanne was so dissatisfied with the state of affairs about her mother's death.

She only shrugged. "I told you, Victoria, your grandfather was hurt. He was never the same after my mother's death."

Which shed a lot of light about why her own mother had made it her life's calling to please the man. Tori tried to imagine what her mother, only six years old at the time, must have felt to learn her mother would never come home again. Tori could only imagine how devastated she must have been, and the thought hurt.

Sometimes when someone dies, the people left behind are so hurt it's easier to drift apart rather than face the pain of their loss. Laura had shared Aunt Suzanne's words.

Tori recognized the truth in the pain evident in her mother's face, in the fact that her grandfather wouldn't speak about his late wife and hadn't allowed his grieving daughters to speak of her, either.

"So what was the argument between Aunt Suzanne and Grandfather about?"

"Your grandfather claimed her wishes had been that if anything ever happened to her that her work be destroyed. Your aunt didn't believe him. She refused to accept that our mother would want those portraits of us growing up destroyed."

"She thought he was lying?"

Her mother nodded.

"Did you believe him?"

"I don't see why he'd lie."

"So you think Aunt Suzanne was mistaken?"

She frowned. "You've got to understand that I was young when my mother died. Your aunt was older and had more time with our mother. I only have vague recollections of sitting for her in her studio. I remember her saying that it was one of the few rooms in the house that caught the light just right. It didn't matter what time of day it was, her studio was always bright. And I remember that she always laughed. That's probably what I remember most—the sound of her laughter." She met Tori's gaze and sighed. "I don't have any answers, Victoria."

"Why are you telling me all this now? I've asked before."

Something was different this time, something that made her mother's eyes grow misty, something that made Tori brace herself to hear the answer.

"Because I won't let you go. I'll do whatever I can to keep you a part of this family. I hate what happened with my sister and you'd break my heart if you gave up and walked away."

And Tori didn't need to ask if her mother would feel abandoned. The answer was in her misty eyes, the way she held Tori's hands, as if she could physically hold her here, stop another person she loved from leaving.

And that was when Tori finally understood. Her mother had lost a beloved parent too young, and her death had ultimately cost her a sister, too. Was it so hard to understand why she clung all the more to the father who was so hard to please?

Or why she'd want to fight for her daughter?

"I love you, Mom." Tori blinked back tears as she leaned

forward to hug her mother, a gesture that suddenly seemed like exactly the right thing to do.

And when her mother hugged her back, a familiar feeling from long ago, Tori knew it had been. There'd been too few displays of affection between them for too long.

"We can figure this out, Victoria," her mother whispered. "Work with me."

"I will," she promised. "I know I haven't given you much to go with here, but I've been thinking a lot about some of the choices I've been making lately."

Her mother didn't say a word, but gave her another squeeze for good measure. Then the moment was over. She fished through her purse for a tissue and dabbed her eyes, in control again, leaving Tori feeling more loved than she had in a very long time, and amazed at how much she needed to feel this way.

She also left her with a sadness of how grief and rigid expectations had pulled her from her family and how much work she faced to bridge that distance. But as she glanced at her mother, found her watching with a hopeful expression, Tori knew she wouldn't be alone. She'd do whatever it took to repair her relationships, because expectations had also pulled two sisters apart, two sisters who'd loved each other so much they still suffered. Aunt Suzanne had filled her life with people to love, but her mother only had Dad and Miranda and a lot of friends, acquaintances and social contacts she kept up appearances for.

And a father who never seemed to approve.

And Tori.

Only as she watched her mother blink back her emotions and put on the face she showed the world, the face that hid the vulnerable woman behind the perfect smile, Tori promised herself that she'd not only meet her mother halfway, she'd find someway to turn this whole situation around.

"So, Victoria, tell me about Adam," she said, an obvious attempt to steer them back onto a comfortable ground. "He seems like a nice, suitable man."

Tori shot her mother a smile and said, "Adam is very suitable. Rutger might even let him through the front door."

Her mother laughed, a genuine sound that made everything okay again. "Well, I trust you'll let me know when you're ready to bring him home to meet the family."

And the fact he'd been invited meant everything. "I will."

Then she escorted her mother out of the inn, to—hopefully—catch some portion of her meeting. And as she watched her slip into her car and drive away, Tori realized that Aunt Suzanne had been right about something else, too—only Tori had the ability to step back from the weight of the family's expectations to view this situation objectively.

If she let her self-righteousness and rebellion go.

Aunt Suzanne *hadn't* said that. She hadn't had to. She'd trusted Tori would understand when she was ready.

And Tori was. The question now became what to do next.

Laura had taken the first step. What happened next was up to her. As she watched her mother drive off in a wink of taillights, Tori knew that whatever her next move, it would be one that would make her strong, heartbroken mother feel love and approval from all around her.

It would be one that would bring her back into the fold again, too. No matter how hard she had to work to get there.

ADAM CAUGHT UP with Tori just as she stepped inside the main lobby. She appeared in the front entrance, looking fresh and beautiful with her bright hair tumbling around her shoulders and her neat linen pantsuit hugging her trim curves.

Without saying a word, he directed her back into his office, where he delayed conversation with a kiss.

She didn't seem that eager to talk anyway, as she slid her arms around his neck and pressed up against him, all those trim curves catching him in places that made him think about when they could break away from work for a visit to her suite.

Her kiss tasted just as eager, and he liked this new place they'd arrived at in their relationship. Last night had convinced him he stood a shot at persuading her to hang around after the grand opening ended.

A shot was all he needed.

She'd accused him of a single-minded focus on work. Just wait until she saw what happened when he turned that single-minded focus onto her.

Tori wouldn't know what hit her.

He finally broke their kiss and said, "You're not scowling. Do I assume everything went okay with your mother?"

He'd been surprised by how much he hadn't wanted to leave her alone to face whatever had brought Mrs. Ford to the inn, which, given the woman's careful interrogation of him in the lobby, he guessed had to do with him.

But he hadn't earned the privilege to stand by Tori's side yet. Perhaps with the Road Hog gang, but not with her family.

Not yet.

"Better than expected." She leaned her backside against his desk and lifted her gaze to his. "Miranda narced on us, but it turns out you made a good first impression."

"Does this mean you won't ditch me for another George because I got the family seal of approval?"

"Oh, you're turning into a regular comedian, aren't you?"

"Last I heard, you wanted me to lighten up."

"Ha, ha. But I wouldn't exactly say you've been approved yet—not until you survive my grandfather."

"But I've taken the first step." He pressed a kiss to her brow. "Or will I get the boot because I survived your mother?"

She exhaled huffily. "No, I won't ditch you just because my mother likes you."

"Excellent," he said, and he meant it. "So what did you tell her was happening between us?"

"That I let you restrain me in our dungeon suite so you could make love to me while I hung from a rack."

"Was she pleased I could satisfy her little girl?"

Tori laughed. Resting his head against her brow, he drew in a deep citrus-scented breath, and was about to reply when his intercom beeped and his administrative assistant said, "Daniel Hargrove is on line two. I thought you'd want the call."

Tori glanced inquisitively up at him and mouthed the word, "Daniel Hargrove?"

"My former boss. Do you mind?"

She shook her head. "Take your call."

And in true Tori fashion, she didn't let him go, but nestled close, resting her face against his shoulder and closing her eyes contentedly, obviously expecting him to conduct business while being distracted by her delicious presence.

Encouraged as he was that she hadn't balked at his references to *them* and the future, Adam reached for the phone.

"Daniel, good to hear from you."

And it was. Adam had a great deal of respect for the tough hotelier who'd given him his start in upper management. But once Daniel stated the reason for his call, Adam disentangled himself from Tori and retreated behind his desk. He needed distance to concentrate so Tori didn't get wind of what this conversation was about. Daniel Hargrove was talking about a multimillion-dollar property that he'd only be interested in acquiring if Adam agreed to invest in it and run.

"You're the only man for the job, Adam," Daniel said. "I'll pass on the deal if you're not interested, because so much will depend on who runs the place, but if you're interested in assuming some of the risk as a partner, I don't need to tell you the earning potential here is astronomical."

To say he was stunned would have been an understatement. "Who do you have in mind for the management staff?"

"You'll put your own crew on board," Daniel said. "And if you're asking me if I'm going to make Vanessa part of that team, I guess you haven't heard that she's no longer with my company."

"I hadn't heard," Adam admitted.

"She accepted a position with a cruise line that gave her a chance to travel the world and have adventures. *Her* words. Last I heard she was sailing the Mediterranean working on her tan."

Adam laughed, pleased with this news. Vanessa had wanted changes in her life, and she'd made them. He wished her all the best and found himself not in the least regretful, not when he'd made changes in his own life that were *very* welcomed.

His gaze slipped once again over his biggest change, and he found his curious beauty had folded her arms across her chest, drawing his gaze to the sleek swell of curves there that had him thinking about sex in the middle of his workday.

During his engagement, Vanessa wouldn't have believed him capable of thinking of anything but work while on duty, but Adam suspected she'd be equally pleased to know that he'd veered from the course he'd been traveling, too.

"Well, I wish her all the best," he told Daniel. "When can I review your proposal?"

"I'll put you in contact with my lawyers immediately. It's a big venture, Adam, but I've got a feeling about this one."

"And I respect your feelings. I'll take a look at the prospectus and get back with you."

"Fair enough." He gave a booming chuckle over the phone. "Glad you're interested."

Adam ended the call to find Tori eyeing him down her nose.

"You wish *her* all the best? Who's *her?*"

Adam leaned back in his chair, pleased she'd chosen this line of questioning. Not only did her interest give him time to figure out what to say about Daniel's call, but he liked that possessive gleam in her deep blue eyes. He liked it very much.

"*Her* is my ex-fiancée. Apparently she's left the employ of my former boss to sail into bluer waters. He's thinking of acquiring a new property and wants my opinion about it."

"So you're still friends with him?"

Adam nodded. Until he reviewed the prospectus and decided if he was interested, he wouldn't mention the offer. At first glance, acquiring a monster property in Las Vegas and partnership with a hotelier of Daniel Hargrove's stature was an opportunity of a lifetime. Even if his fit at Falling Inn Bed, and Breakfast had been optimum.

His fit wasn't, though, and with so many stockholders, Falling Inn Properties couldn't offer him the sort of growth potential Daniel was looking at, with a fifteen-hundred-room property and a casino that averaged millions nightly.

Daniel had known he'd be interested when he'd pulled together this offer, and the fact he wanted Adam back on board meant his skills as a manager and potential partner were valued.

As far as Adam could tell right now, his biggest problem would be the beauty currently staring down her delicate nose at him. He had no doubt he'd lose her if he left town, and he didn't think they were anywhere close in their relationship where she'd seriously entertain leaving Niagara Falls with him. Not when she hadn't gone against her family's wishes to leave town herself.

The trouble was—Adam didn't want to lose her.

15

AT PRECISELY 11:45 a.m., Tori should have been covering Miranda and Troy's departure on a private river cruise. send-off. While Hottest Honeymoon didn't officially begin until next week, the grand opening's focus had switched to her sister and brother-in-law now that Falling Inn Bed had bid farewell to the bridal couple.

At this very moment, the inn staff would be assembling downstairs. Tyler would be there as well, filming the departure, along with her own photographer who'd be snapping shots for tomorrow's article. And Tori hoped he managed some really good ones because she'd be relying on his visual account of this event to write that article.

As much as she hated relying on anything but her own observations to write, she'd decided to skip the event in favor of her own personal interests.

A girl had to have priorities, and Tori was just getting hers straight.

Proving herself to her managing editor had suddenly taken a back seat to getting her life pointed in the right direction, which was why she was still inside her suite. She'd officially reached her limit and resorted to drastic action to find out what was going on with Adam.

He'd been skulking around for the past day, making love to her with breathless frequency as a distraction technique. The making love part wasn't a problem, but whatever Adam was hiding—and he was definitely hiding something—was a big problem.

She'd guessed his current mood had to do with the phone call from Daniel Hargrove, and it had only taken a call of her own to learn what the hotelier was up to. From there, it hadn't taken many brain cells to guess he'd wanted more than an opinion on his next acquisition. Tori suspected the successful hotelier had made an offer to lure Adam back into his employ.

What Tori didn't know was whether Adam was interested.

From her preliminary research, she'd known that Adam would be up for his annual review soon. Falling Inn Bed's stockholders would vote on whether to offer him shares in the corporation. She'd talked to Laura to find out the skinny on his chances of being recommended, only to be unpleasantly surprised.

Adam wasn't a shoo-in. While his co-workers respected him and his work, Laura had explained how his workaholism had made him a rough fit from the start. Tori would have never guessed, given the cohesive way the supervisors worked together, but she'd seen enough evidence to not doubt what Laura said. She also knew that, like her, Adam had been reevaluating the choices he made. But would he want to make those choices here when he could go back to work for his old boss at a hotel that didn't feature sex?

Tori didn't know, and this brought her face-to-face with the fact that she didn't want him to go.

This had been coming on so gradually that she couldn't say when being with him had become so important. But the fault was all Adam's with his talk about seeing where their relationship could lead. Like a seed, he'd planted *fu-*

ture in her head, where it had promptly blossomed. She was used to living in the present and enjoying the moment, which meant she never had these sorts of long-term worries cluttering her head. Or emotions.

Until now.

Damned man. How were they supposed to see where their relationship could go if he wasn't even in the same town?

Then again, all this was pure supposition.

Which was the real problem. Tori wasn't a patient person on a good day; this kind of suspense was killing her. And offending her. She'd been in his office overhearing his half of the conversation, for goodness sake. He had to have known she'd be curious, yet he hadn't said one word. He'd tried to distract her with sex and had succeeded to a certain degree, too, which had only annoyed her further.

The lock clicked and the door to the suite swung wide.

"Tori?" Adam strode into the room and paused to look around. With unerring accuracy, his gaze zeroed in on where she stood in the entrance to the tower. "Laura said there was some sort of problem."

"There is." Motioning to the rack, she launched into her rehearsed explanation. "Since we have tonight free while Miranda and Troy are on their cruise, I was planning this big surprise. But when I came in here to set everything up, I accidentally broke this stupid thing. I'm so sorry."

She delivered all that on one long breath as Adam crossed the room and came to stand beside her. Flipping the padded restraint open, she said, "Here, take a look."

He moved closer. "This isn't a problem. I'll just call maintenance. Dougray will take care of it."

"I was afraid to do that. I didn't know if you'd want him to know we'd been using this dungeon rack. It might damage your reputation. I thought maybe it was something you might be able to fix so it doesn't mess up my plans for tonight."

He frowned, but indulged her.

And the minute he reached for the restraint, she snapped it into place around his wrist.

Tori had to give the man a lot of credit. It didn't take him long to realize he'd been had, but by then she'd sprang away far enough so he couldn't reach her.

"Tori, what are you—"

"You've got a choice to make, Adam. You can step up onto those platforms and let me restrain you, or you hang out where you are, while I head downstairs and get back to work."

"You'd leave me here?"

She shook her head. "I'll send Dougray to spring you."

His frown said it all. Stepping onto the platforms, he positioned his free wrist in the restraint.

Tori made a wide circle and secured him in a quick move, just in case he got any ideas about grabbing her. Her caution seemed to amuse him. She didn't bother with his ankles. The man wasn't going anywhere.

"And just so you don't get the wrong idea, I didn't bring you here to have sex."

"I gathered," he said dryly and, to her chagrin, he didn't seem to be in the least bit disappointed. He only exhaled heavily as if she were testing his patience when he had other, more important things to do. "So what are you doing?"

Tori folded her arms across her chest and eyed him squarely. The only thing he had to do right now was appease her. "I'm restraining you. That much should be obvious."

"Why?"

"So you can talk."

"About what?" His expression of exasperated tolerance began to fray around the edges. "There isn't anything we can't discuss rationally—"

"*We* won't be discussing anything. You *will*, however, explain to me what's going on with Daniel Hargrove. He made you an offer, didn't he?"

"What makes you think that?"

"You mean aside from the fact that I was sitting two feet away when you talked to him?" she asked, sarcasm at its finest. "I'm not stupid, Adam, and I resent you treating me like I am. It took one ten-minute phone call to find out what he's up to in Vegas and guess why he might be calling you."

"I never thought you were stupid." His tone combined with his softening expression started working the edges off her irritation. "I just needed some time to decide how I wanted to handle this."

"Handle me, you mean."

He nodded. "I had some decisions to make. I've got my year-end review coming up with Falling Inn Properties and—"

"If you don't think I'm stupid, then why are you making this into a whole big mystery? I can figure out what you're going to do. Hargrove made you an offer, didn't he?"

Adam nodded.

"Then why didn't you tell me? I might have helped, you know. At the very least, I could listen while you consider your options. But you've been trying to distract me from noticing how distracted you are."

"Did it work?" His dark gaze speared her, potent with the sun streaming through the windows, slicing his strong features with colored light.

"Yes, damn it."

That appeared to amuse him. "So you want me to include you in my life? Be still, my heart."

Had she missed something here? Wasn't *he* the one restrained on the rack at *her* mercy?

The man obviously didn't know what was good for him. "I don't like being shut out, Adam. Something's obviously on your mind, and you're not sharing it with me. Why?"

"The last I heard, you wanted casual, but here you are asking me to share my thoughts and help me make decisions. Sounds like more than casual to me."

Now it was her turn to scowl. "We're not discussing what I want from our relationship—except maybe a little honesty. We're discussing why you felt the need to keep your offer a secret."

"Keeping my offer a secret isn't the problem," he said in that oh-so-rational voice. "The problem is how my career has taken a turn that conflicts with my personal life."

"How?"

"I have to admit, Tori, this is a first for me. Before I met you, my career always got top billing." He gifted her with a smile, one that made her heartbeat quicken, started up a totally unexpected reaction inside—hope. "I needed time to figure out how to reconcile the two."

Something in his smile, something in his words triggered all sorts of feelings inside her, not the least of which was tension. The man was still dragging out the suspense. "I still don't understand the problem."

"I've fallen in love with you," he said in that rough-soft voice, a voice that held nothing back. "That's the problem. If I accept a partnership with Daniel Hargrove, I'll have to leave you and move to Las Vegas to run the Parisian."

"Oh." She tried to look composed when she had to lean back against the windowsill for support. What was it about this man admitting he loved her that sucked all the bones out of her legs? She'd had other men tell her the same thing.

But never when it meant anything, never when she felt it back.

"So," she said, trying to sound completely cool and not managing at all, if that thoughtful expression on Adam's face was any indicator. "What have you decided to do?"

"Well, I made dinner reservations for the Shanghai tonight. I thought we'd get off this property, and I could explain what happened and tell you what I thought we should do about it."

"We?"

He nodded, tugged on the restraints. "That plan's moot now."

Tori might have laughed, but she couldn't get past the fact that he was in love with her, that he wanted to deal with this together, that he thought of them as a *we*.

"What do you think we should do?" she asked.

"We can either stay in town, and I keep working for Falling Inn Bed, and Breakfast until you accept that you want more than casual with me. Or we can go to Las Vegas and you can find a job where they won't pigeonhole you on the municipal beat until you accept that you want more than casual with me."

Tori blinked. It was as if every word had to travel through the clouds in her head to make sense. But even as they did, she kept coming back to the one illustrious point that Adam had made loud and clear.

"You're in love with me?"

He nodded and the hot look in his eyes made her stomach do that ridiculous flip-flopping thing.

"And you're willing to pass up this career opportunity to stay here with me?"

The amusement faded from his expression, and he watched her with a too-serious look that was classic Adam. "I'll do whatever it takes to keep you in my life."

Oh, the utter conviction in his voice crumbled her heart into little pieces. His dark gaze caressed her, and she knew if he hadn't have been restrained, he'd have chosen that moment to take her in his arms and prove everything he said with a kiss.

And she wanted him to. *Something* to drive home the fact that he would set aside his career goals to stay with her in the hope she'd want a future with him. In a job that made him use sex as a selling tool and didn't make him happy.

This was *so* not the Adam she'd met when first arriving on the property that she barely knew what to think.

But Tori couldn't fully grasp that workaholic Adam would put aside his career for her, would put aside his goals because he'd decided she was more important.

Because he believed she wanted more than casual with him.

He asked for nothing. Not a promise. Not a guarantee. He wanted her exactly as she was, knowing that she hadn't thought about the future at all and her past track record with relationships read like the credits on the back end of an action/adventure flick.

And as she stared at him, not sure what to think, her heart melted and her stomach did that crazy swooping thing. She didn't want him to leave. That was really all that seemed important right now.

She didn't want him to leave. Not without her, anyway.

"Las Vegas?" The words popped out, proving she didn't have much impulse control today, because she wouldn't have even realized she'd spoken aloud but for the look on

Adam's handsome face, the pleasure that she was contemplating what he'd said.

"Las Vegas would be an exciting place to live," he offered. "I've been there."

But he didn't have to sell her on Las Vegas, or any other city for that matter. Tori wouldn't consider letting Adam sacrifice his dream. Not when she wanted to be with him. It was that simple. It didn't matter that he was the type of man her family would approve of. Her days of rebellion for rebellion's sake were over.

Thank you, Aunt Suzanne!

"Leaving in itself won't be such a bad thing," she told him. "But I promised my mother I'd try to make things better with everyone."

He smiled. "You can do anything you set your mind to do, Tori. You've got Laura on your side already—"

"Aunt Suzanne and Uncle Russ, too. And I took the first step with my mother yesterday."

"Doesn't sound like you have too far to go."

She gazed at him, feeling warm and stupid inside at the way he watched her, as if the only thing that mattered was helping her sort out the obstacles in their path to being together. He completely believed that she loved him, even when she hadn't thought about tomorrow, let alone about falling in love.

"How can you be so sure I want more than casual with you?" she asked, needing to know.

"My dear Ms. Ford." He chuckled in that throaty, sexy voice that sapped more strength from her already-weak knees. "You've been pursuing me since the minute we met. What else should I think?"

Hm. "I have to admit that I really hate the thought of you leaving town without me."

"See." That look of satisfaction on his face was just too *male*.

"And I wouldn't dream of asking you to sacrifice such a wonderful career opportunity on my behalf. That's terribly selfless, isn't it?"

"Terribly," he agreed.

"Would I be so selfless if I didn't care?"

"Absolutely not."

"And you're right, Las Vegas would be a totally exciting place to live."

"Anywhere will be exciting as long as we're together."

Pushing away from the windowsill, she willed her weak knees to do their job, suddenly needing touch to smooth her through the power of the moment. Since the restraints made it impossible for him to move, and since Tori had no intention of releasing him yet, she slid her arms up the length of his body. She explored the firm contours beneath the custom-tailored suit and trailed her hands along his outstretched arms. She nuzzled her cheek against his too-conservative tie.

The rack had raised him just enough to keep his face out of reach. She couldn't kiss him without lowering the rack into a horizontal position or finding a footstool—neither of which she wanted to do at present. Not when his position left her open to find *other* places to kiss.

Slipping her hands inside his jacket, Tori zeroed in on his waist and unfastened his trousers. She maneuvered them over his hips, delighted to find an erection that sprang free from restraint with gratifyingly enthusiasm.

With his legs spread, she could barely get his trousers to his knees, which left only a stretch of muscular thigh and that wonderful erection exposed.

It would be enough.

She dragged her hands against those strong thighs and was rewarded when his erection bobbed suggestively. Brushing aside the hem of his shirt, she sank down in front of him until her mouth was level with his crotch.

Perfect.

"Tori," Adam said, and a quick glance revealed him watching her with an arched brow. "You do realize I'm on duty."

"I do." Running her fingers under his shirt, she traced the outline of his hips. "But I've got a problem, Adam. If I run off to Las Vegas with you, I'll wind up breaking off a branch of the family tree like Aunt Suzanne did. *How* I leave is going to be the trick."

"Any ideas?"

"Oh, yeah, I've got an idea, but you know me, it's pretty outrageous. I'm going to have to sell you on it."

Spearing her tongue into that crevice between thigh and groin, she smiled when his erection bumped against her cheek. She turned her attention toward it, continued a long wet stroke along this length that made him buck away from the rack.

She remembered how it felt to be restrained, all out of control and dark and daring, while Adam had his way with her.

"Oh, I like this. *A lot.*" She ran her tongue over him again, and this time Adam made that grumbly sound in his throat, a sound that turned her insides all warm and responsive.

Drawing the swollen tip into her mouth, she moistened the taut skin with her tongue, sucked it in a little deeper. When he bucked this time, Tori was ready. Slipping her hands behind him, she palmed his butt and used the leverage to start up a sultry rhythm. She went to work on his will with her mouth and her hands and hot strokes of her tongue.

She relished the way pleasuring Adam pleasured her, a

physical feeling that resounded in all the deep places inside, making her ache. Had both hands not been occupied
with forcing his hips to move exactly how she wanted
them to, she'd have slipped her fingers into her own slacks
and explored the wonderfully needy heat growing between
her legs.

As it was, she could only drive her fingers a little deeper
into his butt, keeping him moving to her rhythm as his muscles gathered and tightened for the impending explosion.
She slackened her pace to prolong his enjoyment, started
the process all over again until his thighs vibrated and
she'd grown all hot and wet in her panties.

"Did you have this much fun when I was restrained?"
she asked, her excitement at the thought of a future to explore the way they made each other feel getting the better
of her.

"I had a very good time," he ground out on the edge of
a growl. "And whatever your idea is, I'm sold."

"Want to come that much, hm?" She drew a few more
long pulls, smiled when he arched hard against his restraints. "Are you sold enough to marry me?"

To Tori's delight, he lost it then, climaxing with a warm
pulsing beat that managed to echo through her body as she
rested against his thigh and savored the feel of his pulse
beating hard beneath her cheek.

He finally relaxed, his arms slack against the restraints.
He opened his eyes and stared down at her. "Marry you?"

She nodded, pressing a kiss to his warm skin. "You
can't pass up this opportunity, Adam, and my family would
freak if I just move away. Miranda moves all over the
country with Troy, but the family approved of him, so no
one has any problem."

"And you think they'll approve of me?"

"Mother already invited you home for dinner. That's a big first step. She'll help us sell the rest of the family, too."

"So you want to get married so you can move away without burning any bridges?" he asked, sounding skeptical. "Doesn't sound like enough to base a marriage on."

"I agree. But I've got another reason, too."

"Really?"

She nodded, enjoying her turn at dragging out the suspense.

His eyes swept over her, a caress. "And what would that be?"

She heaved a dramatic sigh, then rose in a full-bodied motion that brought her up against him. She could feel his fading erection swell and feel his heart pound when she rested her cheek against his chest. "I've been reevaluating the way I've been doing things lately, and have decided that it's not working for me anymore. It's time to move in a whole new direction, one that's not all about proving myself, but about making me happy."

"So what have you decided?"

"That I want more than casual with you."

"From casual to marriage is a big move."

She agreed. "I know I haven't given you much of a reason—"

In one inspired move, he bucked against his restraints, lifting his legs and trapping her between them so she couldn't get away, a slick martial arts move that hinted at just how skilled the man was.

"Adam!"

"You've got nothing to prove to me, Tori. I'll marry you, and you won't ever be sorry you asked."

His gaze captured hers with such pleasure and promise that her breath caught, and as she stared up into his face, his too-serious expression mirroring her own desire, Tori couldn't help but remember her cousin's words about the magic that happened in this inn.

Falling Inn Bed specializes in love, Laura had told her.

Tori had claimed to deal in reality, not fantasy, but as she snuggled close to this man who'd changed everything, she realized that fantasy and reality weren't mutually exclusive.

What she felt for Adam was a little of both.

Laura had converted another believer, and she still had all of Hottest Honeymoons to help her romantic idealist cousin direct some of that magic toward their families.

Most particularly, toward Miranda.

"You won't be sorry, either, Adam. You have my word," Tori whispered. "And my heart."

Epilogue

ADAM STOOD unobserved behind the front desk as Tori entered the main lobby with Annabelle. She'd just concluded an official interview with Falling Inn Bed, and Breakfast's sales director. Judging by the color in her cheeks and the smile on her face, Adam guessed the interview had gone well.

Tori looked delicious today, dressed in a tailored summer suit that managed to hug her curves while remaining stylishly professional. The way she'd pulled her hair back gifted him with a view of her beautiful face, and Adam was struck by how he could *feel* her presence even from across the lobby, a physical sensation that made it impossible not to smile.

And when Tori turned toward him as if sensing his gaze, he felt an excitement that tightened his chest around a breath, and when she motioned him to join them, he was halfway to the door before realizing he'd moved.

Not so long ago, he'd been accused of never smiling at all but now…falling in bed with Tori Ford had meant falling in love, an occurrence that was changing his life. He suddenly looked forward to a future with more possibilities than he'd ever conceived of.

And he'd been thinking a lot about those possibilities the past few days, as he and his attorney reviewed Daniel Hargrove's offer and the financial statements of the Parisian. Tori had joined the effort by researching newspapers and neighborhoods around Las Vegas.

It had been an exciting few days. With the official culmination of Risqué Receptions, Hottest Honeymoons was under way, and Adam looked forward to a break in the event schedule as Miranda and Troy became the focus of events. He planned to use the time to finalize details so Daniel could move ahead with the acquisition.

And he and Tori still had to handle her family.

He'd been formally invited for dinner with the family tomorrow afternoon, and he looked forward to the event, even if he and Tori hadn't agreed yet on how to raise the subject about their engagement and move.

She felt she should talk to her mother first and enlist her aid in breaking the news gradually. Even though she was finally bringing home a man her family would consider suitable, she was still bypassing a lot of steps with their sudden engagement. Adam wasn't convinced gradual was the best approach. He didn't want to hide things that would have to be explained later—especially on his first visit. He'd rather address all the issues up front with Tori by his side. In fact, he was going to insist on it.

Of course, he hadn't told Tori that yet...

By the time he'd caught up with her, Annabelle had run off and he took the opportunity to kiss Tori. Not so long ago, he'd have considered such a public display of affection in the main lobby unprofessional, given their circumstances. But now that Adam had finally gotten into the spirit of things at Falling Inn Bed, and Breakfast, he just appreciated the way Tori's deep blue eyes sparkled in a look meant only for him.

"How'd the interview go."

"Great," she said. "We wrapped things up, though. Do you have a break for lunch?"

Glancing at his watch, he calculated the time until he was due in Ms. J's office for the staff meeting. "Can't do lunch. But I do have some time for a little shopping. Want to pop by Frieda's with me for a few minutes?"

"The Toy Shoppe, hm?" Her deep blue gaze twinkled. "Are we ready for another game book already?"

"Not just yet. There are still a few games in the Sexcapades book that I want to try out."

"Be still, my heart."

Adam laughed as he led her across the promenade and into the store. "I'm just broadening my horizons."

Adam wouldn't say more and, judging by the sudden flush in Tori's cheeks, he didn't need to. He suspected she might be remembering last night, when he'd used those exact same words while affixing nipple clamps on her beautiful breasts in a sexy game called Choose Your Weapons.

Nodding to the owner, who stood behind the front desk, he withdrew his set of master keys as he led her straight to the back of the shop.

"Adam," she said, gazing up at him with surprised blue eyes. "Have you ever looked inside this display case?"

He nodded.

"You're going to totally trash your reputation before you leave for your new job, you know."

"It'll be worth it if I can solve our problem for breaking the news about Las Vegas to your family tomorrow."

She glanced inside the glass display case that housed a variety of high-ticket *objets du sex*, from sculptured glass dildos to artfully crafted vibrating eggs. "And how are you planning to do that with this stuff? I'd bet money I'm the only one in my family who appreciates these sorts of goodies."

Sliding the key into lock, he opened the showcase and

pointed to a double-tiered filigreed gold bracelet on a velvet shelf. "Grab that, please."

Tori did and inspected the delicate workmanship. "It's a bracelet?"

"So it would seem." Adam plucked it from her hand and manipulated the two tiers open to reveal the real trick.

"Jewelry handcuffs. How clever." She laughed, running a finger along the scalloped edge.

"We won't have the rack in Las Vegas, and I've enjoyed restraining you."

"And being restrained, too, I hope." She flashed him a saucy grin, reminding him of when she'd tricked him into the rack restraints and proposed. True, he'd missed an important conference call, but he wouldn't have missed her proposal for the world. Or work, either.

Reaching for her hand, he slipped a gold cuff around her wrist and locked it into place. "I enjoyed it very much."

Then he pocketed the tiny gold key as she dangled the remaining cuff and asked, "Now you've got me curious. How is it you expect *this* to solve our problem with my family?"

"There's another game that I read about in our book. It's called One Good Turn…" He clicked the remaining cuff shut around the door handle of the display case.

Tori pursed her lips and let out a low whistle. "Bondage in a public place, Adam? You really are broadening your horizons. Don't get me wrong, it's turning me on, but—"

"You don't get loose until you agree to my terms."

Tori tossed her head back and laughed. "Sneaky bastard. I walked right into this."

He nodded, unable to keep the smug smile from his face. "You did."

"What terms?"

Adam reached inside the display case and withdrew a square jeweler's box.

"This isn't what I think it is, Adam, is it?"

"You'll have to open it."

He held it out to her and, one-handed, she flipped the top of the box to reveal the heart-shaped diamond ring inside.

"I want to present a united front with your family tomorrow," he told her. "I want them to know that you're mine forever, whether or not they understand how we can make this commitment so quickly."

Removing the ring from the box, he slid it onto her finger, then brought her hand to his mouth to brush a kiss there. "What do you say? Will you go public with me?"

Her eyes shone suspiciously, but she was all Tori bravado when she said, "You'll leave me locked up here until I agree?"

Adam nodded. Reaching up to thumb her cheek, he used touch to bridge the distance, to tell her without words that he would be by her side to face whatever life tossed at them. There was no place in the world he would rather be than with this woman, laughing and learning to lighten up and spending time on the things that were most important.

Savoring life to the fullest with the woman he loved.

Slipping her free arm around his neck, Tori leaned up on tiptoe, and just as their mouths met in that magic they only made together, she whispered, "Yes!"

And Adam knew the future would give them so much to savor.

* * * * *

Don't miss a visit to the next sexy suite
at FALLING INN BED…
Sneak a peek at Miranda and Troy's story
PILLOW CHASE
Blaze #161
coming in December 2004!

TROY WAS ALL HARD muscle and warm skin as he nestled Miranda into the curve of his body. She felt surrounded by him, that hot erection pressing firmly against her lower back. Reveling in the simple feel of skin against skin, she appreciated every moment they could be together.

She missed Troy when he was away, but somehow never so much as when they were together again. Only then could she allow herself the luxury of remembering how his strong arms felt around her, how his body sheltered her in its heat, how she felt loved and protected and so glad they were together.

Sighing, the sound turned into a purr as Troy slid a hand between her legs to coax the sensitive bundle of nerve endings from its hiding place. With her panty hose gone, Miranda was left to enjoy the full intensity of his touch as he idly fondled her, coiling the tension inside until she parted her thighs wider to increase that drive-me-wild friction that was, indeed, driving her wild.

Who knew wearing a blindfold could be so erotic?

She certainly hadn't, but then Troy had always had the ability to shoot her from zero to sixty with the perfect combination of intimacy and exploration. He knew what aroused her because he'd taken the time to learn, and continued to learn, continued to share his likes and explore new ones together.

Each time he returned from duty, the process began over again. They reveled in being together. They appreciated the contrast of newness and the familiarity. They pleased each other in ways only they could. And right now, with her blindfold, Miranda became even more aware of his touches than ever before.

He dragged his fingers through her damp heat, and she nestled back against him, feeling the strong warmth of him surround her, savoring the knowledge they still had another week to play out this fantasy together.

"Trust me?" he whispered close to her ear as he rested his chin on her shoulder, pressed a kiss into her hair.

"With all my heart."

She'd been so preoccupied with her arousal that she hadn't felt him move, so when the first icy droplet trickled between her legs, she gasped and tried to pull away.

"Surprise." He nudged the tip against her aroused skin, a quick touch to test her response. "The see-through vibrator turned out to be a lot more than a see-through vibrator."

"What—" she sucked in another hard breath, eyelids blinking against the blindfold in a rebellious attempt to see "—*is* this? A water torture device?"

"A dual-temperature vibrator." Another quick nudge that made her sex contract wildly as the cold blasted her skin. "The extreme sensations are supposed to push you over the edge."

"Oh, I'll be over the edge all right," she said breathlessly. "Over the edge of this chaise trying to get away if you touch me with that thing again."

"Sure you don't want to give it a shot? You're so hot that cooling off might feel good." He used his cool fingers to up her temperature a few more degrees.

She might be hot, but when another droplet dripped

from the dual-temperature torture device, splashing onto her stomach and dribbling into her navel, Miranda jumped.

Troy chuckled. "How about this to help you decide?"

He finally went for her bra, a one-handed motion that snapped the garment under her arms and let her breasts tumble free. He knew exactly how to arouse her, how to make her melt in his arms so she'd agree to anything. And Miranda didn't mind, not when he rolled her nipples into a frenzy, a distraction before he swirled the vibrator around one peak. The condensation chilled her skin, the sensation shocking in intensity.

"How's that?" he asked.

She took a few deep breaths, willed herself to relax and think enough to describe the sensation. As that ache speared through her, she realized that *torture* didn't adequately describe the feeling. "It's...*different*."

"Too much?"

She shook her head. "Intense."

He touched the tip to her other nipple, and the cold shot another jolt through her, making her arch into his hands, to feed this icy ache.

With his skilled fingers, Troy obliged. He made the pleasure radiate all through her until she leaned her head back so he could kiss her throat, savoring the feel of his mouth on her, his hands, until she knew exactly what she wanted.

"Let's try this." She curled her fingers over his hand and guided his newest toy between her thighs. She started tentatively, testing the feel of that coolness, pausing to prepare herself for each touch.

"Still intense?" He glided the vibrator lightly along her sex in a channel of chilly condensation and hot skin.

"Mm-hmm, but nice. In small doses."

"I like this." He kissed her neck again, pressed the length of the vibrator between her thighs again, catching her everywhere with that pulsating cold.

Miranda didn't reply. She was too busy riding the sensation, and she wasn't the only one. Troy ground his erection against her, a move that conveyed need louder than words. Her pleasure brought him pleasure. What could be better?

Miranda could think of only one thing.

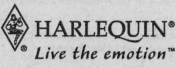

The world's bestselling romance series.

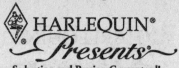

HARLEQUIN®
Presents

Seduction and Passion Guaranteed!

Back by popular demand...

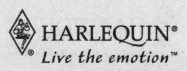

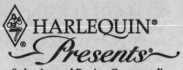

HARLEQUIN®
Presents

Seduction and Passion Guaranteed!

INTERNATIONAL
DOCTORS

**They're guaranteed
to raise your pulse!**

Meet the most eligible medical men in the world in a
new series of stories by popular authors that
will make your heart race!

Whether they're saving lives or dealing with desire,
our doctors have bedside manners that send
temperatures soaring....

Coming December 2004:

The Italian's Passionate Proposal
by Sarah Morgan

#2437

Also, don't miss more medical stories
guaranteed to set pulses racing.

Promotional Presents features the
Mediterranean Doctors Collection in May 2005.

Available wherever Harlequin books are sold.

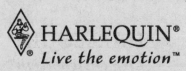

HARLEQUIN®
Live the emotion™

www.eHarlequin.com